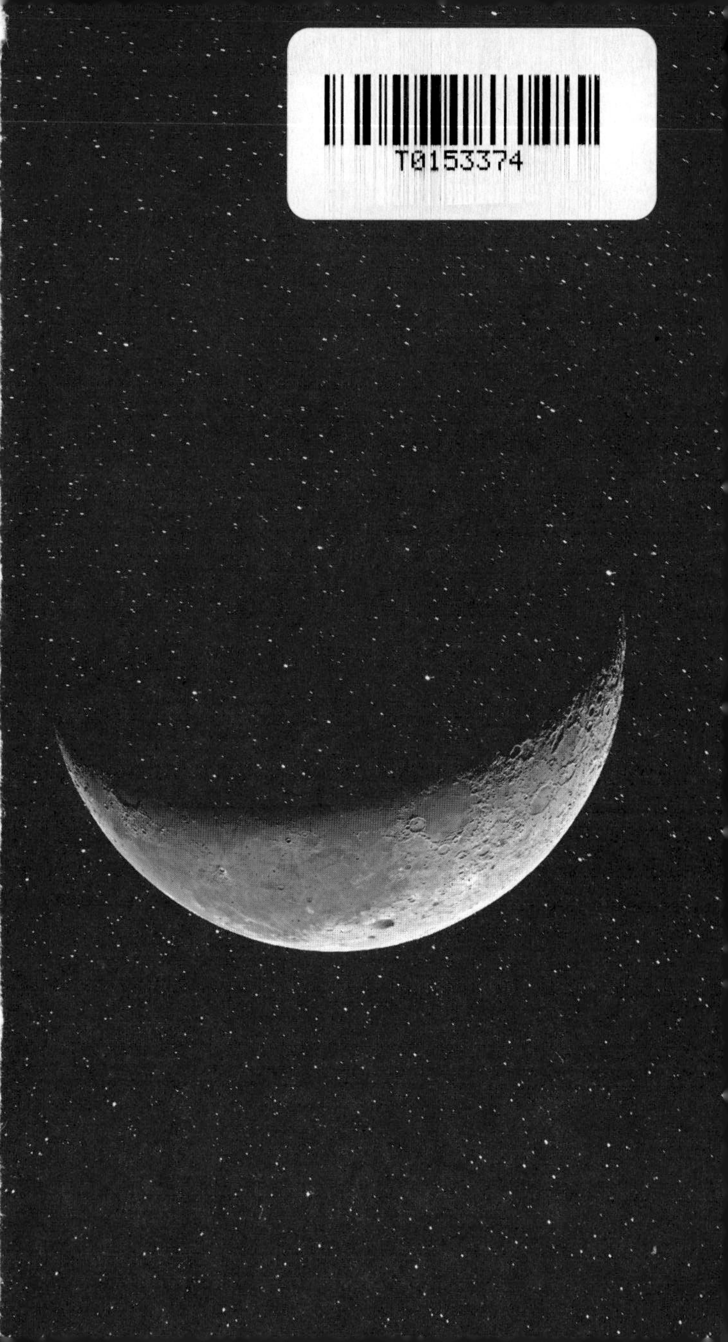

Books by the Same Author!

A PICK·A·PLOT!™ BOOK #4

You Are Alice in Wonderland's Mum!

WRITTEN & ILLUSTRATED BY SHERWIN TJIA

© Sherwin Tjia, 2017
Designed by Sherwin Tjia
First Edition

Library and Archives Canada Cataloguing in Publication

Tjia, Sherwin, author, illustrator
    You Are Alice in Wonderland's Mum! / Sherwin Tjia.

(Pick-a-plot ; 4)
ISBN 978-1-77262-017-7 (softcover)

    1. Choose-your-own stories. I. Title.
II. Series: Pick-a-plot! ; book 4

PS8589.J52Y72 2017   C813'.6   C2017-904620-9

Printed and bound in Canada by Gauvin Press

Conundrum Press
Greenwich, Nova Scotia
www.conundrumpress.com

Conundrum Press and the author acknowledge the financial assistance of the Canada Council for the Arts, the Government of Canada, and the Nova Scotia Creative Industries Fund toward this publication.

for
kitten

READ ME!

Like the horse before the cart,
A little word before we start
About the nature of this art.

You'll discover as you read the rest of me,
That your choices create your destiny.
Choose wisely! Or it'll be the death of thee!

Turn to the pages indicated
To have your curiosity satiated.
Be mistaken, or be vindicated!

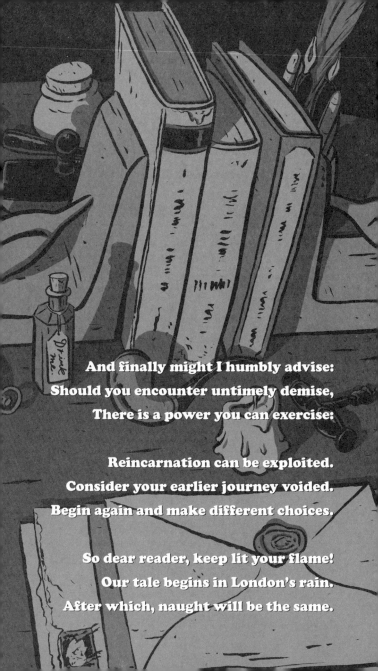

And finally might I humbly advise:
Should you encounter untimely demise,
There is a power you can exercise:

Reincarnation can be exploited.
Consider your earlier journey voided.
Begin again and make different choices.

So dear reader, keep lit your flame!
Our tale begins in London's rain.
After which, naught will be the same.

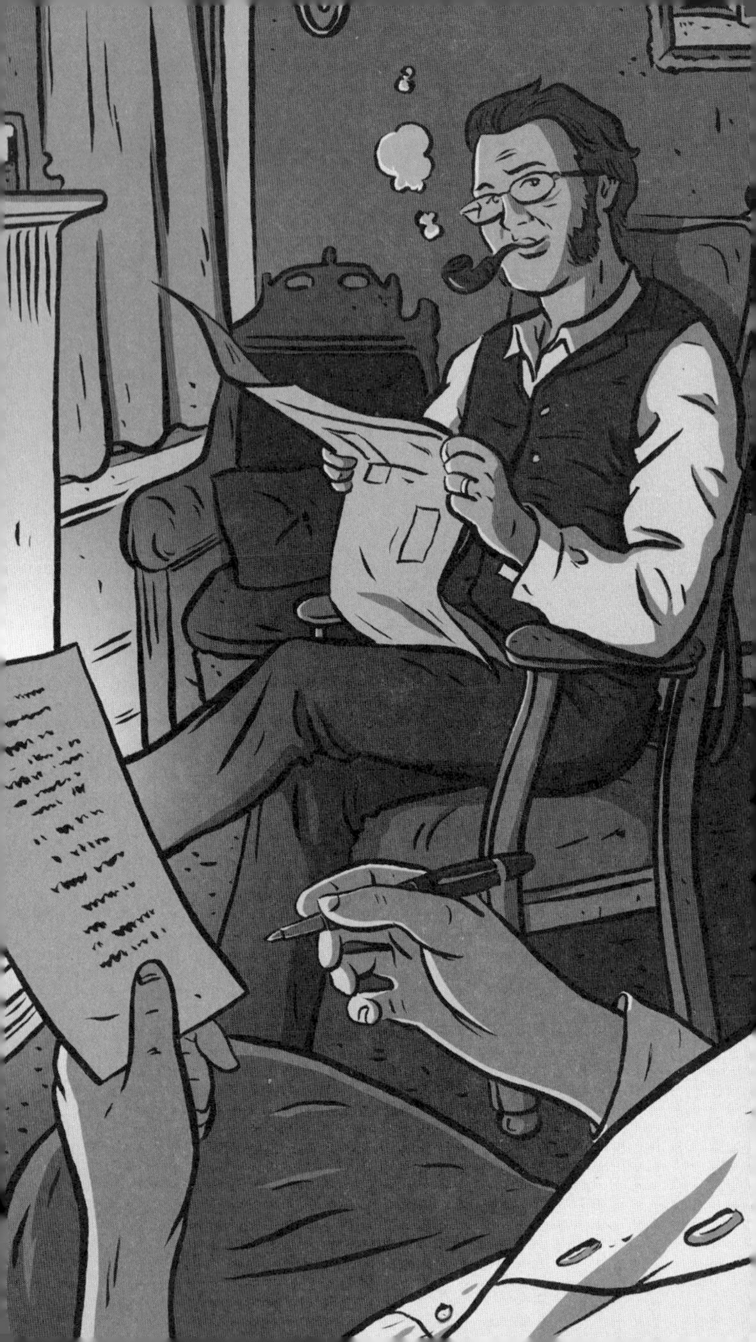

Leaning back in your chair, you consider the list of names in front of you. You'd been at it all evening and think you finally have a quite manageable list of ten to fifteen children. You wonder if anyone's missing.

"I think I have it," you murmur to yourself.

"Eh?" Reg looks up from the paper he's reading, cocking an eyebrow.

"Alice's birthday party," you explain, putting down your fountain pen on your blotter pad.

"Oh, quite right," your husband says, turning back to his paper. He strikes another match and re-lights his pipe, taking a long draw before exhaling smoke through his nostrils.

Outside, another London rainstorm batters the windows, the sound of the drops against the panes mingling with the crackling fireplace.

You take another look at the list. One name nags at you.

Esther Prout.

The Prout girl's father — a watchmaker — was recently jailed for unpaid gambling debts. The family was even forced to take in a gentleman lodger for extra income. It would be an undue burden to invite her to Alice's party, as it would be unseemly for her to appear without a gift. You suppose they could always not RSVP, but why put her in this most embarrassing position in the first place?

You raise your pen to strike her name from the list, but then you reconsider.

You sigh. It might be even more embarrassing for Esther *not* to be invited.

On the ornate Persian rug in front of the hearth, you watch as Dinah uncurls, stretches to her full length, then readjusts her position, exposing her cool side to the heat. She gazes at you for a moment through half-closed eyes and not for the first time you wish you were a cat.

Maggie pokes her head into the parlour. "Girls're all tucked in, ma'am," she says gently. "If there's nowt else?"

"Reg?" You look to your husband.

"No, no," he says. "That's all, Maggie."

The housemaid nods and disappears.

Leaving your list at your writing table, you wander upstairs, first looking in on your eldest, Lorina, who is already pretending to be slumbering.

Fine — you'll humour her, not saying anything to prompt a response. Nevertheless, you give her a kiss on the cheek and a squeeze on the shoulder before you leave.

Across the hall you go to Alice's room. She is reading a picture book with the oil lamp still lit.

"You should be asleep, young lady."

"Mummy, give me a *story!*"

You shake your head. "Tomorrow's washday," you remind her, taking her book. "Get to sleep."

Alice pouts.

"I hate washday."

You laugh. "Everyone hates washday. Yet it must be done."

"But I want a *story,*" Alice repeats.

"Don't fuss," you say, blowing out the lamp wick. "Tomorrow, I promise."

With her hands to her chest, Alice makes a heart symbol with her fingers and thumbs. "Good night, Mummy!"

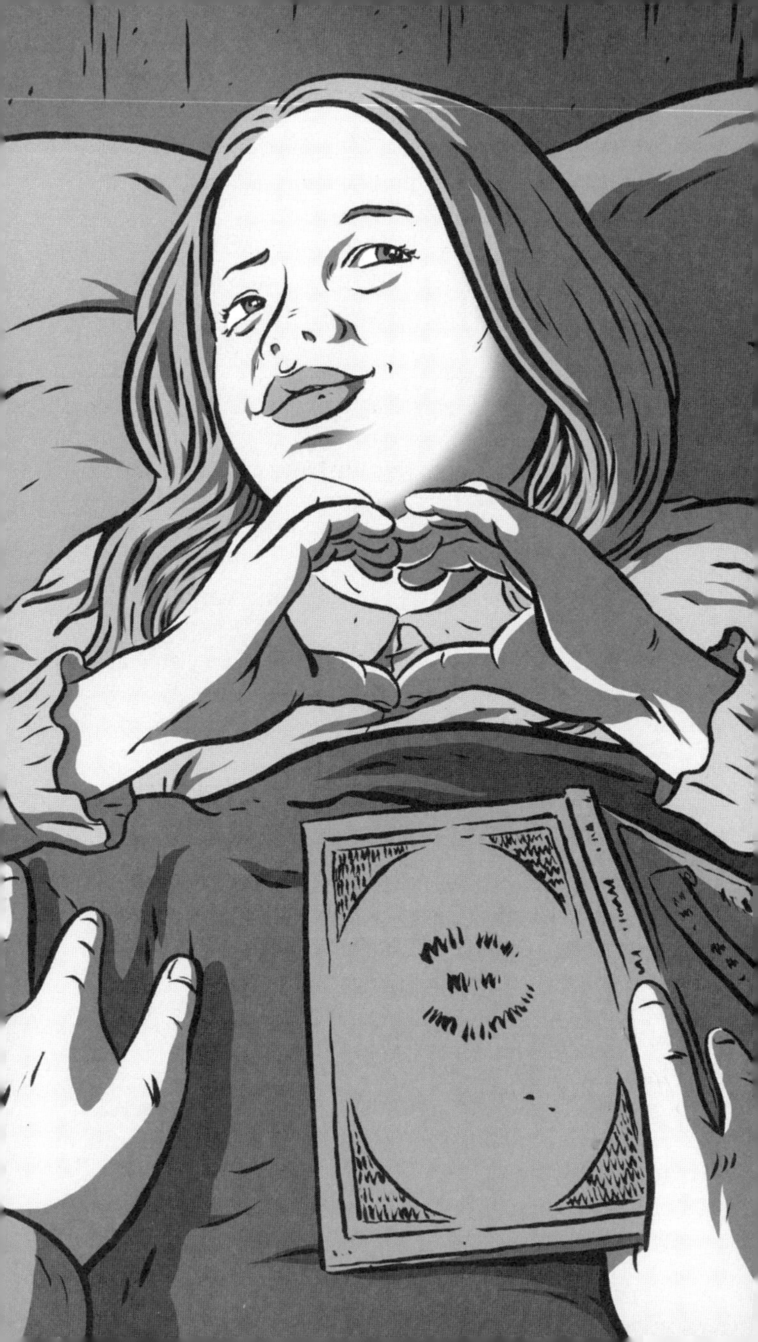

The first thing you feel, even before you open your eyes, is Reg's soft muttonchops against your lips. Then it's his mouth, kissing you.

You squint into the bright morning light. You must have forgotten to draw the drapes last night.

"Fancy a tussle?" Reg whispers in your ear, his hand on your hip.

"You're joking."

"It's no jest," Reg grins, moving his hand up your belly.

Gently, you push your husband away. "It's washday," you say.

Reg chuckles, a deep rumble that you've always loved. "Let Maggie do it."

"Maggie *does* do it! But she can't very well do it alone, can she?"

"Why must you insist on aiding her? After all — what are servants *for,* if not — "

"I can't help it," you mutter. "It's the farm girl in me."

"I'd like to see a little more of that farm girl."

You give your husband a reluctant smile, but no further encouragement.

"I know, I know," he says. With a final kiss, he gets up and pads over to the wash stand. "It's high time I was getting to Christ Church anyway."

As your husband gets dressed, you peer out the window.

It is an absolutely stunning day. Sunlight rakes into the room, warming it.

You sigh. After what must have been a week of rain, to be rewarded with *this* — but on *washday.* It is irony of ironies.

Once Reg is off, you wash yourself, updo your

hair, then get dressed. Maggie has already got morning tea started, as well as the children up. You make your way downstairs and warm your hands with a cup of orange pekoe, gnawing on a biscuit.

Washday is always the worst. It takes over the entire kitchen and scullery. You boil a lot of water, do a lot of heavy lifting, and rub your fingers raw scrubbing all the sheets and linens and clothing from the week. Your arms will ache for the next couple days at the very least.

Already, the kitchen is humid, and the floors wet underfoot.

That's when you notice that Lorina and Alice aren't dressed for washday, but for an outing.

"What's all this, then?" You stare at your daughters, in their frocks and petticoats. You glance over at Maggie for an explanation.

"I'm sorry, ma'am," she says, shaking her head. "The young misses insisted."

Lorina and Alice stand together. It's clear that they'd planned this united front.

"Mum," Lorina says imploringly, "it's been *ages* since we've gone to Hyde Park, and today's such a *beautiful* day. We've been cooped up here for five whole days! Can't we have a proper day outside?"

You fight to control your temper. Washday requires all hands on deck. Lorina *knows* that.

"Even Dinah gets to enjoy the sunshine!" Alice points out a window where Dinah is perched on a fence post.

"Dinah is a cat!" you snap back.

"Don't be cross, Mum," Lorina pleads, "but we've been going absolutely *mad* indoors." She turns to her sister. "Isn't that so, Alice?"

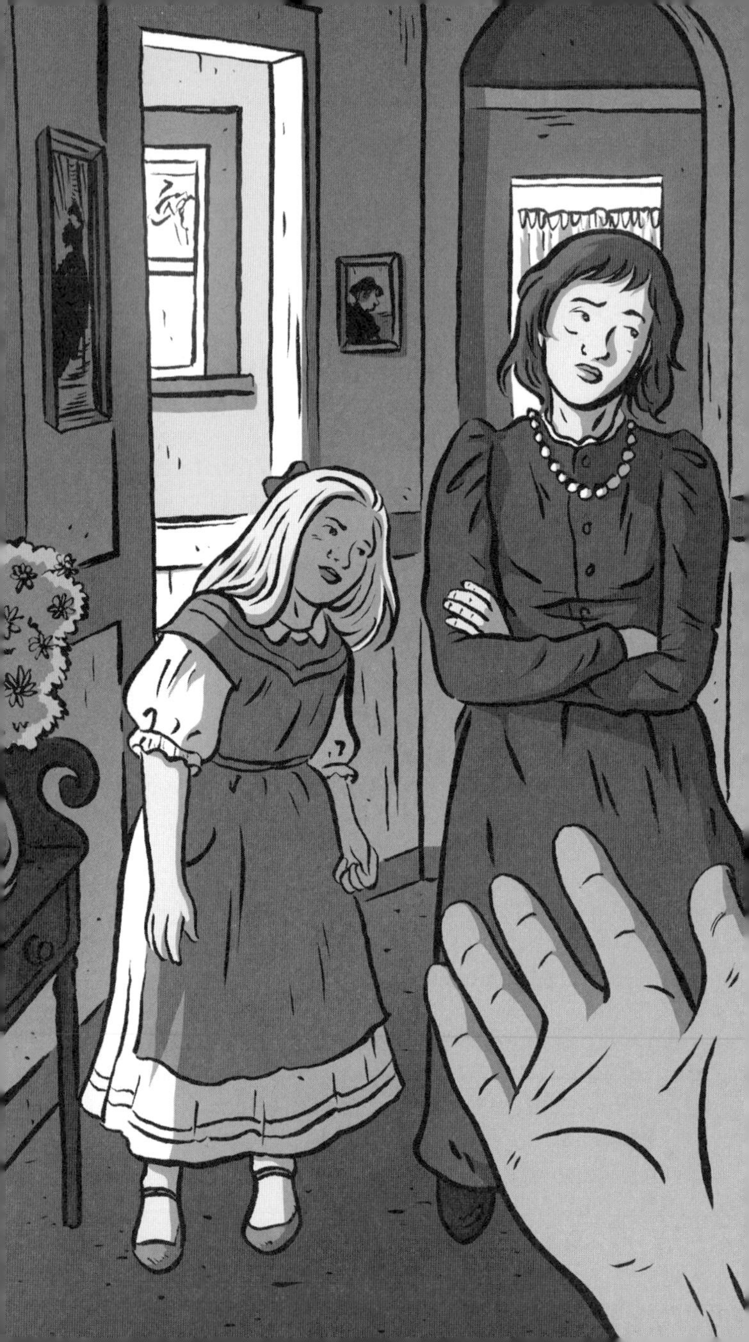

The younger girl nods her head vigorously.

Your two sly children.

It is true that they have been restless. Their bickering had reached an almost intolerable level. Just yesterday Alice had been picking her nose and flicking snotballs at her sister. It was a warm and welcome change to finally see them acting civilly with one another — if only to act in concert against *you*.

The girls need discipline, but you can also feel your resolve melting. Maybe a day outside would allow them to let off some steam.

If you relent and allow the girls to go to Hyde Park, turn to page 24.

If a firm hand is required in this case, forbid the girls from going on page 58.

If you relent, but insist that their governess Agnes goes with them, turn to page 117.

8

You stand close to the door, barking directly into the crack between door and door frame.

"Lorina Elizabeth Liddell!" you scold, in your most commanding voice. "I will brook none of this continued foolishness. You shall open this door and tell me what you know or I shall box your ears and take a switch against your back!"

The sobbing behind the door intensifies.

It's been years since you've used such a threat with either of your daughters. But Alice is missing, and there'll be time for apologies later. Right now you need Lorina to come out of her room.

You try a different tactic.

"Alice is your little sister, and I entrusted you with her care! Where did she get this matchbox? Where would a little girl get such a thing?"

Lorina's voice is small behind the door.

"Maybe she found it? On the street?"

A blatant lie.

"Maggie," you turn to the housemaid, watching from down the hall, "get me a switch."

Maggie blanches. She raises her eyebrows, as if to ask, "Truly?" and does not move.

In truth, you're unsure if you really want the switch. You simply want the threat of it.

"Wait! Wait!" Lorina calls out. "All right!"

The door opens and your daughter appears, eyes and nose puffy.

"I'll tell you."

Turn to page 66.

"I'd rather just kiss you and get it over with," you tell the man, and in the darkness you see the white of his toothy grin appear, as though there weren't even a body behind it.

"As ye wish," the man says, putting the coin away. You hear it clink against his pocketwatch.

For the first time, you are glad it's so dark. You know how this looks.

Apprehensive, you lean in gingerly. The man's rank, bodily odour swarms you. Nauseous, you think you might throw up. You start to pull back. You change your mind.

But the man grabs you like a trap!

He brings his mouth to yours.

You pull back, but his wet lips are already pressed against yours.

Then his tongue darts into your mouth.

You push the man away with all your might and this time he draws back, releasing you, laughing.

"Foul man!" you spit, wiping your mouth with your sleeve.

The man draws his fingers across his lips, as if saving some for later.

"Now tell me!" you shout. "Tell me what you know!"

Smiling, the man nods.

Turn to page 30.

Pushing past Reg, you run into the hall.

"Hey!" your husband yells from behind, grabbing your arm. You push back at him and throw him into a wall. Amazingly, he goes down far easier than you thought he might.

Alice is out in the hall, leaning against the wall, her palms up to her eyes. You scoop her up under an arm and dash as fast as you can down the stairs.

The whole world has gone daft.

As you open the front door, you hear Reg get up with a roar.

You don't look back. You just run. The bare ground is tearing up your stockinged feet, but you don't dare stop. Alice is alternately screaming and sobbing in your grasp.

Then out from an alleyway comes Maggie and a policeman.

"That's the one!" Maggie yells, pointing at you.

You shake your head.

"Drop the girl!" the bobby orders, brandishing his truncheon.

Out of breath, you can barely protest.

"There's been some misun — "

The officer rears back and swings at your temple!

The impact knocks your brain around in its pan and you drop.

Turn to page 20.

The cold creeps into your bones as you step quickly toward the orphanage. A light fog mists the cobble-stoned street, and you worry about your child. Her disappearance maddens you. You want to just collapse right there on the street but that won't help anyone — least of all Alice.

Then you see it, a weathered three-storey brick building squashed between a candle factory and a workhouse. Jutting from the wall is a painted sign.

Lady Plumly's Home & School for Orphaned Girls.

Beside the sign are a few dirty windows, obscured by dark curtains. You go over to the wooden door and give it a rap. You have to knock hard because it's an old door, and thick. The sound barely travels.

You wait a few moments, then knock again.

No response.

Finally, you try the latch, and it opens right up.

Inside is a large open room, divided into various sections. Along one wall is a series of long tables and benches. Presumably where the children eat their meals. Then on the other side of the room is a number of single chairs, all facing a coal-fed range. Then there's a play area, where the children are now.

It's about two dozen girls, all barefoot and in plain brown dresses, each adorned with a large white apron over top. Some play with broken dolls missing limbs. Others draw on sand trays with sticks. But several are cloistered in the corner doing needlework of some sort. When they catch sight of you, however, they grow silent.

A grim, skinny woman follows their gaze and lurches over to you. One of her knees does not bend.

"'Ello, 'ello," the woman nods at you, her smile

tight. "'Ow can I 'elp you?"

"Are you Lady Plumly?" you ask the woman, scanning the girls over the woman's shoulder.

The thin woman cackles.

"I *look* like a lady to you?"

You merely smile politely.

"Nay, I'm no lady," the woman extends a hand and you take her gnarled grip in yours. "Me name's Fanny Jenkins. Merely run the day-to-day. Are you lookin' to adopt?"

You look over at the girls. They are all staring blankly at you.

You don't see Alice among them, but the building has a few floors. From here, you don't see where they sleep. There are certain to be other rooms, and most likely other girls.

If you lie and say you are looking to adopt, turn to page 38.

If you tell Fanny Jenkins the truth — that you are looking for your missing daughter, turn to page 89.

If, however, you insist on speaking to Lady Plumly herself, take on airs and turn to page 79.

Outside, a fog bank has swept in and you step into the familiar moist mixture of the Thames river stench and coal smoke. You sigh and pull your cape close around your shoulders. You look for a cab to take home, but the fog is too thick.

Under the streetlamps, you see faint ghostly figures. With zero visibility, the coaches move excruciatingly slow. Even if you did manage to find a cab, it would take forever to get anywhere. You'd move as fast as molasses.

Out of the dove-grey veil, mere strides from you, a carriage rolls past. A boy walks with the horse, one hand holding its harness, his foot dragging along the curb. It's the only way to navigate in such a pea-souper.

Pausing for a moment, you wonder what you should do next. Should you return to Hyde Park? Alternately, going home might be a good idea. Alice might be there and all this searching would be for nothing. You close your eyes for a second and you can see your daughter making the heart symbol with her hands and giving you that sweet smile. Your heart aches for not knowing her whereabouts.

A movement mere feet in front of you.

A blade slashes through the fog.

"Quickly now!" a man growls, "your purse!"

If you hand it over, turn to page 258.

If you run, go to 188.

If you fight the thief, turn to page 83.

When you get close, you see that the two policemen are not merely dressed identically, but their faces are likewise the same. Not for the first time tonight do you wonder if you are actually trapped in a terrible nightmare.

One of the moustached men leers at you from underneath his tall cap. "Any fish biting tonight, dearie?"

"I do beg your pardon!" you reply, wielding your posh accent like a guillotine. You take some satisfaction from the looks of chagrin on the officer's faces.

"Oh," the officer says flustered, "my apologies, madam." He takes off his cap, and then after a moment, his partner does as well. "We assumed you were out here for more nefarious reasons."

Then his partner levels his gaze at you.

"Most *proper* ladies are not out in Hyde Park after nightfall."

"Be that as it may," you say, not appreciative of the intimation, "every citizen deserves the benefit of the doubt, and the benefit of your protection. Do they not?"

The two men *harrumph*.

One of the officers gives you a little bow. "I am PC Dean Tweed, and this is PC Dunn Tweed. Both of Her Majesty's Royal Constabulary. And we are most humbly at your service."

If the situation weren't so serious, you might almost find them funny. You proceed to ask the officers about Alice. But they are at a loss. They recommend that you go home and check there.

"Truth be told, lots of lasses go astray in a city the size of London."

Despite the discouraging news, you ask them

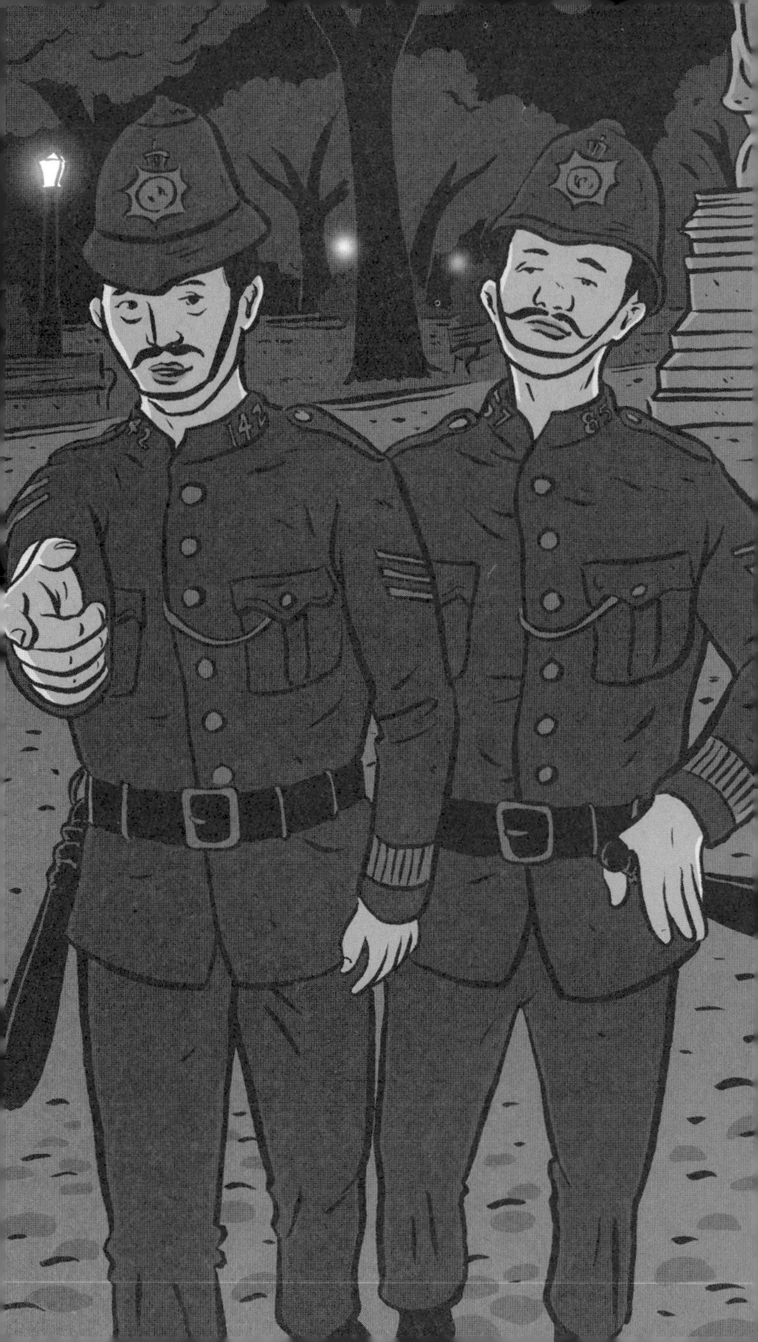

about Bodkins.

"Bodkins!" Dunn says, frowning. "Where'd you hear that name?"

"A vagrant mentioned him. Do you know him? Have you seen him here today?"

Dean scratches his chin. "This vagrant. Did he happen to be carrying a pocketwatch?"

You nod.

The officer laughs. "That *was* Bodkins! The lay-about was pulling your leg, he was."

"Ma'am," Dean continues. "Run back home. I'd wager your wee lass found her way home all on her own."

If you decide to do as the officers recommend and go home, turn to page 71.

If, on the other hand, you decide to investigate Bodkin's hidey-hole in the bushes, turn to page 88.

"Oy," the officer barks, and for the first time a mild Irish accent leaks out. "That's not the tone to take with a lady!"

Reg glares at the man.

"This is my wife!" he shouts. "I'll talk to her however I please!"

"Ma da was a right bastard like you," the officer says, slamming his hand down on the counter, his cultivated cool exterior now completely gone.

For the life of you, you don't understand how this could have gone so wrong so quickly. You grab your husband's arm in order to take him outside, but he shoves you away.

Tripping on your skirts, you fall on your rump.

"Reg!" you mutter in frustration.

Regret immediately fills his eyes and he goes to help you up.

But while you're getting to your feet, the officer has leaped over the counter.

Oh no.

"Sir," the officer jabs a finger into Reg's chest. "You need to calm down!"

Practically spitting, Reg leans forward. "Your father was right to beat you! You are an impertinent ass!"

You need to stop this. Moving forward, you try to separate the men but they are close to blows.

In your peripheral vision you see other officers rushing over the counter to aid their colleague.

Just as Reg goes to strike the officer, the other men grab him by the arms and separate the two. Exhausted, you simply close your eyes.

"How dare you! You've no right!" Reg is shouting.

"You're going to jail!" the officer screams back.

18

They slip handcuffs on Reg. You watch helplessly as they drag him towards a far door. But then, just before they pull him through, Reg seems to come to his senses and he calls to you —

"Dodgson! Go see Dodgson! He has a photo of Alice!"

Then he is through the door and all is quiet.

The other complainants in the room turn back to their business as if the incident had never happened. When you turn back to the officer, he is now back behind his desk, running a hand through his hair, adjusting his uniform.

He turns to you, catching his breath.

"Right," he says. "I think I smelled drink on his lips. He'll have to sleep it off."

"Is he under arrest?"

"No," the officer says, retrieving his previous calm. "I won't press charges, but we will detain him. You can retrieve him in the morning."

"The morning?!"

"Come back in the morning. 9 AM. We will be happy to release him into your custody then."

"But what about my Alice?"

"Ma'am," the officer crosses his arms across his chest, "in a city this size children go missing every single day. You should have kept a better eye on her. I do apologize but we are kept busy enough tracking down killers and thieves."

"So you're telling me you can't spare a single officer?"

The man lays his hand flat on his blotter, and pats it.

"Our officers are busy tonight watching your husband," he says, with exaggerated politeness. "And if you don't want them to be watching you as well, you will leave the premises, madam."

You exhale audibly, then turn on your heels and leave Scotland Yard.

"Worthless shite," you mutter to yourself as you walk down the front steps.

Turn to page 121.

20

A month and a half later you sit in court, accused of one count attempted murder of your husband, Reginald Haysworth Liddell. And, incredulously, one count of first-degree murder of yourself!

"This trial is a sham," you state vehemently, when asked to respond to the charges. "I am she. I am the woman whom this court is accusing me of killing."

"You are no woman," the judge says, his face beet red between the curls of his white wig. "You are Charles Lutwidge Dodgson. Does that name ring a bell?"

"That's the name of the man I visited!"

"*You* are that man."

None of this makes sense. All you did was drink from that vial.

"You poisoned that poor woman, then dressed up in her clothing with the aim to impersonate her. Do you deny it?"

No, impossible. You squeeze your eyes shut and rub them with your balled-up fists. But the judge's voice trammels on like a train.

"You were obsessed with the child. We have the photos you took of her. You followed her. You stalked her. You learned as much as you could about the child's family. Their comings and goings. And then you persuaded the child's mother to come to you, where you poisoned her and took on her identity in some twisted attempt to gain access to the child."

"No," you utter. This isn't how it happened. "There's been a mistake."

"The only mistake is *you*," Reg hisses. He sits in the audience gallery, just to your right. At first you were grateful to see him at the trial, but he too is under the same misapprehension of events.

Quietly, you begin to weep. You look beseechingly at Reg.

"I'm your wife!" you plead.

He looks away, disgusted.

"The accused will direct their comments to the court," the judge reminds you testily.

"I was only trying to save our daughter," you try to maintain eye contact with Reg, but he's closed his. "It was the vial! I drank from a vial. Please go back to Dodgson's room, and check for a vial."

"*You're* vile!" Reg spits. "What codswallop."

The trial ends quickly. The jury finds you not guilty due to reason of insanity. But they drag you away to the sanitarium, where they drug you daily.

The place is all screaming people and burly men and blessed blackouts.

Every night you try to will yourself awake from this nightmare, but you only dig yourself deeper into this intolerable reality.

All you want to do is get back to your daughter. At night, Alice's face appears to you, like a shining lamb of God.

You need to scheme an escape. You need to get back to her. You need to take revenge on Reg. On Maggie. On Lorina. How dare they betray you. Believe those lies about you. You were their wife and mother. You deserved better.

And once you get out they will deserve everything coming to them.

THE END

"Heads," you say.

The man flips the coin into the air. You can barely see it, but he manages to catch it in his palm, which he holds out in front of you.

You bend down to look. If it's possible, the man's hands smell even worse than his body.

"It's heads!" you crow. You look back up at the man, but he is not looking at the coin. He is staring at your chest.

You cross your arms in front of you.

The vulgar man leers at you with his mouthful of missing teeth.

He nods.

"Ye win then."

Turn to page 30.

Taking on your sweetest tone, you lean forward, placing a hand against the polished wood counter.

"I am sure you are very busy," you say with a smile. "A city this large — I simply cannot *imagine* the daily horrors you are tasked with keeping at bay."

The officer shrugs modestly.

"But if you have any resources at all to spare in helping us find our Alice, we'd be ever so grateful. She's just a helpless little girl."

Beneath the cool exterior, you can see the officer melting. You tilt your head toward him in a way you know is coquettishly appealing and set to best advantage.

"Well..." the officer says, "I suppose — "

"But it's also your *job*," Reg interrupts harshly. "Do your bloody job."

You shoot your husband a dark look.

He turns to you. "What?! Don't give me that look!"

Turn to page 17.

Only late in the afternoon do you finally get a chance to sit down with a cup of tea. Most of the chair backs have something — a shawl, a shirt, some trousers — drying on them, but just the chance to sit down eases your aching body.

Dinah, eager for a warm lap, leaps up onto your knees, but doesn't anticipate your spotted and sodden skirts.

The cat pads around your thighs, looking for a dry spot, but on washday there are no dry spots. Sensing her disappointment, you chuckle to yourself and stroke the cat's back.

Suddenly, the front door bursts open and Lorina appears, out of breath. Startled, Dinah pushes off your legs and scampers out the back door.

"Mum!" Lorina cries, distraught.

You are up and moving towards your eldest. From the stricken look on her face you have a sudden, terrible vision of Alice trampled under the legs of horses or mangled under the wheels of a wagon.

"What — " You can barely breathe the question. "What happened?"

"I can't find her."

"What do you mean?"

"I simply can't find her."

You grab your eldest by the shoulders. "Where is your sister?!"

Lorina is crying. "I searched and searched. I called and called for her. But she's simply gone."

Blood thrumming in your ears, you make Lorina sit down. You force her to take a breath, have a sip of water, then tell you everything from the beginning.

The story is simple. It seems that Lorina fell asleep in the sun reading a book while Alice was gath-

ering daisies for a chain.

"She was right beside me as I dozed. But when I awoke, she was nowhere to be found."

In the tabloids, you've read horrific stories about children going astray but you fight the rising panic. It won't do Alice any good if you fall victim to your imagination just now.

Lorina weeps and clutches you for comfort. You cry yourself, in confusion, regret and fury.

Why, oh why, did you let them go unaccompanied today?

Maggie comes in from the backyard, having put up the last of the sheets on the clotheslines, curious what all the ruckus is about. You tell her everything, and she shakes her head.

"What is it ye wish to do, ma'am?"

It is late enough that Reg will be home shortly. Your husband would know the proper next steps. Wait for him on page 98.

However, Hyde Park is massive. Likely, Lorina missed something. Alice could easily still be there. Go look now before it gets dark on page 184.

"Word is that pretty little girls are being plucked from public places. Train stations. Parks. Baths. Unaccompanied girls go missing. Even matchgirls. Disappearing."

You listen to Lady Plumly with growing alarm.

"And what becomes of them?" you ask.

"It's none of my concern," Plumly says, blithely. "I have too many lasses of my own downstairs. However, I have heard rumours and speculations that girls are being shipped out at the port. To where? That remains a mystery. The Orient? Africa? India?"

"Is there a particular dock?" you ask. "A particular ship? I need more information." Lady Plumly's vague hints are infuriating.

The woman spreads her arms wide, shrugging.

"I have no more information," she says. "You're very lucky I told you as much as I have."

"Please," you can feel your chest tighten underneath your corset. "I need something to go on."

"Hump," Lady Plumly says, "please show our guest out."

Before the giant can place a paw on you, however, you've already begun moving.

The port, you think. That's not much to go on.

Possibly it's too vague to be of any use.

If you decide to take a Hansom Cab home to see if either Alice has come home, or if your husband can help, turn to page 76.

If you decide to just head down to the port with no further information, hoping you might gather more clues there, turn to page 50.

Putting on your housecoats, you and Reg get up. Your husband carries an oil lamp, and the two of you tread over to her room. Gently, you knock on the door, then open it.

But it's empty. The bed hasn't been slept in.

Fear clutches your heart.

Your knees grow weak.

Has she been taken again?

This had been a nightmare of yours for *years* — in dream after dream, Alice came home. Alice was back. But you'd turn your head and she'd be gone. You'd have an argument and she'd be gone. You blinked and she'd be gone.

Reg steadies you when you gasp and sway.

"But where is she?" you whisper.

As if on cue, the both of you hear a noise from downstairs.

Turn to page 262.

28

You wander the streets for a spell. Dark and foggy, you follow the glow of the lamps.

If it weren't for the deep stench of horse manure, you'd feel that at some point you'd left the regular world, the world you know, behind. At some point you'd stepped into a queerer world. A world that underlay our own world like a blueprint, like God's secret plan.

You have a hope, based on nothing, that you will simply run into Alice on the street. That by some divine intervention you will stumble upon your child, crying and lost, and that she will see you and run to you and cling to your skirts and you will carry her home, berating her for leaving her sister, but full of the greatest relief you have ever known.

While you and Reg and the girls have always gone to church every Sunday, you have never *needed* God as much as you do now.

As you walk, you pray. You close your eyes and walk blind. You navigate by listening to your beating heart, your footsteps on the cobblestones. The slapping of the water against the wharfs. A distant foghorn. You listen for God's response to your entreaties.

Then you hear new voices.

A language you don't understand.

Around you, the mist is now pierced by rain. Gentle, but steady. Over time, it will push away the fog, but right now it is soaking into your clothes.

You open your eyes and find yourself in the Limehouse district. A whiff of rotting fish assaults your nose.

Suddenly exhausted, you take in a bright, glowing lamp outside of a teahouse.

Why not?

Though you have never been inside a Chinese teahouse before, you think to yourself, I like tea.

Why not step inside and have a nice cup of tea?

As you push the door open, a warm waft of smoke blows over your face.

Inside, it is dimly lit and for a moment you stand on the threshold, uncertain whether to continue or to go home. A gentle conversation in Chinese wends its way through the smoke to you.

*If you want to just go home to your husband,
hopeful that he has better ideas on how
to find Alice, turn to page 76.*

*If however, you go inside and take a seat,
turn to page 144.*

"Aye, I'll tell ye," the man says, leaning back against the tree. He takes a quick glance around, then says, "A right queer fellow he is."

"Who is?"

"Always lurking nearby. Traipsin' about. But he's no cutpurse. He's a gentleman."

"A gentleman?"

"Aye. Wears a waistcoat, he does. But always looks like he's in a hurry. Name of Bodkins."

"Was this Bodkins here today? In the park?"

The man nods.

"If any ill befell yer lass, I'll wager it was he."

"He wears a waistcoat? Do you have any other details?"

"Aye. He's lost his rabbit."

"He has a rabbit?"

The man nods.

"Right beautiful bugger it is, too. Pure white."

"So you've seen it?"

"Aye. A little red ribbon around its neck. A'times he carries it about, shows it off, lets the lads and lasses touch it."

You try to remember if you've ever seen this man. You would have remembered him. A gentleman in a waistcoat with a little white rabbit with a red ribbon around its neck? Hard to forget.

"Of late, however, he comes asking the lads and lasses to help him *look* for the rabbit."

You frown. "The rabbit's gone missing?"

"Perhaps," the man shrugs, then grins. "Perhaps he's eaten it."

You glance across the park and note that most of the gas lamps have been lit already. The vagrant follows your gaze and sees a couple bobbies that are slowly wandering in your direction.

Again, he pulls out his pocketwatch and glances at the time.

"My, my," he says. "How late it's getting."

The vagrant starts moving off, in the opposite direction of the officers.

"Wait!" you step after him. "You're sure his name is Bodkins?"

"Aye," the man calls over his shoulder. He is hurrying now towards a clump of thick bushes, under a copse of trees. "You'll find yer lass," he says reassuringly. "Perhaps she simply fell into some hole."

Then the man disappears into the shadows of the trees.

You stare after him for a moment.

The whole thing seems like a dream, or a nightmare, except that you can still smell the man's pungent scent around you, like he's marked you.

"Bodkins," you murmur to yourself.

Finally, a lead.

If you go ask the bobbies about this Bodkins, turn to page 14.

However, there is another woman here under a lamppost, casting a wary glance in your direction. Maybe she saw something? Ask her on page 46.

Still, you have a feeling that the vagrant knows more than he's telling you. If you follow him into the woods, turn to page 88.

You stab the figure in the back, but he refuses to release Edith. With a great effort, you yank the knife free and plunge it in again.

Your mind races. Have they sent the palace guards to finish the job? It'd been six years. You thought you were free. However did they find you?

The figure drops to his knees, knife still jutting out. Finally Edith is released, and she draws a huge swallow of air. She backs away from the figure on the ground and collapses into a chair, hyperventilating.

The hood falls away from the assailant's face as he drops to his side.

Oh no. It's a *girl,* not a guard.

It's been six years but it's unmistakably her —

"Alice!" you cry. Oh no. Oh no. You struggle to pull the knife out, but it's too heavily embedded in her back. Your daughter struggles to breathe, red foam forming at her lips.

"Mummy," she whispers.

Then, with her hands, she forms the heart-symbol she used to give you every night before bed.

You clutch your little girl's hands as she dies.

You can't believe this. This is impossible.

You don't want to live in a world where you killed your own daughter. Grasping the knife in her back with both hands, you wrench it loose, then plunge it into your own heart.

"No!" Edith's hoarse scream breaks through the blood thrumming in your ears as you fall to lie beside your daughter. Your true daughter. Edith runs over to you, trying to pull the knife out, but you hold the handle with a death grip.

THE END

"All right," you nod, shaking Sing's hand. "I'll owe you a favour."

The man calls out to the woman, and presently she brings him a hot drink too.

"Is that tea?" you ask.

"Caffee," Sing says. Then he scratches his goatee thoughtfully. "Sing hear lots."

"What have you heard, Mr. Sing?"

"Here, at port," he points outside his door. "A lots people. In, out. Very danger. My job — Sing hear lots."

"I would imagine you hear a lot, running an opium establishment," you look around drily.

"No, no, my job — mean to help people."

"You mean the favours?"

Sing nods. "I help people."

"Why?"

"Why not?" Sing smiles.

"And why me?"

"I help every people. Not just you."

The man pulls out a little red leather notebook, with worn gold edging. Then he finds the next available page and produces a fountain pen.

"You name?" he asks politely.

You give it to the man, spelling it. Then he asks for your address, which you deliver likewise, with some misgivings.

"Is that your ledger of favours, Mr. Sing?"

The man nods, then closes the book.

"How many names are in there?" you ask with genuine curiosity. "How many people do you help?"

Sing hands the notebook over casually.

You open it up, but it's largely unreadable. Every page is packed meticulously with inscrutable Chinese ideograms. Some names have been scratched and

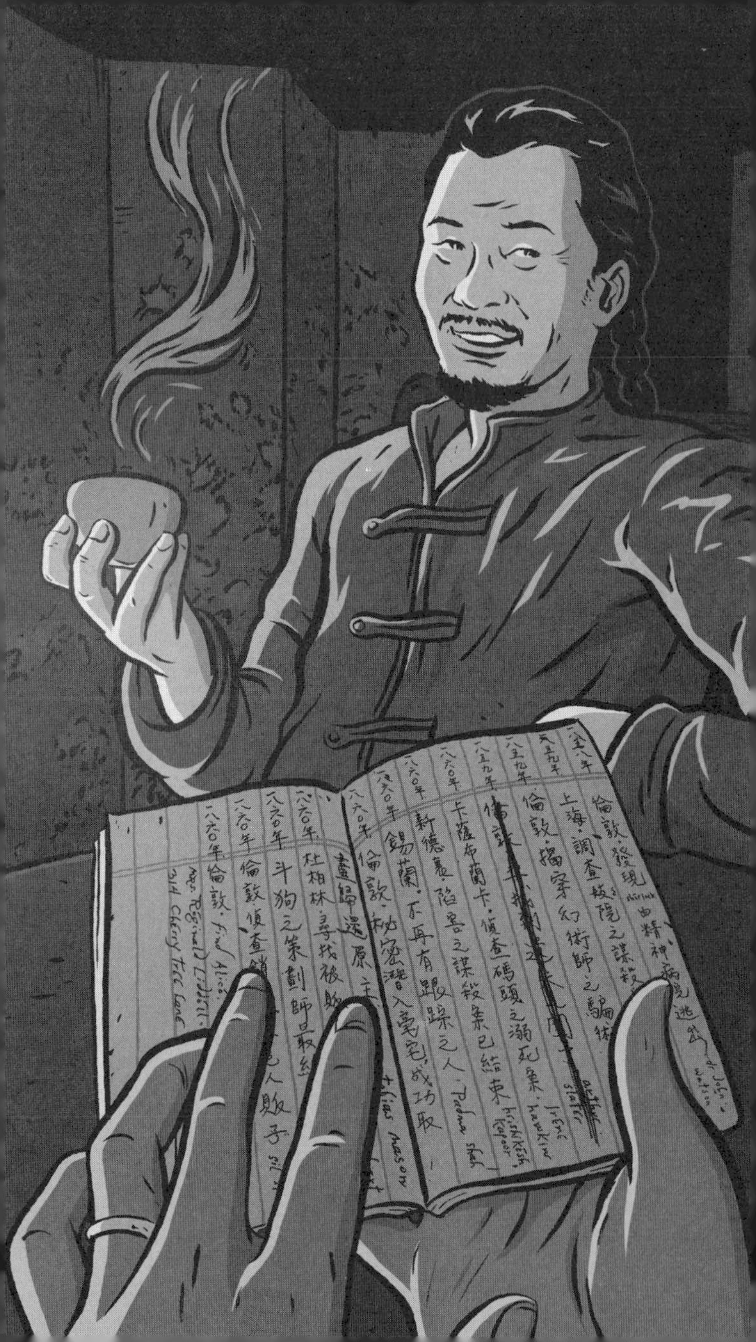
dr John watson
arthur slater
Irene hawkins
hrishikesh kapoor
Padma shah
tobias mason
Mrs. Reginald Liddell. find Alice.
314 Cherry Tree Lane

scribbled out. There are a handful of English names here and there — now including yours. You get the sense that if this notebook were ever lost, that it would be an incalculable tragedy.

"You've helped a great many people, Mr. Sing," you say, handing the notebook back. "I certainly hope you can help me."

"Sing help," the man smiles, tucking the notebook into a pocket. "First, Sing smoke. You smoke?"

"I beg your pardon?"

Sing gets up and beckons you to follow him to an empty booth behind a screen. He sits down on a bench and starts setting up the opium tray. He lights the lamp, and puts a few drops into the hopper.

You have never done anything like this before in your life, but tonight you feel you are venturing into unknown territory. You have lived in London for most of your adult life, but you realize there are entire worlds underlying the London that you know.

Sing reclines and takes a long draw on the pipe. Then he offers it to you.

You are sorely tempted.

If you smoke the opium, turn to page 155.

If you politely decline, lie back and have a nap while Sing finishes his pipe. You are exhausted and could use a break. Wake up on page 90.

"Yes," you say, recovering quickly. "I'm here to audition."

You don't know why you just said that. Maybe you're afraid that if you'd said no, that you'd simply be dismissed. Perhaps if you play along, you might be able to gather more information. Earn her trust.

Lady Plumly looks you over. From crown to calves, she inspects you like a cut of beef. It is deeply unsettling.

"My dear, what's your age?"

"My age?"

"Of course, it'll be whatever you tell your clients," Lady Plumly chuckles, "but you're a mite grey in the whiskers to be getting into the game, ain't you?"

You blush, but bite your tongue at the insult.

"Age is merely a number," you say blandly.

"Hmph," Lady Plumly cocks her head. "Quite so."

Then she catches sight of your wedding ring. "And, you'll want to take *that* off."

"Right this minute?"

The woman gives you a hard look. Then she calls the giant over.

"Hump. Come over here, my love."

The man plods toward you, his heavy steps booming on the oak floor.

He has a big grin on his face. His teeth look as if they've never been brushed, covered as they are in slimy yellow sweaters.

"Happy time," he chuckles.

"Show me," Lady Plumly says, nodding at the man.

"Show you?"

"Audition for me."

"On him?"

"On Humphrey, yes," the woman says impatiently.

This was a mistake. You want to get out of this, but you're unsure how.

This whole evening you feel like you've been entering one room after the other, each subsequent room smaller than the last, each exit closing up after itself.

If you decide to just audition and get it over with, turn to page 74.

If you balk, and try to leave, turn to page 82.

"Why yes," you tell the woman. "My husband and I are looking to adopt a little girl."

Fanny Jenkins takes note of your wedding ring, then eyes your wool cape and your nice leather shoes.

"There *is* a matter of a small adoption fee," she says. "But I trust that won't be a 'ardship for yourself and your 'usband?"

"That's fine," you say smoothly. Then the woman claps her hands three times and all the girls immediately line themselves up from tallest to the smallest.

You're taken aback. You didn't expect something this formal.

As you're led down the row of girls, Fanny Jenkins nods at each of them in turn and every girl states her name and age.

"Vivian, miss. I'm twelve."

"I'm Grace! Age seven and three-quarters."

"Name's Eliza. I'm six."

Your heart breaks as each girl stands up straight and announces herself. One girl is so nervous she is visibly shaking. You want to hug her, but you don't want to make the whole ordeal worse than it already is.

Finally you reach the end of the line without having seen Alice. Fanny Jenkins smiles at you.

"Anyone you fancy?" she asks.

"Is this all of them?"

"Aye."

You take a deep breath. You can feel the stares of all the girls burning into the side of your face.

"Would you like to go back down the line?"

You shake your head.

"No, no," you manage to croak. You turn to the girls. "It was a delight to meet each and every one of you," you say with a sprightliness you don't feel. You turn back to the woman. "I must go home and make a considered decision. I'll bring my husband next time!"

The woman nods. "Be sure you do," she says, walking you out. The line of girls relaxes and they go back to their playing. "Could I get your name? Call on you, per'aps?"

You hurry to the door and throw yourself out into the cool of the night.

"Not to worry!" you call over your shoulder. "I'll be in touch!"

Turn to page 13.

40

"Tails!" you call out as the coin is flipped into the air.

With a soft *plop,* the coin lands in the man's palm and he holds it out for inspection.

Your heart sinks. It's heads.

"Heads, heads, heads," the man chants. "Innit funny that it should be heads or tails? Ain't none of us have tails, only heads. Only tails we have are tales."

You frown at the man. Has he been drinking? You didn't smell any alcohol on him. Of course, the urine stench might have hidden it.

The man pockets the coin, then grins.

"Hide and seek, hide and seek," he sings. "How queer it should be hide and seek, this being Hyde Park and all. Ain't none of us have seeks, only hides."

"Sir," you say evenly. "You are trying my patience. Please tell me what you know."

The man cackles, then nods.

Turn to page 30.

You step into the large red-brick building timidly. It was designed to intimidate — filling a whole city block, tall spires on its corners. It was designed to suggest stability and surveillance. For Alice's sake, you hope they live up to their reputation.

Inside, you're greeted by a long counter behind which several moustached officers stand, dealing with complainants.

One officer takes note of your arrival and beckons you and your husband over.

"What seems to be the issue, sir?" he says in a cool, even tone.

As your husband tells the man about Alice, you take note of another officer at his desk, writing reports. Two other officers huddle in a corner, exchanging gossip about a killer dubbed the Mad Hatter. They are alarmed because there appears to be a new breed of killer who acts in serial, like they are telling a story, but through bodies.

You look away in disgust.

The whole world has gone to hell.

You turn your attention back your husband. Something is agitating him.

"Description?" the officer says in that same, even tone.

"She's a little girl. You need to have officers in Hyde Park right this minute."

The officer doesn't so much as blink.

"Description? Do you have a drawing, or a photograph?"

"A photograph? No I don't have a bloody photograph. She's a little girl. She's seven. Fair hair!"

Reg is practically shouting.

"We *know* where she went missing. *Hyde Park.*

You're supposed to be Scotland Yard! The experts! Now, will you aid us or not?"

A man and a woman a few strides down the counter raise their eyebrows at Reg's outburst, but quickly turn back to their respective officer.

You've always loved Reg for his fiery temperament, but occasionally it does more harm than good. Sometimes you need to gently remind him of this fact.

If you touch your husband's arm to get his attention turn to page 68.

If instead you try to defuse the situation by speaking to the officer directly go to page 23.

Alice is screaming again. It's muffled behind the door, locked as she is in her room, but it still unsettles you.

You're fortunate that no one can hear her out here. You remembered that a friend of the family had an unused cottage by the cliffs of Dover. So you fled here with Alice. But she has gone a bit mad. She is convinced that you are not her mother.

What was in that vial you drank? It seems to have turned the world topsy-turvy.

And while the cottage is on a large parcel of private land, and there's no one to hear Alice's mad screams, Dover itself is a small community and your presence has not gone unnoticed. The neighbours have *definitely* noticed you. You don't know why they should — you're simply going about your business.

Today you're in the kitchen, preparing lunch for Alice and a cup of tea for yourself and pondering the hire of a 'noggin-knocker', which is a speciality of a physician you'd heard rumour of. Through a series of gentle taps, those beset by visions, or taken by delusions can have them dispelled. In a manner of speaking, sense could be knocked back *into* someone.

A sudden pounding on the front door startles you and you drop your cup on the floor, smashing it!

"Open up!" a man bellows. "This is Scotland Yard!"

More pounding.

Oh no.

You run to Alice's room, unlatching it.

Inside, Alice stares, wide-eyed as you rush in and grab her.

"No!" she shouts. "No!"

You head out the back door, clutching a screaming, struggling 7-year old under your arm.

Out of the corner of your eye, you spot men in dark uniforms.

Alice sees them too. "Help! Please help!"

The land is overgrown with tall grass and brambles and the men aren't as adept at clambering over it as you are and you make it to the cliff side with Alice before them.

You aren't sure what your escape plan was here. In the panic you simply wanted to get yourself and Alice away. Turning back to the cottage, you see a tide of men in black uniforms. Why couldn't they simply leave you be?

"C'mon!" you yank on Alice's arm. She's been deliberately dawdling.

But in her struggle, Alice slips!

No!

Alice clutches at the long grass as she slides down over the side of the cliff.

You dive after her, grabbing an errant wrist, but you are now sliding over yourself!

Desperate, your other hand snags an ancient root.

And there you hang.

"M- Mu- Mummy," Alice whispers. "Don't let go!"

Your heart soars. This is the first time Alice has called you Mummy since you returned to her.

"I shan't, my love!"

In what seems forever, the men finally arrive.

"Hand 'er up!" the first man says. With a huge heave, you swing Alice upwards. She screams the whole way, until she is lying on solid ground. The men hustle her away, then two of them haul you up.

But they don't let go of your wrists. Instead, they clap cuffs on them.

"Charles Lutwidge Dodgson," one man intones, "You are under arrest for the murder of that child's mother and father."

You stare at them, confused.

"But *I* am that child's mother. How could I be charged for her murder when I am her?"

The man smirks.

"You make a poor woman," he says. "You put paint on a pig, that does not make it a princess!" The surrounding men all chuckle.

"But I saved her!" you gesture at Alice. "She called me Mummy! Alice, tell them who I am!"

Alice stares at you with hatred.

"You killed my father!" she shouts. "And you killed my mother!"

No. This is impossible.

A stiff wind buffets the cliff side and errant leaves flutter up like playing cards around you.

Could it be true? Could you be Charles Dodgson?

You gaze at the cottage. Dodgson's summer home.

Can't be.

You relax your muscles and step back over the cliff's edge.

"Oy!" one of the men reaches out to grab you, but not, you notice, very hard.

THE END

Stepping off the path onto the grass, you approach the woman. She's well-dressed, with her hair loose under a satin hat.

"Excuse me," you say. "But do you know a Mr. Bodkins?"

The woman frowns. "Bodkins? Why?"

"Do you know him?"

"Are you 'is wife?"

You laugh. "Oh no."

"Never 'eard of him," the woman says, turning away.

"Wait!" You move to follow her, touching her arm, but she spins suddenly.

"Why are you crowding me?"

"I'm not trying to — "

"Get yer own patch 'o pitch," the woman says. She eyes the nearby bobbies warily, who are beginning to take notice of the commotion.

That's when you realize who — or rather *what* — the woman is.

There's only one reason for a solitary lady to be out in the park at night. In your zeal to find your daughter, you'd forgotten.

"Oh goodness," you say, backing away. "You're a prostitute."

The woman's eyes flash in the dark.

"Aye, and what of it?"

You scurry back to the path, underneath the light of the lamp.

"Don't you judge me," the woman growls.

You take refuge under the lamp. First smelly vagrants, and now dirty whores. What is going on? How did you end up here?

"'Oity-toity sow," the woman grumbles. "Sod off.

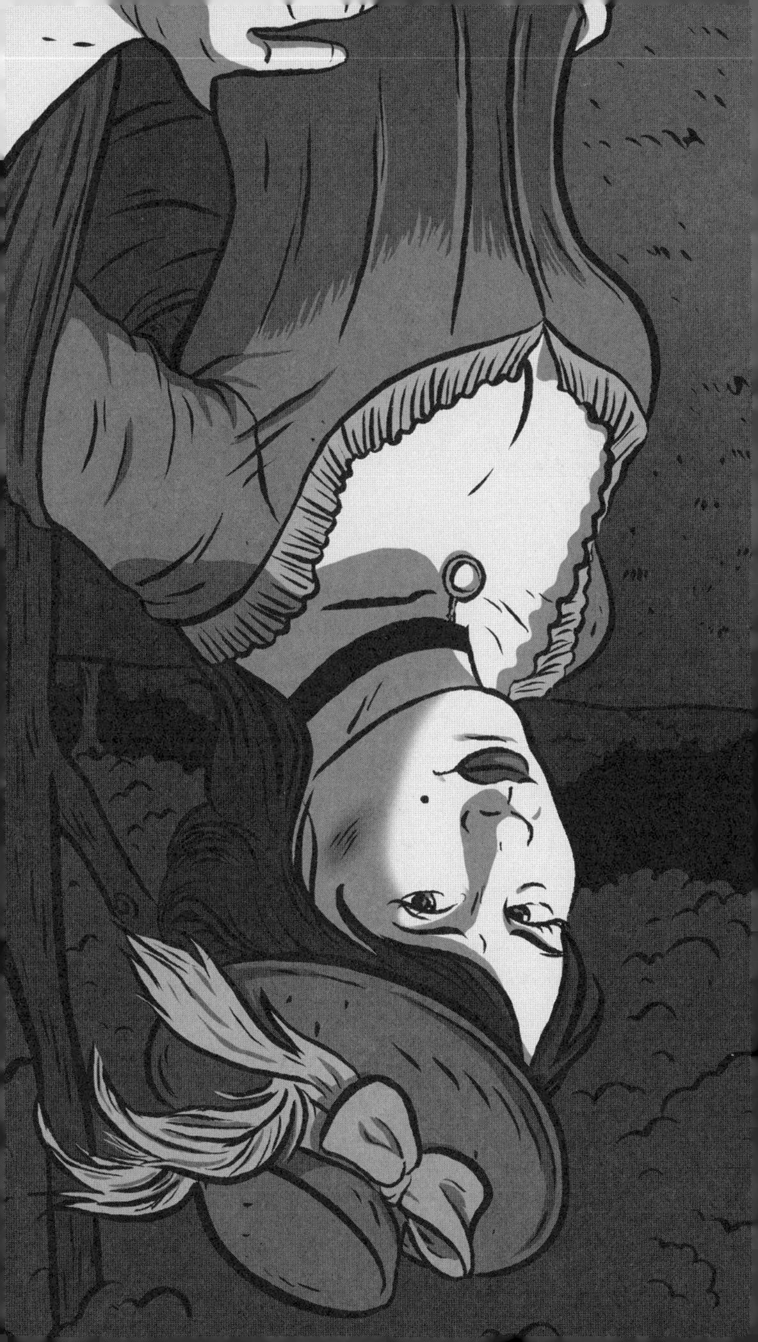

Mark what 'appens when you 'ave 'ard times beset you. When *your* 'usband runs off. When *you've* got mouths to feed at 'ome."

If you decide to speak to the police, turn to page 14.

If you'd rather just go home and see if Alice somehow got home herself, turn to page 71.

But perhaps you were too hard on the woman. Despite her profession, she still might have seen something. If you apologize to her, turn to page 60.

You grab both of Reg's wrists. But he overpowers you, and his hands reach your neck. He's saying something, but it's incoherent. His spittle flecks your face.

As his hands squeeze, the pressure builds in your eyes. Desperate, you throw him into a far wall. Your husband hits, then goes limp, falling awkwardly. You stare for a moment, in shock. Reg's neck is bent. But you don't have time to check him. You run.

Out in the hall, Alice stares at you, eyes wide, as if she doesn't recognize you. As you approach, she faints. Perhaps it is a blessing in disguise as you scoop her up easily in your arms and descend the staircase.

But just as you think you're home free — Maggie appears with a large knife from the kitchen! She takes a terrified swing at you, but you dodge easily, heading for the front door.

Outside, you find the cab that dropped you off earlier still idling, waiting for a fare. What a stroke of luck! But when the driver spots you with Alice, the cigar drops out of his mouth.

"What in the bloody?" he says, and starts shaking his head but you throw your purse at him. It bounces off his chest and into his lap. "I will give you everything!" you roar, a lioness protecting her cub.

From the house, Maggie is screaming. The driver picks up your purse, opening it.

"Well?!" you look back at the house, expecting Maggie and her knife to rush out at any time.

"Get in," the driver says with a curt jerk of his head. "Be quick!"

Turn to page 43.

50

The whole way down to the port, the Hansom Cab cuts through a thick fog. At times, the driver slows the horse down as he attempts to navigate through the clouded streets without incident. Fortunately, by the time you get near the water, the fog has lifted.

The smell of the Thames fills your nostrils as you step out of the cab. In the moonlight, the massive ships glide gently on the water, their distant lamps swaying slowly. But very soon, clouds occlude any moonlight and a steady rain begins to fall.

What luck, you think to yourself. The moment you leave the shelter of the cab, the skies open up.

You look around. Where to start?

But even as you try to make a decision, the insistent rainfall makes it for you. It begins to beat down in sheets.

Soon you'll be soaked.

A warmly lit storefront beckons and you rush over. It's some kind of tea house. You peer at the Chinese letters you don't understand.

Well, you think, Orientals love tea as well. After all, isn't that where orange pekoe tea comes from?

You push the door open and are greeted by a thick wall of smoke that makes your eyes tear up. Despite this, you'd much rather sit in smoke than stay outside in a deluge.

Turn to page 144.

"Can you show me?" you ask the girl.

"Show you what?"

"Where her name is crossed out in the ledger."

Edith walks you over to the book and opens it. Sure enough, the very last name in the book is hers. Alice in black ink, crossed over in red.

You blink back tears.

"Sorry," you say to the girl. "I don't doubt your word, but I had to be sure."

"Of course," Edith nods.

"I have to go now, but would you like to come with me?"

"What?" The girl looks at you with wide eyes. "But there's no escape."

"I have a route," you reassure her.

Edith looks down at her feet. A small farmhouse and silo sit on a table-sized field of green.

"If we're caught, we'll be killed," she says quietly. Then her voice hoarsens. "I mean — how does that even make a lick of sense? We're to be future queens, but if we want to nick out of the palace for a bit of fun, we're to die?"

"You don't believe that tale any more than I do," you say gently.

The girl wrings her hands. "They tell us that wherever we go — they'll send the guards to bring us back."

"You need to trust me. You're only a little girl. They won't send anyone."

The girl licks, then munches on her bottom lip.

"You've been a very brave little girl this entire night," you tell her. "I just need you to be brave one more time." Edith blushes at your compliment, then suddenly throws her arms around you.

"I trust you," she whispers into your apron.

With Edith's help, you make your way back to the cellar where you came in. You know that Sing and his men will have left by now, but there's no way they would let you out with one of their girls in tow, especially their hall monitor.

"Can you swim?" you ask the girl.

Edith nods.

"It's a long way, and we'll have to take breaks. But I saw areas along the way where we can cling to the bricks of the tunnel. It'll be cold and hard going, but we can do this."

However, as you step into the cellar, Sing is there!

"I thought you would have left by now," you clutch him, like an old friend.

And now you see *why* they're still here: a full barrel of wine sits in the belly of the rowboat, alongside several huge wheels of cheese. They have another barrel on the dock, and were figuring out how to make it fit when you burst onto the scene.

"Thick as thieves you are," you smile at the three men. Never have you been so relieved.

Sing shrugs, then smiles at Edith. "Alice?"

"No, this is Edith. Alice is... " You can't finish the sentence.

Sing looks at you with pain in his eyes, then nods.

"Come," he says. "We go."

Six years pass. Edith has grown willowy and lovely and after a period of mourning, even Reg comes around to loving her. Lorina never quite takes to her, but industriously shows the young girl the ropes. For a while it's even the family project to look for Edith's parents, but you learn through dogged investigation

that after a year with no news, Edith was presumed dead. Her family moved, and no contact information was left or forwarded.

So now Edith calls you Mum, and Reg Dad.

But one day as you arrive home, you see the front door open. You wonder if you have a guest. But more likely, someone has been thoughtless. Sighing, you cross into the foyer, but you hear a commotion in the kitchen.

A hooded figure stands over Edith, strangling her on a counter! Edith's eyes flit in your direction but they're glazing over.

Only two weapons are close at hand.

If you whack the figure in the head with a rolling pin, turn to page 163.

If you stab them in the ribs with a cutting knife, go to page 32.

You clutch your purse tightly as you nod at the man. "Actually," you say, "I'm looking for someone."

"Are ye now?" The man withdraws his hand and shoves it in his pants pocket. Or what passes for pockets in what passes for pants. "Just so happens — me too."

"You are?"

"Aye," the man nods. "I've been waiting all day."

What an unsettling response.

You frown, hoping that in the deepening gloom the man can't catch the alarmed expressions that flit across your face. You take a quick glance around. Under a lit streetlamp not far off, you think you see a bobby twirling his truncheon. If need be, you can call for help.

"Sir, would you happen to have seen my daughter? Her name is Alice. She's quite young. She got lost this afternoon."

The man licks his lips. "Mayhap I spied something. A little girl? Hair fair?"

You start at the mention of Alice's blonde hair. You wait for the man to go on, but he only stares at you. Trying not to betray your fraying nerves, you reach into your purse and pull out a shilling.

"No, no," the man mutters. "What do ye take me for? I've not a pot to piss in, but I'm still a gentleman. I'll tell ye what I know — "

He pauses.

" — for a kiss."

What?! Outrageous.

"No," you state. "Impossible."

"Just a tiny peck," the man says, pinching his thumb and index finger together.

"Sir, I am married."

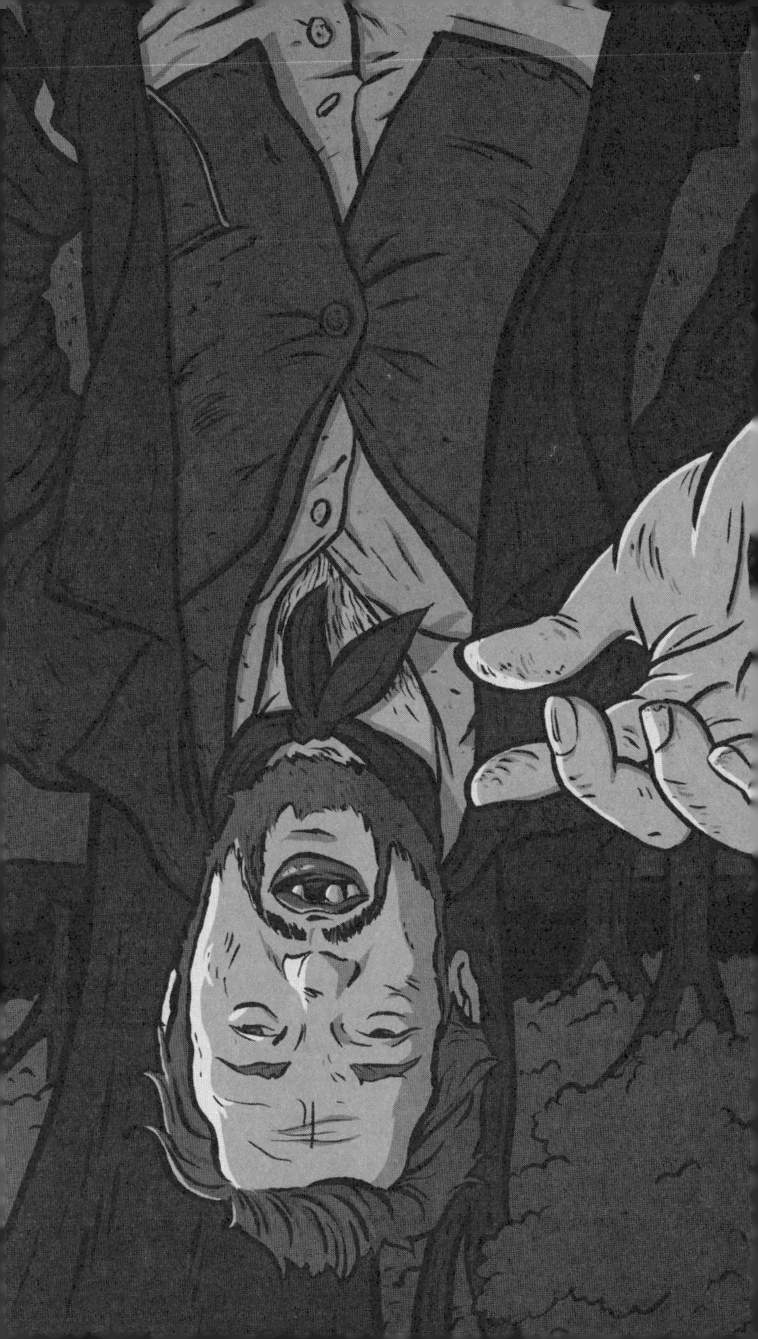

56

The man smiles, reaching into his pocket and pulling out a pocketwatch. It's odd that a vagrant should have such a luxury, but you are reluctant to point that out. He looks up at you, dropping the watch back in his pocket. "I don't have all day."

You shake your head. You are *not* giving this man a kiss.

The man sighs. "Fine, gimme the coin then."

Relieved, you hand the man the shilling. He rubs his fingers over it for a few moments then looks at you. "Call it," he says.

"Call what?"

"Heads or tails."

"Whatever for?"

"If ye call it true, I'll tell ye what I know."

"What if I'm wrong? Do you expect a kiss?"

"No. But I'll take the coin."

"Why don't you just take the coin, and tell me what you know?"

"Now where's the fun in that?"

Daft. The man's daft.

"Sir, please. Just tell me what you know."

But he refuses to be swayed. "Call it," he demands, placing the coin on his thumb.

If you call heads, turn to page 22.

If you call tails, turn to page 40.

If you would rather just kiss the despicable man, and not play his silly game, turn to page 9.

You take a deep breath and bend down by the doorknob.

"Darling," you say, deliberately controlling your tone. "I'm not angry with you."

The sobbing continues.

"But," you say, "Mummy must know — where did Alice get this? Did you give it to her?"

You hold up the matchbox and examine the painting printed on it. A woman with a parasol gazes cheekily at you while the words *The Tiger-Lily* hang in the air. Is that a pub?

"Lory, please," you knock on the door again. "Open up. Come downstairs. Have some pudding with me."

At 15, Lory is all impertinence. It's infuriating. Were you like this with your own parents? They certainly weren't pleased when you married Reg, and left the farm for the big city.

"You'll be cross," Lory's small voice carries through the wood of the door.

"Mummy won't be cross."

"Yes, you will."

"Perhaps. But you'll feel a lot better, in the long run, if you tell me the truth. It'll be better for you, *and* for your sister."

A sudden silence. Then the door opens.

"All right," Lorina says, her face streaked with tears.

Go to page 66.

"Enough of this nonsense," you point a finger at the girls. "Upstairs. Out of those clothes. I want you back down here and ready to work in five minutes!"

Lorina rolls her eyes and sighs audibly while Alice pouts at the floor. They are hoping you might change your mind but you spin on your heels and march to the kitchen.

All morning it's hard, intense work. You set the girls combing through everything for any rips and tears that might need mending while you and Maggie set about cleaning the larger items.

The dirtiest of offenders have been soaking since Saturday in cold water and washing soda, and while Maggie sets about batting them with the dolly stick, you get more hot water from the pots boiling on the range and from the copper in the scullery.

It goes like this for hours. Periodically, you direct the girls to carry outside the heavy basins of dirty water. Alice lifts from one end while Lorina hefts from the other. Their difference in heights leads to a lopsided gait that sloshes water onto the floor as they navigate out the back door and into the yard. Later you'll set them to work mopping it up.

But you are heartened by their efforts. And by noon, you decide to reward them for their hard work. You tell the girls that they've worked enough for one day, and that you'll send for Agnes, their governess. Once she arrives, they can have their day in the park.

Hair tangled and matted against their sweaty foreheads, the girls cheer.

Perhaps you are an easy touch, you chide yourself, but the delighted looks on their faces is worth it.

"Mind you, all you've got for a picnic is some bread and cheese. A little jam. A few biscuits."

But that doesn't seem to deter them. With re-newed energy, the girls bound up the stairs to change. A firm hand, you think, leavened by love.

Turn to page 117.

"Wait!" you follow the woman as she saunters down the path, away from the officers.

"What now?" she snaps.

"I'm ever so sorry," you say, keeping pace with her. "I do apologize. I don't — well, I'm inexperienced in the ways of the world. I meant no offence. You have children at home?"

The woman slows her gait and turns to you, her face softening. Underneath all the paint, you can tell she's actually quite young. The only thing that isn't painted over is a prominent dark mole on her left cheek.

"Aye."

"Who's watching them?"

At this, the woman goes silent.

"I mean," you stammer, "I was merely — "

"Me young'uns are safe enough," the woman says. "I give 'em a drop of Dalby's. Puts 'em right to sleep. A'times I take it meself, after a long night."

You're familiar with Dalby's Calmative. You used to use it yourself with Lorina, but grew suspicious when her pupils remained dilated.

"Actually, I have children myself. That's the reason I'm out here," you confess. You explain about Alice, and ask the woman if she's seen anything.

The woman is quiet for a long time. She shoots glances at you, as if deciding whether she trusts you. Finally she stops underneath a lamp.

"Lissen 'ere. Talk to Lady Plumly."

"*Lady* Plumly?" You snort. "Is she royalty?"

"Royal pain in me arse," the woman grins, "but any'ow, all of Hyde Park falls under 'er sway. She pays the bobbies to leave us alone. And they do, mostly. Any of the goings on 'ere — Plumly'll know."

"And where might I find Lady Plumly?"

"She runs an orphanage on Ravensworth Road."

"An orphanage?"

"Ground floor's the orphanage. Action's all upstairs. Who knows? Yer lass per'aps ended up there."

"Are these orphans treated well?"

The woman hesitates before answering. "Best ye go see for yesself."

Your gut clenches. You don't like the sound of any of this.

"Now off ye go," the woman says, waving you off. "I've said my piece." You watch as the woman removes her shawl and opens her coat to reveal her décolletage.

"Thank you so much," you give the woman a friendly touch on the shoulder before you set off towards the park's exit.

Ravensworth Road isn't so far from here. It's a brisk walk.

Though you are dreadfully exhausted, you feel in your heart that this is the right direction. You worry how this looks — an unaccompanied woman moving through the night — but you hold your head high and very soon you are out of the park.

Turn to page 11.

When the dizzy spell has passed, you find yourself reclining on a chaise lounge and for the first time you take a proper look at the establishment you have entered.

The room is cloaked in velvet. High up on the walls are mirrors, reflecting the fuzzy fabric.

The woman who caught you comes over with a glass of water, which you take gratefully.

"Thank you," you murmur between gulps, "this is very kind of you."

"Not at all," the woman says, with a Russian accent. "My name is Irina Nurmagomedov Blatskya, and you are most welcome here."

You take in other details of the room. A crystal ball is prominently displayed on a round table in the centre of the room. Tarot cards are on another table. Every lamp is covered with lampshades fringed in beads.

"You're a mesmer?" you ask the woman. You've heard a great deal about these so-called spiritualists who perform séances and readings. All of it quite disreputable. Reg dismissed it all as trickery and nonsense.

"I am a psychic medium, yes," Irina says, taking a seat across from you on a three-legged stool.

"So, you can read my mind?" you smile.

The woman, dressed in a dark, flowy dress, shrugs.

"Your mind is not in peril," she says. "Your heart, however, is in pain."

You frown. What does this woman know?

"What do you mean?"

"If you would like — I can give you a reading."

You start to shake your head, but reconsider. If

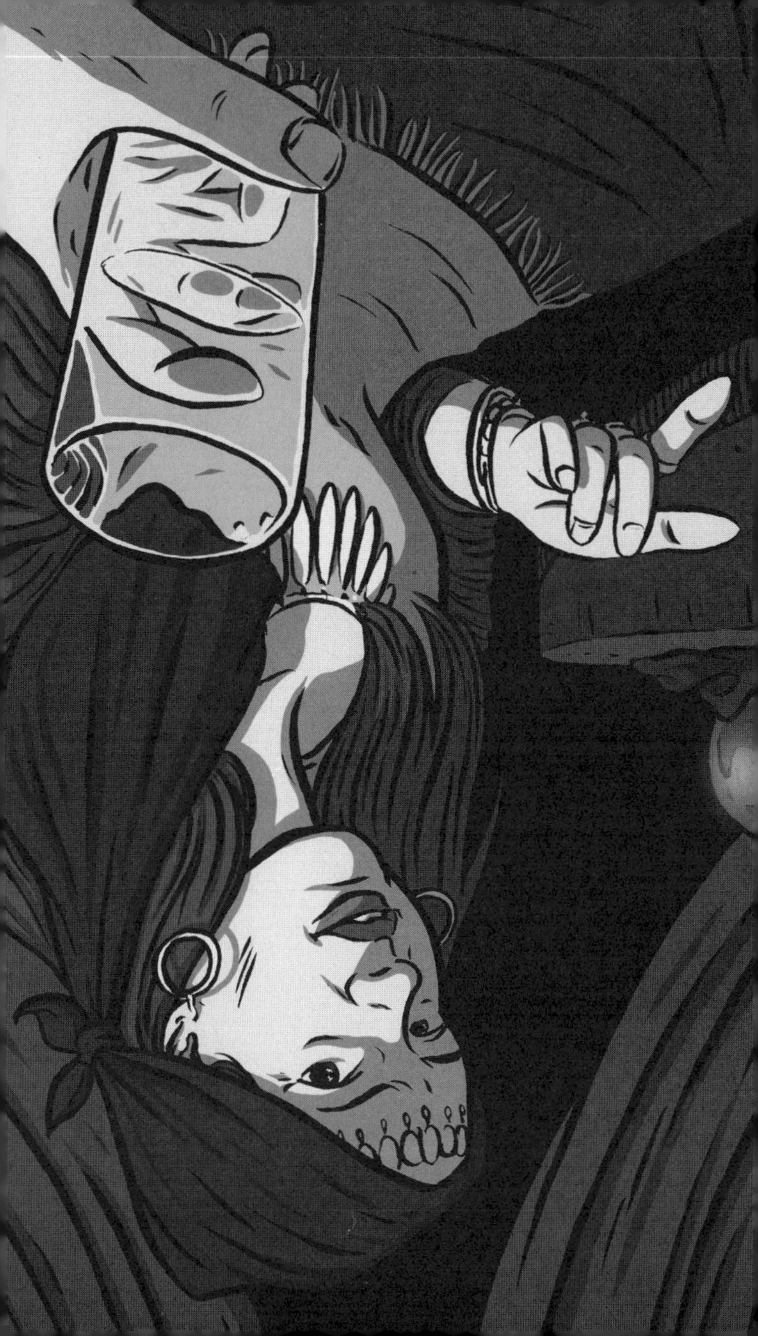

the woman has knowledge about Alice, you must find out. But it might be a confidence trick. Irina knew you were in pain from the way you arrived. After a moment, you shake your head no.

"I'm sorry. I'm appreciative of your hospitality, Madame Irina, but I have no money."

"Free of charge," the woman says, waving a hand covered in gaudy, cheap rings.

You take another gulp of your water, considering this.

"I see a girl," Irina says, gazing up at one of the black mirrors on the wall.

You sharply inhale.

"What do you know?" you say, perhaps more aggressively than you intended.

Irina continues to gaze into the mirror. You look up, searching it yourself.

"A sad girl can look into a mirror and escape her body in this world," Irina murmurs.

"What does that mean? Is Alice — sad?"

"Ah yes," Irina nods. "The girl's name is Alice!"

Wait. That was information you *gave* to her. Deeply skeptical, you're unsure if you're being had. Perhaps this Irina Nurmagomedov Blatskya is merely attempting to gain your confidence for some larger scam.

"I see Alice gazing at another girl. No — not another girl. It's Alice herself. It is her reflection. I see her walking into the mirror."

Into the mirror? How can one walk into a mirror?

"And the girl in the mirror walks out of it. And one day, the girl from the mirror will pass herself off as your daughter. But the real Alice still lives."

You blink your eyes, trying to make sense of the

riddle Irina just proposed.

"You must go," Irina says, meeting your gaze.

"Go? Go where?"

The woman gets up and from some hidden pocket takes out a small change purse, which she hands to you.

"What is *this* for?"

"To help you. Find your daughter," Irina commands.

"Thank you, but where must I start?"

"Every choice we make splits the world entire into two," Irina intones. "A double of you appears in a copy of this world. In that world your double lives her own life, encountering her own weal or woe. And it matters naught what happens to her in that one. What matters is what choices you make in this one. You make the right choice, and you get to live in the world you make."

"But where do I start?"

"With yourself," Irina says, taking you by the arm and escorting you to the door. "Know yourself."

Once back out on the street, you half-think you must have just imagined the last fifteen minutes.

The door locks soundly behind you.

Continue to page 28.

"There's a music hall," Lorina says tentatively.

"Where?"

Lorina sits in the kitchen, eating a bowl of pudding while you try to tease the information out of her.

"On Gryphon, in the East End." Lorina taps the matchbox, which is on the table next to her. "The Tiger-Lily."

"What kind of music hall would let a 7-year-old inside?"

"I'm not *stupid,*" Lorina says, insulted. "Alice waited outside."

You almost slap her.

"When did this happen?"

"In August. When you allowed us out to look for a present for Grammy."

"Why a music hall?"

"I wanted to see a cabaret."

"A cabaret? Why would you want to see such a thing?"

You imagine your daughter in a dark, smoky bar. Half-naked painted ladies serving drinks to leering, lustful men.

"I'd heard about it," Lorina says. "I wanted to see."

You sigh. You'd believed you'd raised your girls to have more refined tastes.

"So Alice stayed outside?"

"Yes. But the show wouldn't start for hours. So I went back outside. And there was this man talking to her."

"A man? What sort of man?"

"I don't know. I'd never met him before."

"Well, was he a policeman? Did he work at the bar? Why was he speaking to your sister?"

"I don't know!" For the first time, Lorina expresses frustration with your line of questioning. But you
can't relent. Not yet.

"How did she get the matchbox, then?"

"I don't know! All I know is that I saw a man in
this enormous top hat talking to Alice."

"What about?"

"I've no idea. She wouldn't say. But Mummy, the
top hat was extraordinarily large."

You lean back in your chair, exhausted. A top hat.
Extraordinarily large. This is not much of a clue. But
it's the only one you have.

Turn to page 77.

68

When you touch Reg's arm, he flinches.

"Leave me be!" he mutters, shaking you off.

Is that a whiff of drink on his breath? You know that he occasionally goes out to a pub with a few of the Oxford dons, but this is the worst possible time for him to be sauced.

"This won't help Alice," you hiss at your husband.

Reg points a finger at the officer. "He needs to know his place!"

"Calm down!"

"I will do as I please!" Reg grouses.

Turn to page 17.

The dinner is a lavish one. Smoked pheasant. March hare. Boiled snowpeas. Yams and custard pie. Two fine bottles of red wine. And a specialty orange sherbet. Reg balked at the expense, but you argued, "This is the man who aided me when no others would."

"Fine, fine," Reg grumbled.

Lorina was unable to attend, but Alice is there. You're uncertain if she remembers Sing, but she betrays no sign if she doesn't.

Ethel comes in and tops up the glasses that require it.

The dinner so far has been cordial. Sing's English hasn't much improved since you met him the first time, but then, you think, neither has your Chinese. And actually, you've discovered in the intervening years that Chinese has two very distinct dialects: Mandarin and Cantonese. You haven't a clue which one Sing speaks, and are too embarrassed to ask.

But your impulsive daughter Alice has no such reservations. After she has another glass of wine, she leans conspiratorially toward Sing and says, "Mr. Sing, is it true what they say about the Chinese and dogs?"

Sing leans forward and frowns.

"What say?"

You have no clue what Alice is about to ask, but you're full of apprehension. In the intervening years since the palace incident you'd made a concerted effort to get books about China, and introduce Alice to Chinese culture. If they ever met again, you wanted Alice to be a well-educated young woman, cultured and refined and tactful. But she has always navigated by her own star.

"That you *eat* them," Alice says, a grimace on her lips. "Do you eat puppies, Mr. Sing?"

Sing gets an enigmatic look on his face, then shrugs, "Dog bite Sing — Sing bite dog."

A shocked expression on Alice's face.

"Is that a yes?"

Sing grins.

"Eat dog once," he says, sticking out his tongue in disgust. "No tasty."

"Ew!" Alice howls, "Mr. Sing!"

Sing laughs out loud and shakes his head. "I push your leg."

"Don't you mean, 'pull your leg,' Mr. Sing?"

"That too," Sing says, tossing back his wine, his face glowing beet red. "No dog," he continues. "But Sing like cat."

Alice frowns, offended. She can't tell if Sing continues his jest.

"*We* have a cat!"

"*Had* cat," Sing says, edge of his lips quirking upwards.

Just then, your cat Dinah appears, ruining the fun. With a measured pounce, she jumps up into Sing's lap and rubs her nose into his neck. The man laughs and digs his knuckle into her cheek. Your pussy purrs with pleasure.

THE END

The moment you step in the door you call out for her.

"Alice!" you bellow through the house.

"Goodness!" Maggie comes out of the kitchen. "Didja find the young miss?"

You shake your head. "She's not home?"

A sharp crease appears between Maggie's eyes. "Nay. I'm sorry, Ma'am."

You gallop up the stairs. Maggie's been in the kitchen all afternoon. Perhaps Alice arrived home and went straight to her room. Maybe she was frightened she'd get in trouble.

At the landing you poke your head into every room. Perhaps Alice is hiding, or playing a game. In Alice's room, you drop to the floor, searching underneath her bed frame. But the only thing under it are some wooden blocks and Dinah, the cat, staring at you with her yellow eyes.

You collapse on the bed, exhausted.

In the tabloids, you'd read about children going astray — drowning in the Thames, crushed by a cart wheel — but you always thought you could protect your children. If you raised them proper they would thrive, grow into beautiful, loving women, who would find wonderful husbands, and one day perhaps make you and Reg into grandparents.

Tears spill onto your cheeks, hotly.

You can barely keep it together.

You become aware that both Maggie and Lorina are standing at the doorway, watching you, uncertain what to say.

Like a sleepwalker, you let your gaze drift over Alice's things on her shelf. Among the dolls, the blocks and the books you see something queer.

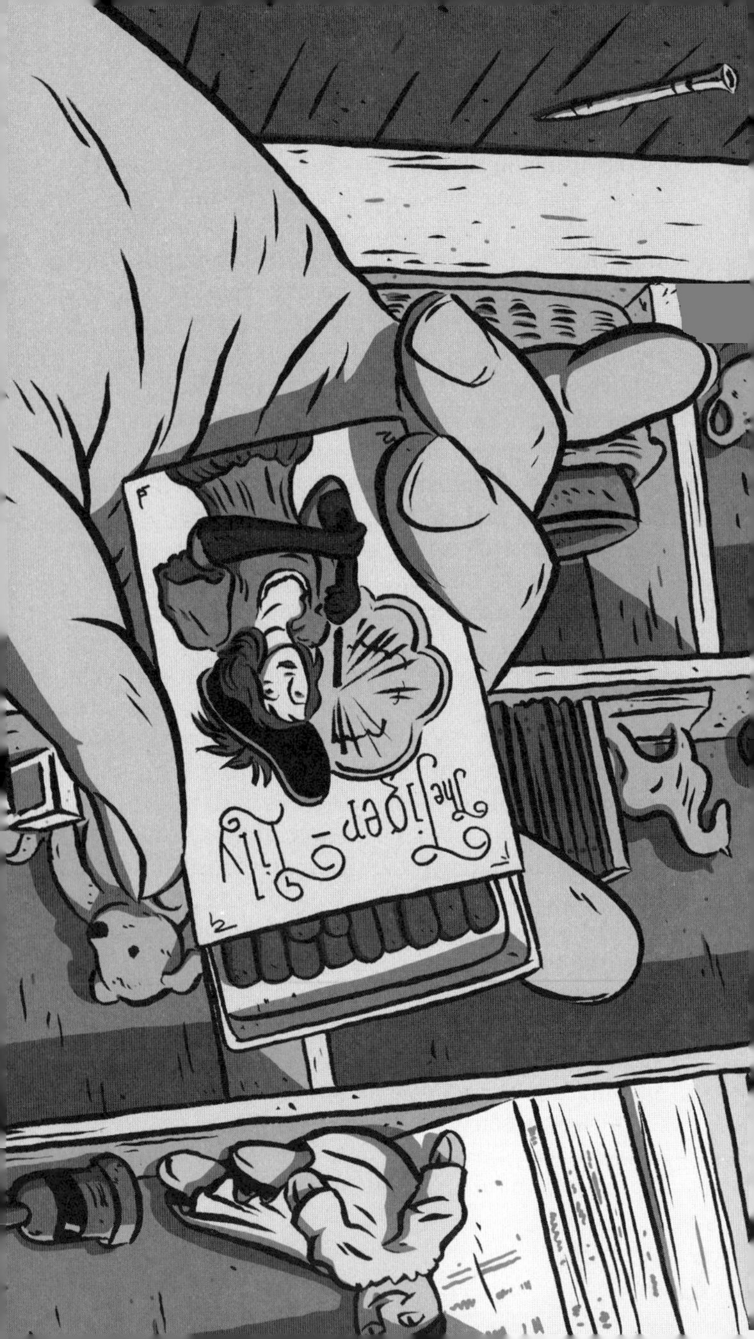
The Tiger-Lily

What *is* that?

You get up and examine it. A matchbox. Where in God's name would Alice have acquired such a thing?

You turn to Lorina, intending to inquire, but she immediately blushes and turns away.

You know that look, and she knows that look, and knows you know.

"What do you know about this?" you say, a low threat in your voice.

Lorina turns and runs to her room, slamming the door.

You chase after her.

"Lorina!"

But the damned girl has locked her door. You and your husband had forbidden the girls from ever locking their doors. While this isn't the first time Lorina has done this, it is the most important.

You hear her sobbing on the other side.

"Where did your sister get this?" you yell. "What do you know?!"

But Lorina continues to sob.

You take a deep breath. You need information and you need Lorina to give it to you.

Do you try honey or vinegar?

If you decide on a sweeter approach, turn to page 57.

If you decide an abrasive approach will get answers more quickly, go to page 8.

Trembling, you get down on your knees. You remove your wool cape. The last thing you want to do is get it soiled.

Giggling, the giant undoes his trousers. You can tell he's already excited under his breeches.

But then the stench hits you and you grimace.

As the giant's fat fingers struggle to untie his underwear, he laughs happily and spittle flecks your cheeks. Then Lady Plumly's perfume mixes with it all and —

That's it.

You can't.

You just —

Involuntarily you gag.

You get up off your knees, hand over your mouth.

You need to leave before you vomit.

You start for the door but the giant moves to block your way.

"You don't go before happy time," he orders. He's struggling to hold his trousers and reach for you at the same time.

"Girl — " Lady Plumly says from behind you, her voice a dark threat, "what game are you playing at? Who are you? Who do you work for?"

Panicked, you run. In the opposite corner is another set of stairs and you rush to them.

"Hey!" the giant yells.

You clamber up the steps and burst out the door at the top, finding yourself on the roof.

The giant is behind you, thudding up the stairs.

You run, but there's nowhere to go.

At the roof edge, you stare down at the cobblestoned alleyway, misted in fog, three storeys below.

There's no other way down from here. You turn

when you hear the man's heavy breathing behind you.

Face red with anger, the giant snorts and wheezes from the chase.

"Why you run?" the man pants. Despite his size, he sounds like he's going to cry.

Several strides behind him, Lady Plumly steps onto the roof.

"What now, Mum?" the giant says.

"She'll just be trouble."

"No, wait — " you say, but the man is already advancing.

"Humphrey Plumly sat on a wall," he chants, "Humphrey Plumly had a great — "

"Stop!" you raise your arms, but the giant is implacable.

He shoves your breast, crushing your breath, and suddenly you feel weightless.

Above you, the clouds part, and for a single second you glimpse the half-moon, like a giant open grin, beatific against the faded celestial bodies behind.

It is the last thing you will ever see.

THE END

Flagging down a Hansom Cab, you direct the driver back to your neighbourhood. Thankfully the fog has begun to dissipate and you make good time.

As the horse trots along the streets, you wonder what you will tell Reg. You wonder if he's even home yet. While his position as Treasurer of Christ Church at Oxford is not an onerous one, it *does* involve many long meetings and long hours.

You needn't have worried. Reg is there, pacing along the front walkway when you arrive home.

"Where the devil have you been?!" he says, charging toward you.

You pay the driver, then turn to your husband.

"Didn't Maggie tell you?"

"Hyde Park, of course. But that was hours ago."

You begin to tell him about your adventures, but he gets into the Hansom Cab you just vacated.

"Reg, what?"

"Get in," he says.

"But where would we be going?"

"Scotland Yard," he says decisively. "Leave it to the experts."

After a moment's hesitation, you join him.

It is a tension-filled ride to the police station. Reg spends most of it not understanding how this could have happened, and how you could have let it happen.

You try to explain, but he's having none of it.

"Let's just leave it to the experts!" he exhorts.

Finally you arrive at the station. A couple bobbies come out the front door as the cab departs.

"Now we'll get to the bottom of this," Reg says, as the two of you enter.

Turn to page 41.

You wrap your wool cape tightly around your shoulders as you step out of the hug of the Hansom Cab's confines.

The horses pull it away and you look up at the hand-painted Tiger-Lily sign, hanging from a steel arm sticking out of the white-brick wall.

It's been years since you've frequented such a place. The last time was before you and Reg were married, and it was by accident. Long ago you'd decided that such places were for degenerates.

You push through the door into the dark, humid interior and a woman in black evening gloves with astonishing cleavage smiles and steps toward you.

"Are ye 'ere for the show?"

Involuntarily, you take a step back.

"Ah — "

"It'll be two quid."

"I'm, well, I'm just here for a drink."

"Still two quid. Show's 'appening whether you drink or no."

You sigh. Reluctantly, you hand over the coin and the woman hands you a ticket.

"Much obliged," she nods. "Sit anywhere ye fancy."

You thread your way among the tables full of raucous patrons. It's so dark that you can't imagine how they'll have a show there later. But as you venture further into the room, you become aware that there is something queer about the people here.

You take a hard look at a woman laughing with a man over steins of beer — is she... a he? Only when she glances back do you turn away.

What else isn't as it appears?

Taking a seat, you do a quiet survey of the rest of

the bar.

In a series of booths along the far wall, you spy a man sitting close to another man, his hand on that man's knee.

Still other men have tattoos lining the length of their forearms. Could he be a pirate? The Tiger-Lily isn't too distant from the docks. Now you imagine gypsies sitting at every table, waiting for a moment of your inattention to strike. You clutch tighter to your purse.

Truly there are no good Christians here in this den of depravity.

You watch a woman on the arm of an African carry their drinks to the stairs and ascend to the upper floor.

Taking deep breaths, you steel yourself.

This is for Alice, you remind yourself. You need not befriend these folks.

Find out about the man in the top hat.

If you go to the bar and ask them, turn to page 229.

If you decide to search the premises yourself, turn to 183.

Fanny Jenkins takes exception to your request, biting her lip.

"The Lady don't see jus' anyone," she says. "Very busy, she is. Who did you say you were again?"

You square your shoulders and lift your nose.

"I have very important matters," you say coolly, "that can only be resolved with the Lady."

A look of uncertainty flashes across Fanny Jenkins' face, then she jerks her thumb at the stairs.

"Go on then," she says. "Top floor. But it's *your* 'ead if the Lady don't wish to see you."

Once you're up the first flight and out of the woman's sight, you allow yourself a moment to take a breath. As you guessed, the second floor is lined on either side with beds. But there are no girls here. You venture up the final flight of steps where you're greeted by a closed door.

Working up your courage, you knock.

You hear heavy steps on the other side.

The door swings open and a huge, pink face appears. Its owner is giant, with a squashed pig nose. One eye is completely white, but the other peers down at you.

"Aye?" he mutters.

"I wish to speak with Lady Plumly please."

"Hump!" a woman calls from inside the room. "Who is it?"

"It's — " The man searches your face, as if looking for a crumb. "I dunno."

"Is it the new girl?"

"It's — a girl."

"Well, let her in then."

The door swings wide and the giant man retreats. Inside is an office lit warmly by lamps. At a far desk a venerable older woman sits. Her face is round and kindly, but her bearing is no-nonsense. Dressed for a station far fancier than her surroundings would suggest, she beckons you forward, and as you step into the lamp light you hear the giant close the door behind you. She reeks of a powerful French perfume.

"Welcome," the woman says, smiling. "Are you here to audition?"

"Audition?" you say, uncertainly.

"Yes."

"For?"

Her eye glinting like a blackbird's, the woman's gaze sharpens. She gets up from behind the desk and goes to the window, the chatelaine of keys hanging on her skirt jingling as she walks.

Carefully, she peers out at the street below. After a moment, she turns back to you, arms folded across her chest.

"To be one of my girls? Isn't that why you're here?"

If you say yes, turn to page 36.

If you tell her the truth, turn to page 120.

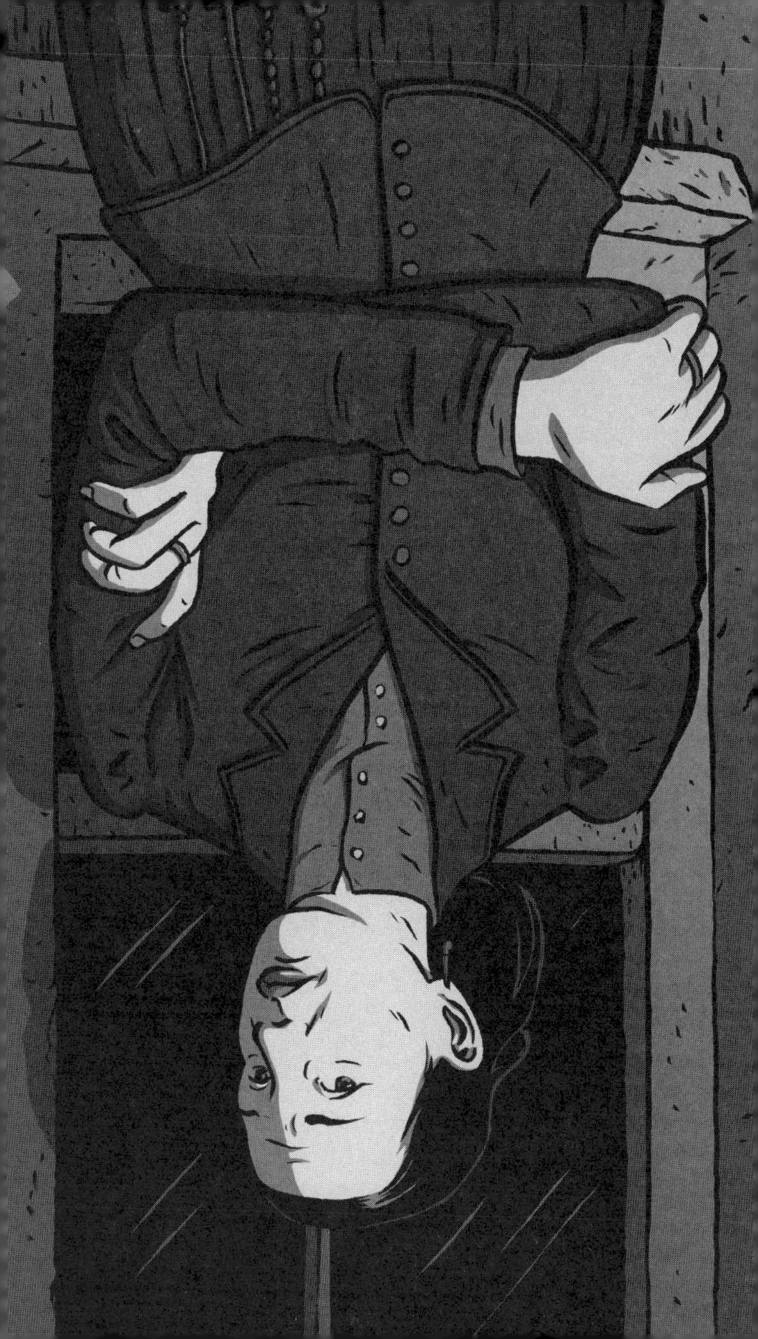

"No," you back away from the giant man. "I'm sorry. I've changed my mind."

The man's nostrils flare and he turns to Lady Plumly.

"Mom!" he whines.

Shocked, you mutter, "You're his mother?! And you wanted me to audition for you? Here? Right in front of you?"

"Get out!" the woman snarls at you.

"Gladly," you spin on your toes and head quickly to the door before she changes her mind.

Turn to page 28.

You grab the grimy wrist of the cutpurse's knife hand, attempting to shake the weapon loose, but he is very strong. He kicks you in the crotch, doubling you over.

This was a bad idea, you realize.

You back away, but the man follows you like a demon through the fog.

He slashes at your chest, but miraculously, the knife edge skips off your corset boning, leaving you unharmed.

Quickly, you spin and run through the darkness.

But the man chases you!

Turn to page 188.

You thank Edith, who has been your constant companion throughout this night.

"I'll thank you not to raise any alarms as I take my leave," you say to her, giving her shoulder a squeeze. She seems to drink in your attention, and gives you a sudden hug.

You wonder how much affection the girls here get. Meagre amounts, you suspect. Little girls need lots of love.

Taking a chance, you wander back down to the cellar, but Sing and his men are gone. Left with few other options, you venture out the servant's entrance. Fortunately, no one gives you a second look. Just a "Farewell, Mary-Ann!" to your back as you tread towards the gate.

Once home, you relate your story to Reg, and at first he is incredulous, but the numerous details of your account soon persuade him, and when a package of your clothing arrives from Mr. Sing, he is convinced.

You mourn Alice for many years. A parent who loses a child never *truly* recovers. When you see little girls in the streets, it touches an open wound in your heart that always brings you to tears.

Eventually, to get your feelings out, you take pen to paper and write a book. An extraordinary narrative detailing your descent into London's underland. A colleague of Reg's has contacts with publishers, and puts you in touch. They are rapt and eager to sign you. A year later, after revisions and edits, *A Daughter Disappeared: Little Girl Lost* appears in the bookstalls.

It is a sensation.

On the cover is a photo of Alice that that same colleague of Reg's — Charles Dodgson — took of her one lazy Sunday afternoon when the days were still sunny. And in fact, a year later, in Alice's honour, Dodgson, under a pseudonym, releases a book detailing *Alice's Adventures in Wonderland,* a fanciful and beautiful fable about where Alice may have disappeared to that awful day. In fact, you much prefer his version to the truth. You love that book because Alice always wakes up from the nightmare and comes home.

In your book, you describe everything just as it happened. From your initial investigations, to the deal with Sing, to your explorations with Edith. Unfortunately, your editor re-writes your arrangement with Sing to portray him as a demonic Shylock offering you a deal "akin to one with the Devil himself." But when you return to Sing's den to offer an apology for the mischaracterization, the man only smiles and says, "Sing no offend. You smoke?"

While the sales of your book are high, the reviews are less stellar. They say that your story about the world inside the palace are "unfounded and irresponsible," and your slanderous lies "close to heresy." Yet for all your accusations, the Crown does not comment.

With your royalties, you start up the Alice Pleasance Liddell Foundation & Concern, a charity that deals seriously with the issue of missing children. Over time, the focus of the foundation evolves from being merely a lobbying arm, to hiring its own investigators.

A few years later, you and Reg celebrate Lorina's betrothal to a barrister who came to work for the foundation, and a few years after that you get to meet your new granddaughter, whom they name Alice.

Then, just as your foundation manages to successfully lobby Parliament to significantly stiffen penalties for those caught trafficking children out of the Port of London, your foundation begins to be approached by survivors from the palace.

Though still in hiding, the Misses Littles, as they've come to call themselves, begin to speak out anonymously about what happened to them.

It was a scheme that encompassed most of London. The Prince sent his men out looking for the young, the pretty and fair-haired. These girls were to be taken quietly, if possible. And when that was not possible, the families were told that the girls were involved in "important royal projects." They were paid a stipend, and if they became unruly — threatened.

A guard who'd left the service, and went into hiding, revealed the criteria. "Aye, they were to be petite. No scars or blemishes. Pretty, fair-haired, with a soft, feminine voice. And a virgin, though young as some of them were, that weren't a problem."

In the palace, they were taught piano, singing, poise. And at fifteen, when the Prince lost interest, the girls were to be "retired". Usually that meant they were married out to the Prince's friends, generals, lieutenants, loyal servants, and the King's Guard. Occasionally, these girls were allowed to go home, but under threat that if any of them revealed the Crown's secrets, that they and their loved ones would all be executed.

When these accounts emerge, you count the years since Alice was taken. But at the eighth and ninth years, when Alice does not appear, you have to accept that she is gone.

You continue to run the foundation, and accu-

mulate victim testimonials and accounts, serving as a resource and sanctuary for escaped girls. You could never prove anything, but your reputation as a defender of the rights of young women grows, and over time you become known as the Florence Nightingale of missing juveniles. If nothing else, Alice's fall has given rise to a foundation full of good people doing good work and saving countless girls from lives of oppression and pain.

Then, in an ironic quirk of fate, you learn from one of the Misses Littles that Alice was indeed alive after you escaped the palace, having given them the pseudonym Dinah. But that after your book came out, the Prince was incensed at the public scrutiny of his private Wonderland. He lined the girls up, and using the cover photo for comparison, uncovered Alice and had her executed.

THE END

Cautiously, you approach the wooded area where the vagrant disappeared. Pausing at the perimeter, you spy a well-worn path through a patch of wild grass, which you follow.

Ugh! A cobweb in your face!

You duck down into a crouch, and wander in. Bushes close in around you. Despite the cool of the evening, you are sweating.

Finally you arrive at a small clearing with a campsite. It's well-hidden in the overgrown bushes.

You scan the area for the vagrant, but don't see him. Possibly he heard you coming and left.

In the murky light, you see an inordinate amount of trash and detritus around the campsite. Random bookshelves, empty picture frames, a rickety chair. Peering closer at the shelves, you see rolled-up maps, empty orange marmalade jars. How in the world did the vagrant manage to haul all this out here?

Then, in the very centre of the camp, you see a hole. In the gloom, you'd assumed it was a fire pit, or a dark rug, but as you approach, you notice a shovel stuck in the grass beside it.

You grow cold. Something bright is in the hole.

Is that Alice's shoe?

"Like I says — " the voice behind you is sharp, as is the reek of urine. "Perhaps she fell into a hole."

You start to turn but the vagrant shoves you. Tripping, you fall into the hole, breath knocked out of you.

In whatever light that's left, you watch the vagrant grab the shovel, raising it high above you.

"Nighty-night now."

THE END

"Miss Jenkins," you say. "Allow me to be perfectly frank with you. I am actually seeking my own daughter, Alice. There was a — a lady in Hyde Park that recommended I come here."

Fanny Jenkins frowns. "A lady?"

"Well, a lady — how shall I put it? A lady of the night?"

"Ah," Fanny says, with a nod of understanding. "You didn't manage to catch 'er name now, did you?"

You shake your head. "No. I'm sorry."

"No matter," the woman says. "Now, when did yer lass go astray?"

You explain to Fanny Jenkins that it would have been earlier that day. Then you start describing Alice but the woman puts a grimy paw up, stopping you.

"No need to blather on. Pity is — the last child turned in was a fortnight past. We's ain't seen your Alice."

You scan the girls again, hoping that Fanny Jenkins is mistaken somehow, but the woman would have no reason to mislead you.

"Good luck to you and yours," the woman starts walking you to the door. "And perchance, if you see that 'lady' in Hyde Park — be a dear an' pass on a message to 'er, will you?"

"Of course," you nod.

"Tell 'er to shut 'er gob."

If you leave quietly, turn to page 13.

If instead you stand your ground and insist again on seeing Lady Plumly, turn to page 116.

When you wake up, there are two blurry figures standing between the screens, shaking hands.

For a moment, you're unsure where you are. Then you remember.

"Sang-Song — tsieh tsieh," one man says to the other, then walks out the front door.

The remaining man walks over to you. It's Sing.

"Good," he says. "You wake."

"How long did I sleep?" you drop your legs to the floor and stretch.

"Not long. But now we go."

"I heard that other man call you *Sang-Song*. Have I been pronouncing your name incorrectly?"

Sing shakes his head.

"Sing name is Sing Sang-Song. In China, you say family name firstly. Sang-Song is name. Sing is last name."

There must be something mispronounced or lost in translation. To you, Sing Sang-Song seems a preposterous name, but it's most likely pronounced Singh Tsang Soong, or something similar.

The Chinese woman reappears and leads you back behind the changing screen, but you don't find your clothes there — instead, you find those of a maid.

"What's this?"

"You wear," the woman instructs.

"Yes, I know. But why?"

"Disguise."

"But where are we going that I would need such a disguise?"

The woman just smiles and shakes her head, then disappears.

Sighing, you strip off the robe and don the maid's blouse and apron.

When you step out from behind the screen, Sing is there, beckoning to you. He guides you through the opium den, past numerous slumbering individuals into another room. There is an altar of some sort. A high table with fruits and vegetables arrayed on it in bowls, along with plates of dried fish and a bottle of wine. And in the centre of the table is an ordinary tin can, filled with rice and sticks of incense. Sing lights two candles, then takes a few sticks of incense and lights them.

He stands, a few strides from the table, with eyes closed, holding the sticks before him.

He looks deep in thought.

You want to ask him what this is all about, but are afraid to interrupt.

Then he makes a bowing motion three times with the incense, and walks forward to stick it in the rice can. When that's done, he returns to where he was standing and claps his hands three times. Then he looks at you, and nods, as if to say, "Your turn."

"What is this all supposed to be about?"

"We ask for luck."

"Mr. Sing, I am a Christian. We don't believe in luck. We believe in God."

"We ask ancestor. You no ancestor?"

You are about to argue with Sing when the Chinese woman sticks her head in the doorway and says something to him, before disappearing.

"Come. We go," Sing says, pointing toward another doorway.

"Wait!" you say, and decide to go through with the lucky ritual after all.

You feel slightly foolish as you stand with the incense sticks streaming their grey smoke. You're not certain what you should be thinking. But in that moment, you simply ask God for luck in getting your daughter back home safely.

Sing leads you out the back of the building into an alleyway. It's still foggy outside, but thankfully the rain has halted. You move quietly down various laneways and sidestreets. While you are completely lost, Sing walks with the sure-footedness of a cat in its home territory.

Finally you arrive at a minor dock, where a small rowboat is moored. In the moonlight you can see two men already onboard at the bow and stern. Sing whispers something to them in Chinese and they whisper back.

Sing helps you aboard and then climbs in himself. Silently, the oarsmen kick off and row you out into the Thames river. At this time of the night, traffic is sparse, but you do run across the occasional rowboat or barge, with lamps ablaze. The oarsmen do their best to steer clear and stay in the shadows.

In the darkness, you hear a splash.

"Why would anyone be dumping garbage at this time of night?" you wonder aloud.

Sing shakes his head. "No garbage," he says, then taps his chest. "Is body."

You continue on for a while, then Sing signals for the men to pull up to a small dock, with stairs leading up to the street.

"Are we here?" you ask.

"No," he says, clambering onto shore. "You wait. Ten minute."

"Wait, Mr. Sing — " You start to protest, but the man is gone.

The oarsmen have already pulled out their matchboxes and lit cigarettes. They chat amiably over your head about something or another. You wonder how long it would take you to learn Chinese. You suppose it could be done. If you put your mind to something, anything is possible. At least that's what you tell your daughters.

Big Ben chimes four in the morning when Sing returns.

He climbs into the boat, and you set off again. Sing lights a match to see, opening his book of favours. He flips to a name and scratches it out.

"Mr. Sing, did you just call in a favour? On my behalf?"

Sing smiles.

"I help him. He help me. I help you. Everyone help."

You travel on the water for another half hour when Sing halts the oarsmen. They slow near a massively overgrown part of the wall bordering the Thames. Vines cover a giant swath, its leaves dipping into the water.

Sing stands precariously on the boat, bracing his foot against the gunwale, patting at the leaves. Finally, he pulls aside some of the greenery, revealing a dark hole, black as pitch.

"What is that?" you ask, astonished.

"Tunnel," Sing says, then instructs the oarsmen in Chinese.

When they steer you into the tunnel, everyone is forced to bend down. Though the growth is pliable, the vines threaten to trap the boat, and there is much shoving and levering with a spare oar on Sing's part. Eventually you wrench through and the men paddle down a small secret tunnel, lined with brick, that twists like a serpent.

Sing lights a lantern and they mount it on the short front mast. It feels like this tunnel has gone unused for hundreds of years. The walls, covered in algae, close in around you, making you feel simultaneously safe and claustrophobic.

Finally the boat reaches a small dock. It too, is covered in algae, and when the men step onto it to tie up the boat, they have to watch their footing lest they slip.

Sing gets out, helps you ashore, then produces a pocketwatch. He glances at it, then tosses it to an oarsmen with muttered instructions.

Turning to you, he holds up four fingers. "They wait four hour. Then go."

"Wait four hours? But for what?"

"You find Alice."

"But Mr. Sing. I don't even know where we are."

"This is palace."

"*Buckingham* Palace? Are you mad?"

Turn to page 112.

"What about you?" you whisper to Edith as you throw your leg over the well's low wall. "Where will you hide?"

"Wait!" she cries. "Don't go in there."

But it's too late. Because there was no winch, rope or bucket, you'd assumed that the low, pretty well was altogether decorative, meant to add charm to a garden. But as your feet struggle to find a bottom, you realize this is something else!

"What is — ?" You hang from the edge, one forearm over the wall, but you can feel your weight pulling you down. Already the strain on your arm is immense. Edith grabs your wrist, struggling to pull you out, but in moments you'll have to let go.

"Help!" you scream hoarsely. "Help!"

Your only hope is that the guards will hear you and pull you out. Anything is better than falling into this well of unknown depths. What's more — a terrible stench has crawled up from the bottom like a living thing and is now curling its way into your nostrils.

You slip again, and now are hanging by your fingertips.

"Girl!" a guard barks. You see light on the lip of the well. "What are you doing?"

Edith's face appears, she tries to grasp you, but her tiny hands are too small. Then she's yanked away, and the mask of a guard appears like a strange moon.

"Who's this?" he yells. "Mary-Ann, is that you?"

But just as his arms appear over the lip, you fall!

It is a long fall.

And when you hit, something in your body snaps below you. The pain is so sudden and overwhelming that you don't even remember passing out.

It's the pain that rouses you. You wake up with your heart beating, chest heaving like you'd been sprinting for your life.

You're sheathed in darkness, but high above you is a tiny sphere of light.

At first you thought it was the moon, but your eyes eventually focus and it coalesces into a small circle of sky.

You paw around underneath you. Whatever's under you must be responsible for the immense stench that threatens to make you vomit. But after you've touched the slime of rotting skin, you don't want to know.

Above you, the masks of two guards appear over the edge.

"Oy!" one cries. "Anyone alive down there?"

"Help!" a weak yell escapes your lips.

"Who are you?" his voice echoes its way down to you. "Are you a spy?"

"I'm no spy."

"I reckoned you were Mary-Ann, but the *real* Mary-Ann's in the kitchen. So who are *you?*"

"I'm looking for my daughter."

"Oh, you're one of them, are you?"

"Is she here?"

"What's your lass' name?" the other guard asks.

"Alice."

"Alice?" A moment of silence, then, "Aye, she's here. She's an unruly one, she is."

"Can I- can I see her?"

The guard laughs. "She's down there with you!"

Then the masks disappear and as you scream up at them, a wooden well cover is dragged over the circle of light leaving you in complete darkness.

The next few moments are confusing to you. You beat the walls, and you beat yourself against the walls. You're not sure which, or if it matters.

Eventually, however, your mind grasps onto the only thing that can reunite you with your daughter — the knife.

You retrieve Sing's knife from your apron's pocket and slit your own throat.

If Alice has fled to the Maker's embrace, then you shan't hesitate to follow.

THE END

You pace about the house, drinking endless cups of tea.

Where is he?

While your husband's position as Treasurer of Christ Church at Oxford is not an onerous one, it does involve many long meetings and long hours.

Finally, you take to standing by the front door. As you gaze into the clouding sky, you think that perhaps it was a mistake to wait for your husband. Every moment you're standing in your front garden is a moment you could be looking for Alice.

Then a Hansom cab pulls up.

As Reg steps out, you run to him.

He drops his bag, surprised. But one look at your face has him clutching your shoulders.

"What is it? What's happened?"

You start to cry. It all comes spilling out.

Reg's face passes through a constellation of expressions. From bewilderment, to surprise, to anger, to incredulity.

"Oi!" the driver of the cab has dismounted and stands with his gloved hand out. "Are ye gonnae pay or what?"

Reg tosses his bag back in the cab and jerks his head at the seats.

"Get in," he says to you.

"But where would we be going?"

"Scotland Yard," he says decisively. "Leave it to the experts."

After a moment's hesitation, you climb in.

"Change of plans!" Reg tells the driver. "We're rerouting to the Met, at Whitehall Place."

It is a tension-filled ride to the police station. Reg spends most of it not understanding how this could have happened, and how you could have let it happen.

You try to explain, but he's having none of it.

"Let's just leave it to the experts!" he exhorts, doing his best to light his pipe.

Finally you arrive at the station. A couple bobbies emerge from the massive front doors as the cab departs.

"Now we'll get to the bottom of this," Reg says, as the two of you enter.

Turn to page 41.

100

Opening the stiff leather portfolio, you uncover a trove of photographs.

It's beautiful work, and you recognize many famous faces. As a fan of poetry, you are delighted to discover the bearded face of Alfred Lord Tennyson.

Some of the photographs are inscribed on the bottom right hand corner.

"From the artist," one reads, "a drawing in light, Charles Dodgson."

You pore through more photographs. Actors. Musicians. Politicians. Many of them you don't even recognize. Finally, nearing the end of the stack, you find various photographs of little girls. They wear myriad costumes, masquerading as sirens from Greek myths. You search the faces for Alice and Lorina.

Finally you find them, posing with a grand chair, in simple shift dresses.

You flip through more photographs and frown.

More young girls. Some tasteful nudes, but others where artistic merit wears thin.

Then you hear a knock.

Startled, you shut the portfolio, putting everything back the way you found it.

You look to the doorway.

There is no one there.

The knock comes again.

But it comes not from the doorway, but from inside the steamer trunk!

Turn to page 218.

In the end, you decide to decline Mr. Sing's kind offer. His trustworthiness has yet to be proven, and you're uncertain he can really help you. After all, he is a foreigner, and what do the people of China really know about England?

"No thank you, Mr. Sing," you say genially. "I must decline."

Sing nods, then again offers you a smoke.

You laugh. "Just my clothes, if you please."

They're returned to you, merely damp now instead of sodden.

When you exit the smokehouse, you find that not only has the rain stopped, but the fog has lifted as well.

Back home, Reg is waiting for you. Immediately, he takes you to Scotland Yard to file a missing persons report. They manage to spare a few officers, and at dawn, you all go back to Hyde Park and give it a thorough search. But no Alice, and no leads.

You are gutted, but you carry on. For months after, every weekend, the whole family searches for Alice. In your writing desk, you have a comprehensive map of London, and section by section you take your family out on excursions to new places, increasing your search area.

In the newspaper, you clip out articles on other children who have gone missing.

Over the next several years, Lorina comes of age and begins accepting and declining gentlemen callers. Reg takes to drink. The two of you consider having another child, but in the end the both of you agree that you don't have the heart for it. The disappearance of Alice is a mystery that surrounds your life like a fog. It's a nightmare you fell into from which you never awoke.

Then, one evening, while you are sitting by the fire, darning some socks, there is a gentle knock on the door.

You peer through the window and it's a girl in her late teens with a simple bag.

"Hello?" you say, opening the door a crack. "Can I help you?"

"Mum?" the girl says, close to tears. "It's me — Alice."

"What?!" Is it really her? She looks similar. But it'd been so long. Nevertheless, your arms open automatically and you embrace your daughter.

"Reg!" you call over your shoulder into the house. "It's Alice!"

Your husband comes running into the foyer and there is a very tearful family reunion.

Lorina is off tonight in the country with a friend and her aunt, but you will send word in the morning.

You bring Alice into the parlour by the fireplace, and sit her down, asking her what happened all those years ago.

"Well," she says, shrugging her thin coat off. "I was very young at the time. Parts of my memory are missing. If I'm to be honest, much of it is in a fog. The last few years I'd been working in a lace factory. But I'm very tired. I'm certain more of my memory will come back once I've seen my room."

Reg frowns. You know that look. He wants to know more. And you do too, but you feel like you are walking on eggshells. You are afraid that if you push too hard, that Alice will disappear again.

"Your room! Of course," Reg says, getting up, "You remember the way, don't you?"

Alice's lip quirks. "Are you testing me, Daddy?"

The girl gets up, and moves quickly out into the hall, heading to the staircase. It's Reg and yourself that have to hurry to keep up.

At her room, Alice opens the door.

You'd never touched it. Over the years, you'd left it as it was. You'd instructed Maggie never to go inside. Even after Maggie left, you'd left it alone.

Alice goes over to the window and opens it.

"It's a trifle musty in here," she complains.

In truth, it gratifies you to see her so at home.

"I'm very tired," Alice says, "and the two of you have been very patient with me. And being here, being in my room, seeing you both has brought back such a torrent of memories. And in the morning I'll try to unearth them all for you, if you will both extend me just a little more patience."

You look at your tall, beautiful daughter, speaking so eloquently.

Of course you can do her that courtesy. Of course you can.

Hours later, lying beside Reg, you can tell something's bothering him. He's tense. His body is as taut as an overwound watch.

"I can't shake the feeling that something is amiss," he whispers to you.

You're turned into his body the way a koala hugs a tree.

"But it *could* be her, couldn't it?"

"She's the right age. Hair's correct. Seems to know her way around the house. Could be her, certainly."

But you know what Reg means. When you've loved a child into being, you know them intimately.

104

The tilt of a body. The cast of a head. Their smell.

Something's off.

You need more information from this girl.

If she's *not* Alice, she may know where the real Alice is.

Do you confront 'Alice' right now?
Turn to page 27.

If you wait till morning, go to sleep on page 170.

"You're quite right," you say, patting the girl on the shoulder as you head back upstairs. "There's nothing down there. It's all junk."

Back in the Dreamery, you ease the palace model back into place, and Edith is visibly relieved, though a little curious.

"What else did you see down there?"

"Musty boxes," you say breezily. "Old bottles."

If you haven't yet investigated the Secret Garden, go to page 158.

If you haven't yet checked out the Performatory, turn to page 106.

But if you've seen everything, and want to consider your next move, turn to page 180.

Edith leads you by the hand through a series of hallways and tiny foyers, finally entering into a theatre by a side door. You sidle in amongst theatre seats towards a central aisle.

"Why would girls be here, at night?" you whisper to Edith.

"Oft times they are building sets, or rehearsing. Deadlines can come down from on high at a whim."

"What sort of deadlines?"

"For instance, one day the Prince wanted to see a staging of Don Quixote the next evening. The girls were working all night, the next morning, and right up until curtain on that request."

"The *girls* are building the sets? Are there no masons? Carpenters?"

"The Prince prefers it when we do it."

As you approach the stage, the girl runs off to the side.

"Edith?"

"I shan't be long!" she calls over her shoulder as she ducks behind a curtain.

For a moment you worry that the girl is off to get guards, but all of a sudden an entire array of lamps at the base of the stage burst alive and you can see the set in all its glory.

"The gas lighting is new!" Edith says proudly. "They were installed last summer!"

You stare, amazed at the set before you; or rather — *sets*. Along with a bare stage there is a multi-storey series of sets behind it, depicting parlours, bedrooms, kitchens and ballrooms. Some rooms even depict the outdoors, with the walls painted a sky blue.

You clamber onto the stage and follow the giddy little girl as she leads you on into a dining room set.

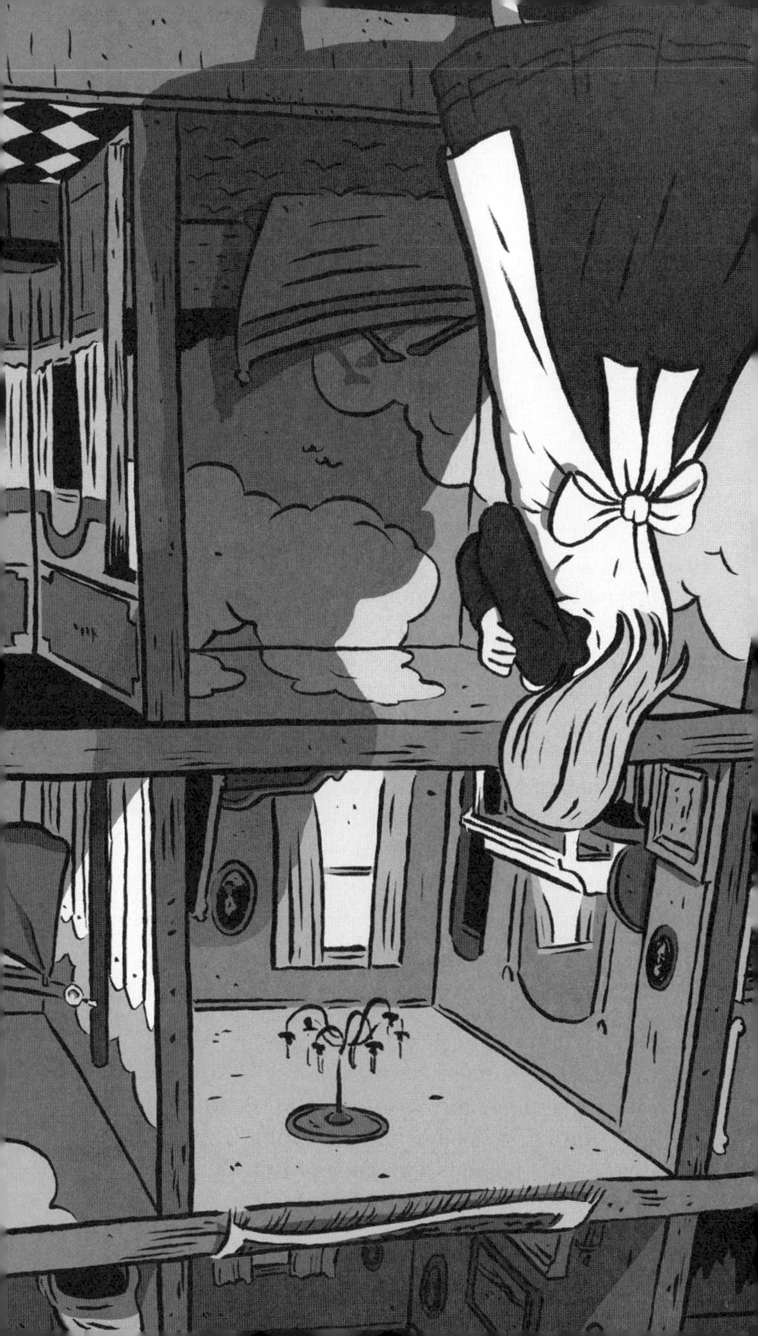

"All our classes take place here," she explains. "New girls watch instructional plays, so they know what's expected of them." She points at the dishware, and the careful arrangements of cutlery. "It's important to know how a table should be properly set."

Then Edith opens a door, and takes you one room deeper into the set. This one depicts an elegant bedroom.

"Hold on," you say, confused. "Why is *this* set here? Surely no one in the audience can see it."

Edith smiles impishly, then goes to a large mirror on the wall. She reaches behind its ornate frame, and opens it like a door, revealing a small carpeted hallway that runs along the length of the sets.

"Go on," she urges. "Go ahead."

Amazed, you step past the looking glass and into the tiny hallway. Edith follows and shuts the mirror behind her. Ahead, the thin hallway is illuminated by holes cut periodically in the walls. As you reach each one, you peek through and see a different set. Tea party in a garden. Swimming hole. Pastry shop. There are dozens.

You gaze down the hallway and imagine how deep the sets must extend. They must go back as far as the theatre seats extend out the front!

"So you perform for the Prince, who scurries in here and watches through the spy-holes," you mutter.

"Yes, that's right."

"But you know he's watching. So why does he need to hide?"

"He prefers it."

You are getting mightily sick of the Prince and his preferences.

As you move from spy-hole to spy-hole, you notice something queer.

"Edith — can I get into that set there?"

The girl nods, finds a small latch along the wall and opens up another door into the room. This one depicts an outdoor camp, and as Edith closes the door behind you, you see that it's actually part of the trunk of a tree, and that the spy-hole is hidden cleverly in a knot in one of the branches.

Whereas when you first entered the sets, everything was life-sized, the deeper you go, the smaller everything gets. Or at least that's how it appears to you. Even the ceiling is lower.

You move through a clump of bushes and enter another set, this one depicting a first-class rail car. You lift up a teacup and examine it. Yes — much smaller. You even try to sit in one of the booths, but can hardly fit your rump in.

Heading to the end of the car, you slide open the door and find yourself in a library. You pull a book off the shelf and it fits in the palm of your hand easily.

"Everything's getting smaller."

"Exactly," Edith grins. You look uneasily at the girl. A grin has been fixed on her face for some time now.

"What's so pleasing to you, Edith?"

"I'm sorry?"

"You've been grinning like a cat who's found spilt milk for the last five minutes. What's so pleasing?"

"Oh," the grin fades. "The Prince likes it when we smile. It's habit, I suppose."

"Why is everything getting smaller the further in we go?"

"It's sized to change as we change."

"You mean — as you grow up?"

The girl nods.

You look at the doorway to the next set and it's so small you are uncertain you can even fit. So you turn and start back.

When you walk through the tea party set, Edith grabs a wreath of white flowers and puts it on her head.

"All the misses littles wear flowers in their hair!" she chants.

"Is that another one of the Prince's preferences?" you ask, trying unsuccessfully to keep the contempt out of your voice. "Like the grinning?"

"When you smile," Edith says, the grin reappearing, "it's so bright, it's like no one can see anything else."

You pass into a fancy dress shop and Edith stops by a table laden with accessories. "The flowers are merely the first step," she says.

"The first step of what?"

"Everyone gets flowers when they first arrive," the girl says dismissively. "That's what all the pawns get. Later, you graduate to white gloves. Then a fan. Handkerchief comes next, then your necklace, and corset."

"To what end?"

"A white garter. A red rose. Then a golden tiara. And then you are the Queen to a kingdom of your own!" The girl says this in the cadence of a chant, as if it's something she's repeated many times over.

You step out of the last set and back onto the bare stage, turning to the girl.

"Edith, how long have you been here?"

"This'll be my third year, and my sixth month as hall monitor."

"How did you end up here? Did you have a life before this?"

The grin reappears on her face.

"It was folly," she says. "But I'm happy to be here now. This is an unprecedented opportunity for us low-class girls to become queens."

"What folly?"

"I sought sweets. And the Queen's men brought me here."

"Have you tried to leave? To get home?"

The grin.

"This is a great opportunity," Edith repeats.

"Has your mother or father come looking for you?"

Edith falls silent, still grinning.

Then you see why.

The grin holds back tears like a dam.

You look away and take a deep breath, telling Edith that you'd like to look for Alice somewhere else now.

If you haven't looked in the Secret Garden yet, go to page 158.

If you haven't yet investigated the Dreamery, go to 124.

If you've already been to both, consider your next move on page 180.

Leaving the dock behind, you and Sing advance up a small set of steps to a rusted gate which is secured by a padlock. From his tunic, the man pulls out a slim, metal bar, which he uses to wrench the ancient padlock open.

Without a lamp to navigate by, Sing lights match after match as you move through cobwebbed tunnels.

Finally, you reach another gate, likewise secured by a rusty padlock, which Sing cracks open. It leads to a cold, musty cellar. You see casks of wine and wheels of cheese, covered in dust. Sing spots some stairs, then urges you ahead.

You're halfway up the steps when you realize he's not following you.

"Mr. Sing," you whisper, "why are you dawdling?"

He waves you ahead. "You go. I stay."

"You're not coming? Surely you're joking."

You're rather vexed by this. All along you'd assumed Sing would accompany you in getting Alice back. Isn't that why you hired him?

The man points at your outfit. "Disguise." Then he points at his face, his almond eyes, high cheekbones. "No disguise."

You sigh. He's right. Quite reasonably there would be no cause for a Chinaman to be in the palace, even as a servant. You'll have to find Alice alone.

"You're certain she's here?"

"No certain."

"Then why are we here?"

"We try."

"And if she's not here?"

"We try again tomorrow. Other palace."

"Another palace?"

"Other place," he corrects himself.

In the light of Sing's match, you can see tiny shadows moving at the base of walls. Mice, probably. Sing follows your gaze and smiles at the little creatures. He slips a small knife out of one of his myriad pockets and digs into the hard wax covering of a wheel of cheese, digging out a sizable chunk. Then he tosses it to the mice.

They scatter, but a moment later, are devouring it.

"Well that's foolish," you tell him. "You could have eaten that cheese yourself."

The man taps his belly and shakes his head. "Sing eat cheese, Sing sick." Then he wipes the knife on his sleeve and hands it to you, handle first.

"Four hour," he says.

You take the knife and smile grimly. You'd been dawdling yourself. You drop the knife into your front apron pocket and turn without another word, advancing up the stairs.

At the top, a door leads to a larger pantry, which is less dusty, and has seen more use. Light spills in from a hallway, and you creep towards it.

This is insanity, you think. Sheer insanity. Why would Alice be here? Whatever gave Sing the merest notion that she might be here? You'd never even clapped eyes on the Queen.

Cast-iron wall sconces hold paraffin oil lamps at periodic intervals. But it is still so dark. You almost want to wait for daylight to search, but that would be untenable. The oarsmen would be gone by then.

A voice from behind you.

"Mary-Ann, is that you?"

You turn. Down the hall is a little girl.

You catch your breath; for a split-second you

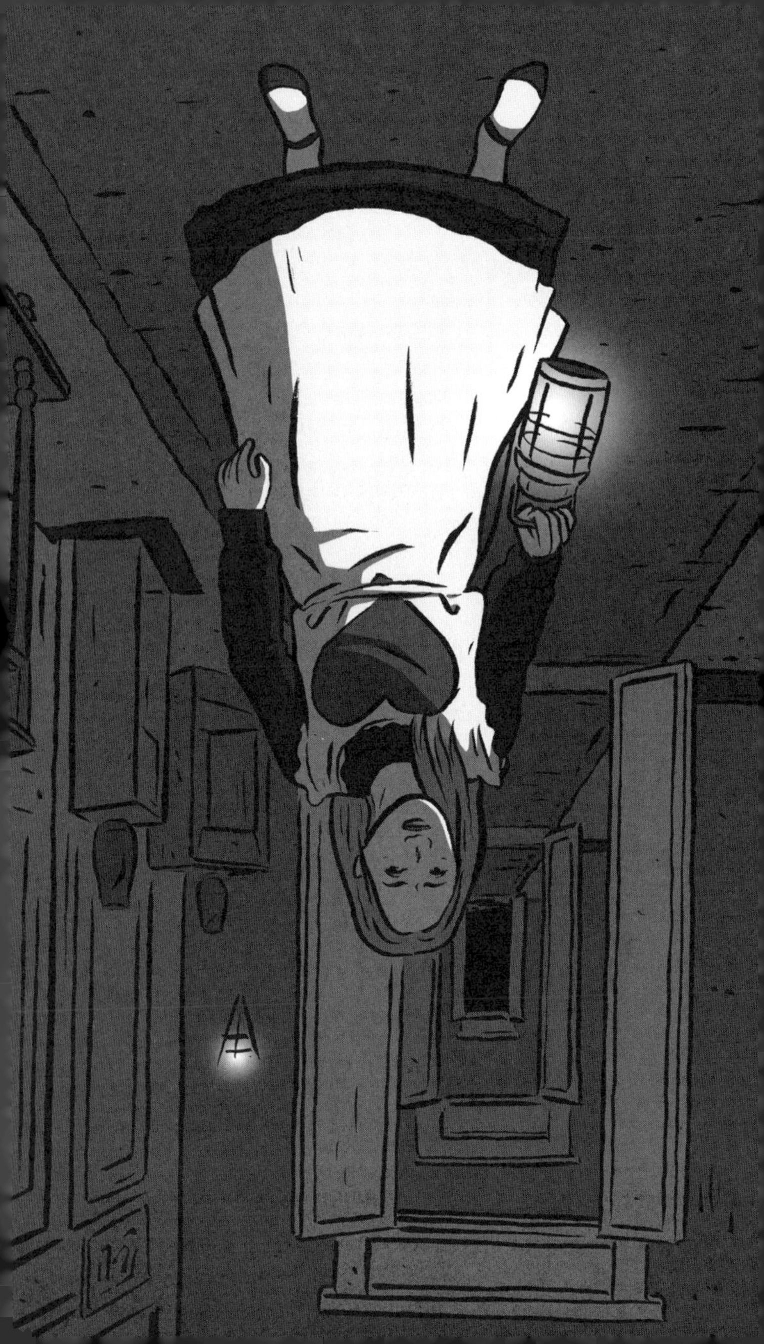

thought it *was* Alice.

Long blonde hair. Pretty nightgown. Slippers. The girl carries a small lantern.

"Mary-Ann?"

If you lie, and say yes, turn to page 138.

If you tell the girl the truth, go to 269.

At the door, you stop and square your shoulders.

"Miss Jenkins," you say, looking her in the eye, "I really must speak to Lady Plumly personally."

There is a momentary look of confusion over Fanny Jenkin's face. Then she bursts out laughing. "Who do you think you are? The Lady don't see jus' anyone."

You feel your cheeks redden, but you refuse to move.

"All right," the woman says quietly, "'ave it your way." Then she takes a tiny brass bell off a high shelf and shakes it.

The sound fills the room and the orphans scatter, cowering behind tables and chairs. Some cover their ears while others cover their eyes. One older girl helps a younger girl by covering her eyes for her. What on Earth is going on?

From upstairs, you hear heavy plodding footsteps.

From the staircase descends a giant of a man. You have never seen a man so large. In the lamplight you see that one of his eyes is fully white while the other swivels in its socket to focus on you. The most charitable assessment is that he is a monster.

"Fanny — what is it?" he says gutturally.

You are either about to faint or scream. You're uncertain which.

Without a word, you open the door and exit the orphanage.

You move quickly away on shaky legs.

Turn to page 13.

As you affix the last of the sheets from your basket to the clothesline, you stretch and gaze up at the sky. The sun is low above the neighbouring houses. You've been blessed by this rare nice day. The gentle breeze should have everything dried by evening and Maggie can probably take everything in by bedtime.

You run your tongue over your dry lips and call over to your housemaid.

"Maggie, I'm on my way in. Fancy a cup of tea?"

"Aye, ma'am. Very kind 'a ye."

You take one final look over the day's achievements — long lines of clean billowing sheets in the sun — and duck back inside the cool of the house.

Not everything could fit on the clotheslines out back, however. You deftly navigate shirts and shawls hung on the backs of chairs on the way to the range. Opening it, you shovel more coal into its hungry mouth before placing the kettle on top. You're grateful there seems to be enough water inside for at least two cups. That'll save you some pumping.

You hear the front door open, and you move to greet your daughters and their governess, but when you get there, something's amiss.

Agnes, a tiny woman to begin with, seems tinier all of a sudden. Her stricken face doesn't dare meet your gaze. She's panting, as if she'd been running.

Lorina is braver, her wide eyes catching yours. She doesn't speak, though her face is similarly ashen.

A fear grips your heart.

"What?! For God's sake, somebody say something!"

It's Lorina who starts the tale. They'd settled down in a spot under a tree, by the lake. They'd been grateful it was a Monday. If it were the weekend, surely that nice spot would have already been taken. In the drowsy afternoon sun, Lorina started reading a book. Sleepy, she tried to persuade Alice to read it to her, but Alice was having none of it. She wasn't interested in a book without pictures. Instead, Alice was gathering daisies, to make a chain, or a garland.

"And the sun, it was so nice against my skin. I simply fell clean asleep," Lorina finishes. "And when I woke up — Alice was gone!"

You turn your gaze to the girl's governess, who looks as if she wants to shrink into the walls.

"And where were you when all this occurred?"

Agnes shakes her head, as if clearing it. She's trembling, weeping into her scarf. If you weren't so incensed, you might even feel sorry for the woman.

"Ma'am," she mutters, barely above a whisper, "I must confess — I weren't nearby."

"Weren't nearby?" you repeat incredulously. "Where *were* you?"

Agnes is silent, but Lorina supplies the answer.

"She was over on Stanhope street — "

"Hush, child!"

" — window-shopping!"

You are taken with a sudden fury. All you want to do is hit this old woman. You take a step forward and Agnes flinches.

"Window — " you can barely choke the words out. "Window-shopping?"

The woman nods in mute assent.

You hear the kettle in the kitchen, boiling over. For a moment, you think you might actually lose your mind, but Maggie takes it off the range and now all you hear is the blood beating in your ears.

"Ma'am," Agnes says, "I- I- know I've bunged this

up. Created a right mess, I did."

"Hush!" you snap. "Did you search the park?"

"Aye!" the old woman says. "Scoured it, we did. Checked every hidey-hole. Me throat's all sore from calling out her name. Alice! Alice!"

You can't stand the sight of the woman any longer. You point at the door.

"Out! Out!"

Agnes stands there, uncertain. But as you take another step forward, she flinches, then leaves.

Once the old woman is gone, you almost faint.

"Mummy!" Lorina cries. As you find a chair to settle on you reflect idly that Lorina hasn't called you "Mummy" in years. It's always the much more formal "Mum" now.

You feel old.

Right now, you wish your own mother were there to take care of everything. Strict as she was, this would never have happened under her watch.

You picture Alice in Hyde Park — lost, scared.

The sun will be down in a few hours. But you know Reg will be home soon, and two heads are always better than one. He will certainly know what to do.

If you go look for Alice now, turn to page 184.

If you decide to wait for your husband to get home, turn to page 98.

"Actually," you confess, "to be perfectly honest, that's not why I'm here."

Lady Plumly doesn't blink. "Is that so?"

You tell her about Alice, and about the prostitute in the park.

"She told me," you continue, "that all of Hyde Park falls under your domain. That anything that happens there you're aware of."

"Is that what she told you?"

"Will you help me?"

Lady Plumly examines one of her fingernails.

"What was the name of the girl who recommended you to me?"

"Well — " you say, "she never actually told me her name." You get the awful feeling that the prostitute in the park spoke out of turn, and that if you identify her, that she might well get into terrible trouble.

There is a fire in Lady Plumly's eyes.

"Then what did this girl look like?"

If you tell her about the prostitute's prominent mole, turn to page 169.

If, however, you tell her that you forget, turn to page 150.

Your husband's words echo in your head as you flag down a cab.

"Dodgson! Go see Dodgson! He has a photo of Alice!"

It's true. Now you remember.

Charles Dodgson is Reg's colleague. An instructor of mathematics at Oxford, the man is a little odd, but great with children. Just a few weeks ago, your two girls went on a day trip with him. In his pockets he's always got a magic trick, or some other amusement. He's also one of the only persons you're aware of who has a camera. While the girls were there, they posed for a few portraits, which could prove very useful right now.

It's not easy to get to Oxford. It's an hour's train ride. You don't know how Reg does it every day. When he first got the position, you'd suggested to him how much easier it would be if you'd all simply move there, but Reg's father had taken ill last year, so it made sense to be close to him in the city.

You direct the driver to Paddington Station and acquire a ticket. It being quite late, you're catching one of the last trains of the day out of London. You're not sure how you're going to get back, but you'll cross that bridge when you come to it.

As you make your way onto a carriage and into a compartment, you glance out the window at the dark, clouded-over sky. Though late, Dodgson should still be up. Normally, you wouldn't call on him without warning, but these are pressing circumstances. And if he is as fond of your daughters as he so often expresses in his thank-you letters, then he will want to do everything he can to aid you.

When you finally arrive at Oxford College, you

make your way to the library, where you know the bachelor don resides. You think back to the last time you were here, about a month ago — the early autumn garden party, to celebrate the last gasp of summer. You hope that Dodgson is home. Could he still be at dinner?

You've only been to the library once before on a cursory tour a few summers ago. You suppose this is the right door, but your recollection could be mistaken. You knock.

Silence.

You knock again, then enter the room.

"Mr. Dodgson!" you call out. "It's Mrs. Reginald Liddell! Alice's mother! I do hope you'll forgive this unannounced visit, but I come under unusual circumstances."

You move through a nondescript alcove where numerous hats and umbrellas hang, then step further into what looks like his office.

"Mr. Dodgson?"

By a window is a sizable telescope, standing beside a massive writing desk, covered in papers. Stacks of letters rise precariously, tied together with twine. Books of all sizes pile against the walls, where shelves are also overflowing with books. In the centre of the room is a large, oak table. On the table itself is a leather portfolio, while just below it is a giant russet steamer trunk. Also on the table is a small glass vial with a tiny tag tied around its neck which says, simply, *Drink Me.*

The whole room is indicative of a fascinating mind.

In the stillness there is a sudden movement and you spot a crow — an inky black patch against the shadows high above — perched on the edge of a book-shelf. It must have gotten trapped inside.

"Oh, hello," you greet it.

It turns its glassy eye toward you. How queer that it should be here and not Mr. Dodgson.

If you decide to open the leather portfolio to see if it contains a photo of Alice, turn to page 100.

If you decide to follow instructions and drink the small vial on the table, turn to page 147.

If, however, you decide to wait for Dodgson to return, find a book to read on page 192.

Edith leads you through a series of back hallways that finally deposit you in front of a thick, purple velvet curtain. "This is the Dreamery," she says. You push through it and stop immediately.

You don't understand how this is possible. Before you, London sleeps. You are suddenly a hundred feet in the sky. It's as if you walked into the room and were floating in a hot air balloon.

"What — ?" you whisper at the scene before you.

You are afraid to move. Afraid that if you wake, you'll fall from the sky.

It takes a full half-minute for you to recognize what you're seeing.

"Why," you murmur in astonishment, as you venture further into the room, "they're scale models."

The outer edge of the city dissolves into countryside, and that is where you start, but soon you step into the city proper, shuffling along the streets.

You marvel at the fidelity. The streetlamps are even lit by gas! Above the city, you stare at the 'night sky', which is a million tiny holes punched in the wall, lit dimly from behind. Letting your gaze drift back to the city, you find that you can navigate with notable landmarks.

Big Ben. The Thames. There's even Buckingham Palace.

That's when you start noticing something queer. Tiny limbs. Arms and feet sticking out of windows and doors of the houses and buildings. Out of a pair of double-doors, you see a head. It's a little girl.

You crouch down onto the floor to get a better look, in case they are manikins. But indeed, they are children.

"My God," you whisper. "Are they all right?"

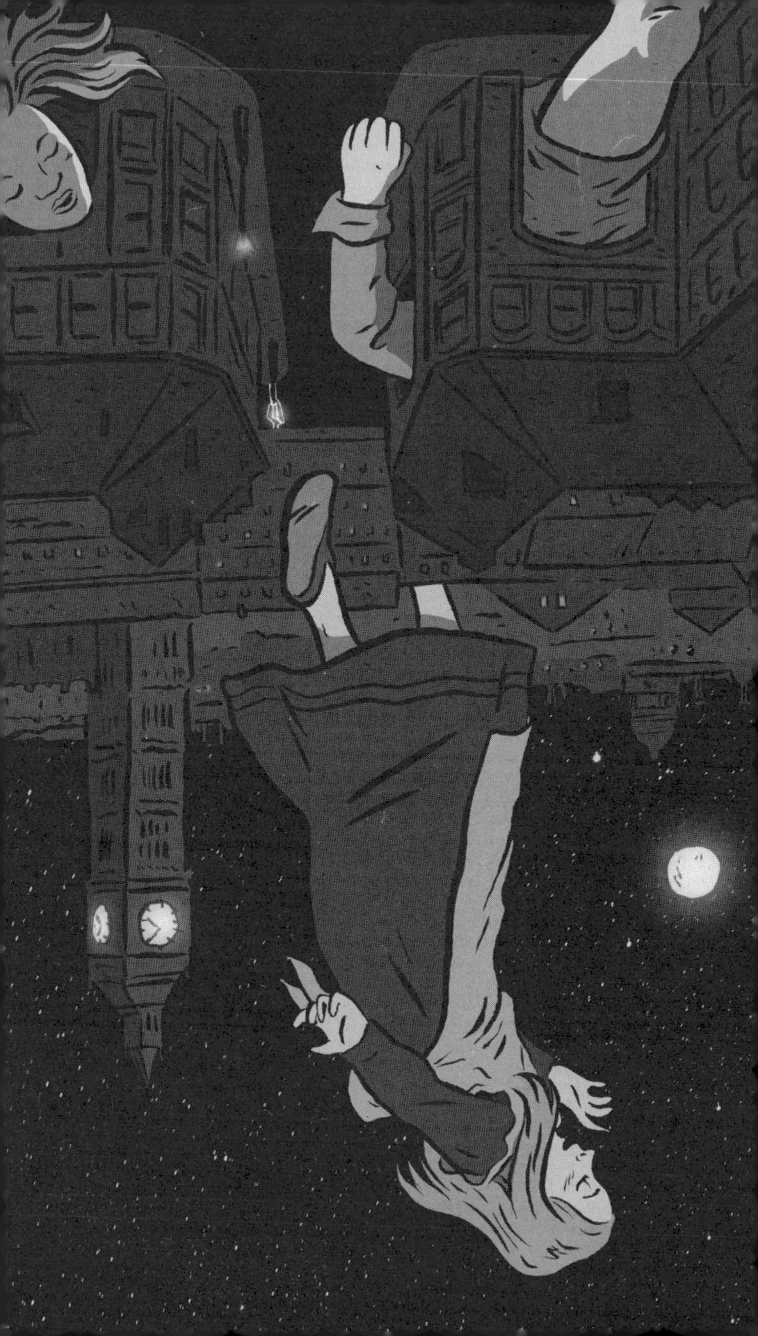

"You needn't whisper," Edith says in a conversational tone. "They're completely asleep."

You begin seeing heads and limbs everywhere.

"How can you be sure?"

"We all take our medicine before bed. It makes us very drowsy. We practically can't keep our eyes open."

It would have to be strong medicine, you think — likely Laudanum — in order for these girls to sleep in such uncomfortable straits. How did they even manage to get inside?

Edith moves nimbly over rooftops, then along a country road to the corner of the room, where set on a hill is a massive leather-bound shopkeeper's ledger. Under a lamp that resembles a moon she flips through pages.

"Your daughter's name is Alice?"

"That's right. She would have come in yesterday."

Edith frowns. "There's no Alice in the last day. Or the day before. Sometimes new girls give made-up names, though. Is there one she likes?"

"Maybe Lorina? Lory?"

The girl runs her finger down the pages of handwritten names and shakes her head.

"Occasionally Alice likes to pretend to be a girl named Florence."

Out of the corner of your eye you see limbs shifting unsettlingly. It is outrageous that the girls should be pinned so. Caged. You glance at Big Ben to check the time, but even Big Ben's clock is frozen, stuck in time.

"I'm sorry — there's no Florence either."

You move through the city streets, glancing down at every head. They are uniformly fair-haired, pretty girls. Some wear blindfolds and night masks but most do not. Could Alice be here? Asleep? You are intimidated by the giant task ahead of you. The room is as immense as a warehouse.

"Alice might have been taken by the Jabberwock," Edith says, closing the ledger. As she stands up, she bumps into the moon, which swings like a pendulum.

"The Jabberwock? What's that?"

Edith explains that when a girl disappears at night and reappears in the morning, sometimes she is taken by the Jabberwock, which is a demon that the Prince tries to protect them from.

"But even the Prince can only do so much," she says sadly. "That's why we must learn our roles, become proper young Englishwomen, so we can be Queens of our own kingdoms one day."

You step over the tiny Thames river, burbling at your feet, and follow Hammersmith toward Hyde Park. When you get there, you try to identify the exact area where Alice was taken, but while the model comes close, even this re-creation does not correspond exactly to real life.

Close by, you look at Buckingham Palace. For the life of you, it's hard to imagine where the Dreamery would be located physically inside the palace. Could you be underground? It's the only thing that makes sense, though none of this makes sense.

"It's odd that the palace has no girl sleeping inside," you say. "That courtyard is a perfectly good bed." Bending down, you look inside the lit building. That's when you notice hinges running along the back wall.

"Is this — ?"

Grasping a window, you heave the building up

like a trapdoor, revealing a lit set of stairs.

"Goodness!" you exclaim. Edith comes running over to you, deftly dodging streetstalls and carriages in her slippers.

When she sees the stairwell, she grabs your hand and urges you to close the palace back up. "I can't imagine we're allowed to go down there. Let's look for Alice somewhere else."

If you insist on heading down the stairs, turn to page 179.

If you haven't yet checked out the Secret Garden, turn to page 158.

If you haven't yet investigated the Performatory, turn to 106.

If you've already seen everything, turn to page 180 to ponder your next move.

As you begin undressing, you watch the three-panel changing screen in front of you to ensure you aren't being spied upon. At any moment you half expect to see the Chinaman's slitted eyes peering around its edge.

You're unsettled — and you have every reason to be. But minutes later, you are as naked as the day you were born as you slide the silk gown on. Despite being cool to the touch, once on, it's surprisingly warm.

Against the wall there is a large mirror and in the Chinese robe, you almost don't recognize yourself. You have been through so much tonight, you almost *feel* like a different person.

Also reflected in the mirror is the screen, and absently, you admire it. You wonder if you might be able to acquire one for your own room. The brush painting on it depicts a flock of birds, above a river, chased by a rabbit. Beautiful, you think.

When the Chinese woman appears again you sharply inhale.

"Goodness!" you half-shriek. "Don't surprise me like that!"

"Sorry," she smiles, then reaches past you for your clothes.

"Oh, where are you taking them?"

"Fire."

"What!? You're going to burn them?"

She frowns. "Burn?"

"You're going to burn them in the fireplace?"

She shakes her head uncomprehending, then pantomimes hanging the clothes up.

"Ah," you say. "You're going to *dry* them."

"Fire," the woman nods, then takes them away.

You emerge to sit at the table you first sat at when

you came in. The woman comes out and places a mug of piping hot tea in front of you. You expected orange pekoe, but it's not that. It's full of green leaves.

You sigh. This isn't what you're used to, but when in Rome...

You take a sip of the brew, and it is simultaneously sweet and bitter, if that makes sense. Hints of pennyroyal, you surmise. Maybe barley?

"You like?" the woman asks, coming round again.

"Yes, thank you," you say. "This'll do just fine." You reach into your purse, which you'd kept on your person, and pull out a shilling which you place on the table.

The woman picks it up, then bites it.

"Oh," you say, surprised. "It's quite real, I assure you."

Then she slips the whole coin under her tongue, and wanders off.

You have several more swallows of the green tea when the first Chinaman comes back. Rudely, he grabs the back of another chair, then pulls it up to your table, sitting down uninvited across from you. You try not to bristle at his forwardness.

He taps his chest. "I am Sing."

"Well, hello," you extend your hand to the man and he shakes it. "I am Mrs. Reginald Liddell."

"Why you come?"

You blink.

"You nice lady," he says, "in my shop. Why?"

You're unsure what to tell him. Sing is all business all of a sudden. As if he knows more about you than you think.

"You need help?" he asks, one eyebrow raised. "You need favour?"

"Yes," you admit. "I need help."

You tell Sing about Alice, and the daft circumstances that led you here, to sit in a Chinese gown drinking green tea in an opium den. The whole time he watches you carefully, nodding. Though his English is pidgin, you have the sense that he understands better than he's letting on.

"Girl missing. Sing can find."

"You can help me?"

"Maybe find," he shrugs.

"Is that a yes?"

"Maybe," the man says again, infuriatingly vague.

"Well, I suppose that's better than nothing."

"If Sing help — you make me favour."

"A favour? But I can *pay* you Mr. Sing," you say, tapping your purse.

Sing shakes his head.

"No money. You make Sing favour."

"But- but what *sort* of favour?"

You don't like the deal that Sing is trying to strike. The terms are too nebulous for your tastes.

Sing shrugs. "One day, Sing need favour. You do."

You look askance at the man. What sort of favours would he be asking for?

"Mr. Sing," you say, "I cannot agree unless I know the particular nature of the favour you will be asking of me."

As if reading your mind, Sing nods. "No sexy," he says. "No break law."

Well, that clears things up. But you think it's queer that in this transaction, Sing is trusting that you'll do the thing he asks of you in some hypothetical future.

"But Mr. Sing," you say, "what if I agree to your

terms now, but refuse to do the favour later on?"

"Then you say no," he says, with a small shrug. "Sing go away."

Really? Is it that simple?

The man nods, then holds out his hand for you to shake.

If you agree to Sing's terms, shake his hand and turn to page 33.

If you disagree, and decide to go home, turn to page 101.

As the guards surround you with swords drawn, you crouch over Alice protectively.

The Prince strolls over and glares. "What were you doing? Mary-Ann, isn't it?"

The announcer walks over as well. "Wait, sire. This isn't Mary-Ann."

"This is my daughter!" you put your hands on her shoulder and try to rouse her, but she remains stubbornly asleep. "Alice. And she belongs to me."

A slow smile creeps across the Prince's lips, but his eyes — two dark coals — remain fixed on you.

"Everything here belongs to *me.*"

The Prince drops his broadsword tip-first into the grass, where it stands motionless. Then, beckoning to his aide, he retrieves his rifle.

Stepping over to you, he aims it at Alice's unconscious head.

"No!" you scream, grabbing the barrel and pushing it aside.

The Prince wrenches the gun out of your grip, then swings it, so the butt comes around and hits you on your temple.

It's such a blow that you are unconscious before you hit the ground.

Turn to page 172.

The girl grabs your hand, then pulls you behind a tapestry hanging against a wall.

"Don't move," she whispers to you, extinguishing her lantern.

The castle wall is cold against the thin cotton of your maid's uniform, but you remain silent and still. From where you're hiding, you have a narrow view of the oncoming guards.

As they approach, you get a good look at them. The two men saunter down the hallway, voices muffled, and you now see why. Large white masks cover their faces, with only a thin slit for seeing. The rest of their uniforms are also white, except for large black club symbols on their chest, like the ones on playing cards. Each man has a sword sheathed on his hip.

"Why do you think they call him the Jabberwock, anyhow? I mean, — what's it mean?"

The other guard snorts. "Always thought it was 'cos he jabbers while he walks!"

"He does a lot of that!"

The men continue on, their lamplight barely grazing your shoes, sticking out from under the tapestry.

"Awright then — Bandersnatch. Do that one."

When their voices have faded, you stir, but the girl clutches your hand and stills you. She is trembling. Finally, after a few moments, she allows you to draw her back to the hall.

"Oh my poor dear," you say. "Are you quite all right?"

In the hall light, you notice that the girl has a giant red playing card heart on her nightgown, also. What's next? A diamond? A spade? A joker?

The girl nods, and you bend down, giving her a hug, which she accepts.

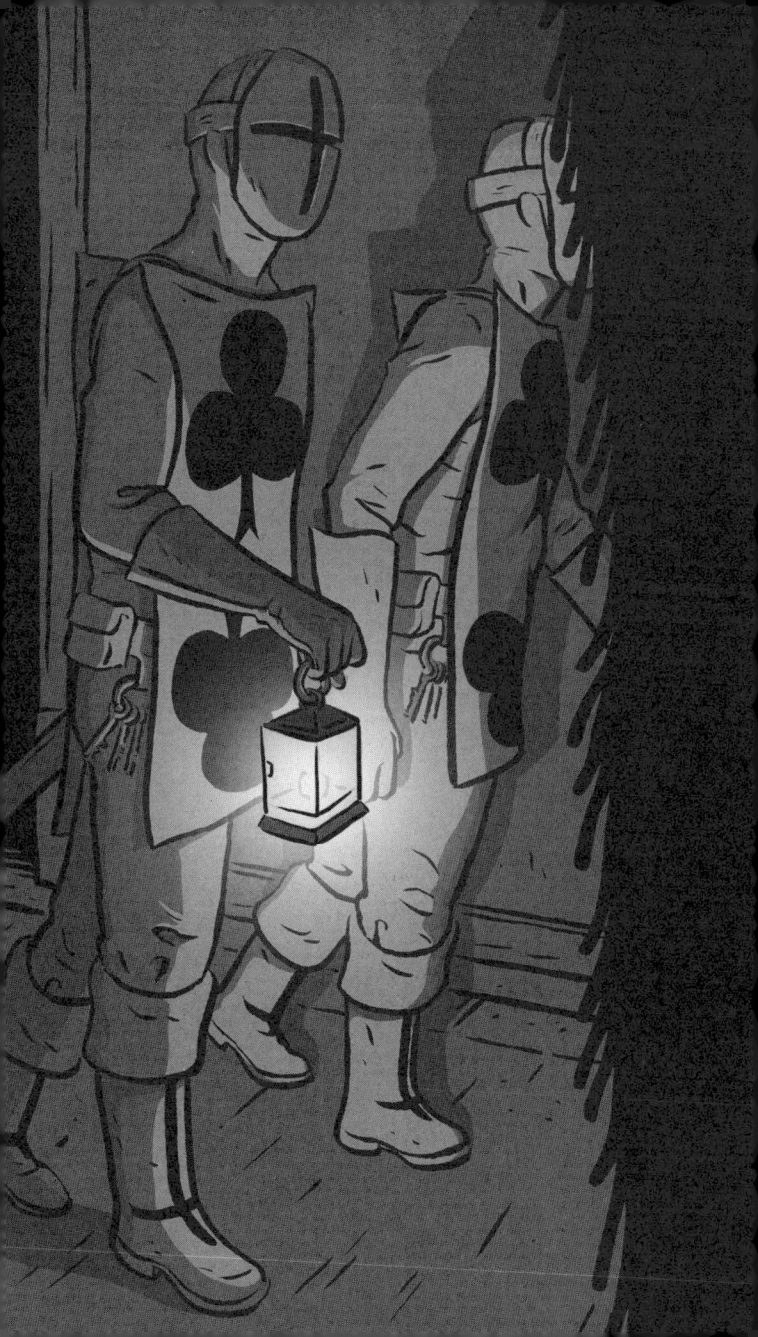

"Now," you say, "before we were so rudely interrupted, I was about to tell you about my daughter, Alice, who I am desperate to find. She's about your age, and about your height. And I am curious if you might be able to help me."

"Alice, Alice," the girl mutters to herself. "I've never heard that name before."

"Alice? You'd never heard that name?" You'd always assumed it was fairly common.

"No. What's it mean?"

"It was my grandmother's name. I'm not entirely sure what it means. What is your name?"

"Edith."

"What a perfectly splendid name. Edith, I am Mrs. Reginald Liddell."

"Reginald? Why do you have a boy's name?"

"A boy's — ?" You laugh. "Well, I'm now married, but Hannah is my maiden name."

"I shall call you Hannah then, because we are all maidens in the Prince's Wonderland."

You don't quite understand what she means, but you nod and smile all the same. "All right, then." You decide to change the subject. "My dear, it's quite late."

"You mean, it's quite early."

"Quite. But most little girls your age need a lot of sleep."

"I'm hall monitor," she says, matter-of-factly. "I'm to ensure that all the other little girls who should be asleep are *not* up."

Your heart leaps at this information.

"So there are other little girls? My daughter is small and blonde, like you."

"So are all the others."

Your mind races with questions you are afraid to

learn the answers to, but you ask the most important one: "Where are they now?"

"Hmm. Alice in the palace, Alice in the palace..." Edith scratches her chin thoughtfully. "In one of three possible places," she says.

If you try looking in the Dreamery,
turn to page 124.

If you look for Alice in the Performatory,
go to page 106.

If you start in the Secret Garden, go to page 158.

138

"Yes, child," you say, trying to keep your face in shadow. But the girl comes near and her lantern lights you up. She stops abruptly.

"*You're* not Mary-Ann," she cries. "Who are you? You don't belong here."

"Oh, my apologies," you say, mind racing. "I thought you asked me if I am merry, which I am not."

"No, I asked if you were Mary-*Ann.*"

"Merry, and — ?"

"Mary-*Ann.*"

"And what?"

"And...?" The girl looks confused, as if she'd forgotten what you were discussing in the first place. Which indeed, was your intention.

From the end of the hall you hear heavy footsteps coming down a spiral staircase. Low voices and a glow portending the imminent arrival of palace guards.

Oh, no.

Turn to page 134.

You wake up, back sore from the thin straw mattress. Rubbing your neck, you wonder how much longer they're going to keep you in the cell. It's been three full days already. You tried to talk to the guards, but with their masks on, they remained maddeningly impassive.

You hear footfalls in the hall, and a nervous-looking middle-aged man with white hair in a grey waistcoat appears at the bars of your cell. He checks his pocketwatch.

"There's yer client," a guard says, shadowing the man. "You'll meet with her after sentencing."

"Wait!" you say, getting up. The rough stone floor is shockingly cold on your bare feet. "That makes no sense. I need to meet with my lawyer before the *trial,* much less sentencing!"

You don't even know what you're charged with — but at this moment, you feel you have to fight for every inch, or everything will be taken away from you.

"I don't make the rules," the guard replies gruffly.

"*That's* clear," you say, perhaps with more insouciance than you intended.

"No lip," the guard warns. "Now turn around."

You're about to argue, but you bite your tongue and do as the guard orders.

You hear the key turn in the rusty cell door lock, then the squeak of the hinges as it opens. The guard manacles your wrists together, then puts a black hood over your head.

You panic for a moment, then force yourself to calm down as you're led out of the cell, down the hall, up a flight of stairs, then down another hall.

Finally, you're seated on a hard wooden bench. The manacles are removed, and so is the hood.

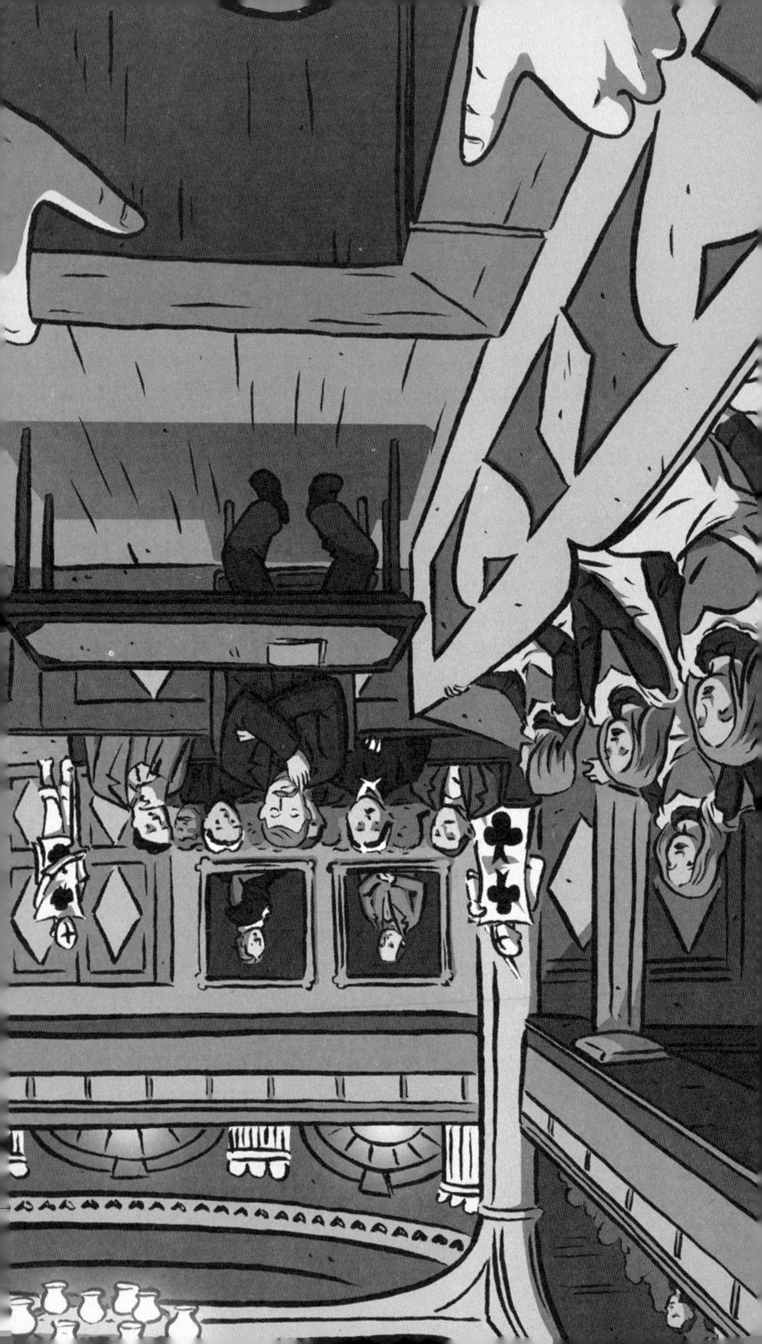

You gasp.

You're in a courtroom. It's packed with people, but they all remained silent as doormice as you were led in. Indeed, until the moment the hood was removed, you thought you were alone.

As it is, you're sitting in the interrogation box, facing the crowd. The gallery is filled with servants, and dozens of little blonde girls. Elevated to your right is the Prince. He wears a white judge's wig and spectacles and glances blandly your way. To your left is the jury's box. It's likewise filled with little girls. A mixture of older and younger.

But you note, with a tiny jolt, that one of the girls is *Alice!*

She makes eye contact with you, nodding slightly. Then she brings her hands up to her chin. Under the guise of scratching her lip, she makes the heart-symbol with her hands she always gives you before bed. Your own heart leaps. You need to survive this. For Alice.

"My subjects," the Judge says. "My objects. Ladies and gentlemen. Animals and minerals. We are gathered here today to part this woman from her head."

"Here, here!" a cry goes up from the gallery.

"There, there," an inconsolable woman, sobbing into a handkerchief, is being consoled by another woman beside her.

"Objection!" you cry out. "What am I charged with?"

"Silence!" the Judge gavels his desk. "Corruption of youth." Then he turns to the jury box. "How does the jury find? Guilty?"

"Objection!" you say again. "Too soon! Evidence

has not yet been presented. Everything here is all topsy-turvy."

"Well, did you bring me any?" the Judge asks.

"Bring you what?"

"Presents."

"Presents?! Are you daft?"

"I see you've nothing gift-wrapped except for your lies!"

None of this trial makes any sense. For a moment you think you're still sleeping. This 'judge' takes every opportunity to twist your words, and twist the rules so that they are stacked against you.

"I am innocent of any charges against me," you say.

"Silence!" the Judge whacks his gavel again. "If your soul is innocent, then your weighed heart shall be as light as the feather of truth. Let's cut out your heart then, shall we?"

You don't have a response to that. Who would?

"I say again," the Judge says, "how does the jury find? If the prisoner is found guilty, you shall all get plum cake for your services."

Some of the jury members break out into grins. One by one, they stand, saying "guilty". All except Alice. The Judge gives her a baleful look, then clears his throat meaningfully.

"Ahem!"

Alice remains sitting.

"Ahem!"

Alice crosses her arms.

"Ahem!"

"I will not stand!" she states, defiant. You have never been more proud of your daughter than at this moment. And never more fearful for both of your

lives.

"The prisoner is guilty!" the Judge screams.

Alice gets to her feet. "Not guilty!" she roars back.

"Then *you* are guilty!" The Judge looks over to the corner of the room, where a guard begins cleaving his way through the crowd to get to the jury box.

Oh no. This will not end well.

If you change your plea to guilty, to draw attention away from Alice, and perhaps spare her, turn to page 172.

If you spring out of your seat, rush to the jury box, grab Alice and run out a side-door, go to page 208.

The instant you enter you feel you've made a mistake. No cheery bell sounded when you stepped in the door, and a blue cloud of smoke hangs everywhere, as if the city's misty fog followed you inside.

Though it looks warm and cozy through its windows, the light in the room is actually quite subdued. Every lamp has a shade or muslin cloth over top. Inside, light is a whisper.

The room itself is a mystery, as most of it is screened off from you. From where you're sitting, at this low, ornate table, it's difficult to get a sense of its dimensions.

Just as you're about to get up and leave, a Chinaman shuffles by. He sees you and frowns.

"You are who?" he mutters. It takes you a moment to adjust to his thick accent.

"I beg your pardon?"

"You want smoke?"

"I ah — " You swallow. "I'd like a cup of tea, please."

The man shakes his head.

"No tea. You smoke?"

With a start, you realize that you're inside a Chinese opium den. You'd heard of such establishments, but didn't recognize the smell of opium smoke, having never been around anyone who'd ever smoked it.

"Ah — "

"You smoke," the man smiles. "Very relax."

You want to tell him no, that the last thing you want to do is to have a smoke of his wretched drugs, that you are wet and tired and you'd pay a king's ransom for a simple cup of hot tea with a little bit of sugar and milk. But you ask him something else.

"Is there anyone here who speaks English?" you

ask him.

"I speak."

"No," you say. "I mean — better English."

"I speak very better," he says, slightly louder.

"No, I mean — "

A call comes from the other side of the screen. Another Chinaman, saying something you don't understand. The one you're talking to moves off immediately, his long braid swinging behind him.

You sigh, exasperated, and get up off the wicker chair. By now you can hear the rain beating a steady patter on the roof. You don't look forward to stepping back out into it, but you don't want to stay here.

From where you're standing, you can spy the scene behind the screens and out of curiosity, you take a peek. The Chinaman moves quietly, like a nurse, tending to his patients. He re-lights a lamp for one man lounging on a bench covered in silk pillows worn rough. Pairs of benches flank square tables, each of which holds a most beautifully-detailed tray, containing an elaborate assortment of strange smoking implements. You had no idea that smoking opium required such complicated tools.

You're about to turn away from the scene and head back outside when you feel a hand on your arm.

A Chinese woman in a light green, silk dress nods at you.

"Tea?" she says.

"Yes!" you almost laugh in your gratitude.

The Chinese woman takes her hand off your wet sleeve and clucks disapprovingly. "You change," she says, guiding you over to another screen. There are no benches behind this one, just a chair and a mirror. But on the chair is a towel and a sumptuous robe.

"You change," the woman says again. "Then tea."

This worries you. Why is she so insistent on you changing? This is certainly beyond the pale, expecting you to disrobe before having a simple cup of tea.

You fear they have plans for you after you've changed. You know that the whole area of Limehouse is ridden with prostitution, gambling and drugs. The room you're in is filled with unknown numbers of Chinamen. They could overpower you.

And no one knows you're here — not even your husband.

Perhaps you should leave now before it's too late.

If you decide to change into the robe,
turn to page 129.

If you leave abruptly for home, go to page 76.

You lift up the vial and uncork it. Rotating it under your nose, you attempt to discern what it is, but there is no readily apparent scent.

You toss the liquid back into your throat and swallow, as if it were a shot of Reg's scotch. It is only then you taste... something. A curious mixture of ginger and — could it be coriander?

Placing the vial back on the table, you wonder if you'd made an error. Feeling a little out of sorts, you sit down on the chaise lounge in the corner of the room. Suddenly you are terrifically sleepy.

Oh no, you think. What did you drink?

You wake up with a start hours later, still on the lounge. It's quite dark, and you listen for the sound of snoring. Did Dodgson return? Perhaps he snuck past you.

Lighting an oil lamp, you walk around the labyrinthine warren of rooms that makes up this part of the library, but there is no sign of Dodgson. Perhaps he never came home.

As you wander around, you become aware that your clothes don't fit as well as they used to. They are a little tight. Again you wonder what it was you drank. You feel a little bloated, like you do that time of the month.

Well — you certainly don't have time for this. Once more your thoughts drift to Alice, and where she might be.

Moving quickly in the moonlight, you head to the front gates of Oxford and board a Hansom Cab that is idling there.

"I'm headed to London," you alert the driver, who is sitting on his raised chair, high on the back of the cab.

The cabbie grins at you.

"Are ye?" he asks.

You frown at the man. You don't like his tone.

"Will you take me or no?"

"Who's the lucky chap in 'is ivory tower?" the cabbie nods back towards campus.

The cheek! He takes you for a prostitute! You turn away, walking down the road, searching for another cab.

"Oy!" the driver calls after you. "My apologies!"

You continue walking. It is only after the driver draws his cab up beside you, and apologizes again do you deign to step into the cab.

You pay the driver, but you refuse to tip him. His insolence should not be rewarded.

It took you longer than usual to direct the driver home. What was in that vial? Your mind is unusually cloudy.

You fish around in your purse and find your keys. So addled are you that you can't even remember which key fits the front lock. You have to try them all before you're finally inside.

It is only as you are slipping off your tight shoes that you have a shock — Alice's shoes are there!

In your stockinged feet, you hurry up the stairs.

Alice is home! Alice is back!

You can hardly believe your eyes, but Alice is asleep in her own bed. You rush to her.

"Oh my precious child!" you whisper. "My darling!" You get on the bed and take her into your arms. Sleepily, the girl's eyes flutter open. Then she catches sight of your face in the dim light cast by the moon through her lace curtains.

"It's me, darl- "

Alice screams.

Aiiiiiiiiiiiiiieeeeeeeeeee!

"Hush! Hush!" you whisper to your daughter but she continues screaming. "You'll wake your father up!" You clamp a hand over her mouth but she screams into your palm.

Footsteps out in the hallway.

Reg appears at the doorway in his nightgown. "Alice? What?" he mutters. Then he catches sight of you and his mouth opens into an O.

What is going on? What is wrong with everyone?

Reg turns to someone in the hallway.

"Maggie!" he cries hoarsely. "Go get help! Get the police!"

"Reg," you implore him. "Whatever is the matter? Why the police?"

Reg raises his hands, as if someone has him at gunpoint. "What do you want?" he asks. You have never seen him like this. "Please," he says, "just let her go. Just don't hurt my girl."

"Have you gone mad?"

Alice takes this opportunity to leap out of bed and run out the doorway.

"Alice!" you start after her but Reg stands in your way, a mean look on his face.

"I'll kill you," he snarls. He runs at you, hands reaching for your neck!

If you decide to flee, turn to page 10.

If you'd rather fight, go to 49.

You tell Lady Plumly that you forget what the girl looked like.

"It was terribly dark," you elaborate, "and we only spoke for a few moments. I'm so sorry."

The woman is still as a snake, staring at you.

You blush, and look down at the floor.

The silence lengthens until you think you might burst.

"Your attempts at deception are hopelessly dilettante," Plumly states, with a wave of her hand. "But that's quite all right. I both admire and encourage loyalty."

You look up, surprise on your face.

"Here," Plumly continues, "everyone lies. I lie. You lie. You'll have to lie even more to get by."

You try to bring the topic of discussion back to your daughter.

"So, about my — "

"Aye," the woman interrupts you. "Girls on the streets don't always end up in orphanages, living off the charity of the Church. The fair-haired and pretty ones, as you describe your daughter, have lots of interested parties."

You frown.

"Of whom do you speak?"

Turn to page 26.

Edith leads you to the Garden, but stops at the threshold.

"I'll enter first," she tells you. "I'm sorry, but if you're caught, I cannot be seen with you."

You nod. "I completely understand." You know that the little girl has taken a big risk in aiding you as much as she has already.

She pushes open the door to the Garden and heads in. A few moments later, you enter yourself.

It's a brilliant day outside. Sometimes London can rain for weeks, but when it dries out, the light is sharp as a pin. You shield your eyes against the piercing sun. It feels like forever since you've seen daylight.

As you move along the outer perimeter, taking in your surroundings, you don't look out of place. There are other similarly-dressed servants. Some busy, others simply standing, attending the event. But you stay a careful distance from them.

Many are busy keeping the Prince's birthday celebration steaming ahead. Gardeners with playing card spades on their uniforms are busy putting out flower arrangements and trimming hedges. Roses bloom everywhere. Girls with red hearts on their white dresses run here and there, carrying platters of fruit and bottles of wine. Guards stand at attention in the Garden's corners. You wish they didn't wear masks. You want to see their faces.

You edge closer to the epicentre of the party and in a small clearing you spot a very curious beast. At first you weren't certain what it was, but now you see it's a lion. But not a real lion. In truth, you have never beheld an actual lion with your eyes, but this creature is clearly two little girls in a lion costume. One controls the head and the forepaws and the other girl is in the back, swishing its tail.

Then the lion makes an attempt at a roar. You stifle a grin when you hear it.

Paces away, hopping out from behind a bush, two other girls are in similar costumes, but these are vultures. Neither of them are Alice.

"A hunt!" A voice intones sonorously. Upon a short pedestal, a man stands in a suit of green. He looks almost like a manicured bush himself. Perhaps that was the point. "In darkest Africa," he continues, "the fearsome lion, king of all the beasts, gives a mighty roar, proclaiming his dominion over all these lands." The girls roar again.

Curiously, a man dressed in a beige hunting outfit sneaks from bush to bush. Giant red playing card diamonds emblazon his outfit, and he carries a musket.

"But there is *one* creature who will prove *mightier!* And it is man. Entrusted by the Maker to take dominion over all of Earth's creatures, man shall prove once again that God's trust is in good hands."

Boom!

You gasp at the ear-splitting noise.

In one elegant motion, the hunter had rounded a bush, aimed at the lion and fired.

The front half of the lion sinks to the ground. The back half is momentarily still, then frantic, trying to flee. To all the world it looks like the lion is sleeping, but some strange force animates its hind legs.

"Got him!" the man in green howls triumphantly. "Foul devourer of men!"

You recoil in horror. Your eyes dart from servant to servant, guard to guard. None of them react. They are acting as if this is normal.

Even the little girls forming a ring around the

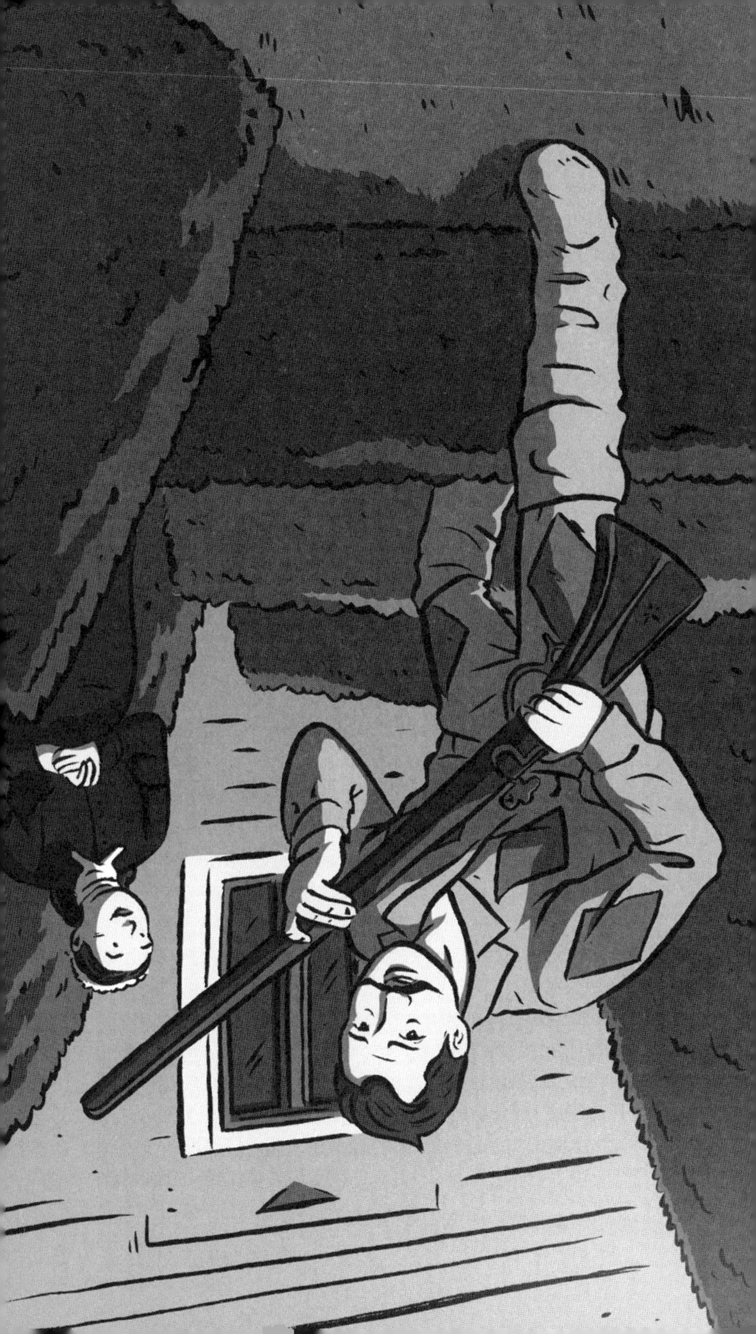

proceedings all applaud.

"What a tremendous shot!" one of them cries.

"Truly amazing aim!" someone else says.

The hunter, for his part, looks around, smiling and nodding. But you note the terrible fact that blood seeps through the chest of the lion costume.

Once he's done drinking it all in, the hunter moves closer to the downed lion and aims his musket carefully once more.

"Finish him off!" a girl yells.

"No monster worthy of the title ever goes down easy," the announcer continues. "Again, our hunter must brave the dangers of a land where death lurks behind every rock, tracking down his injured prey."

Your heart beating, you wonder to yourself, what if Alice is in the lion? What if the next shot will kill her?

If you intervene, and try to save the back end of the lion, turn to page 161.

If you decide the moment is too fraught with danger, hold your tongue and see what happens on page 211.

If your heart is breaking, and you decide to leave the Garden and look elsewhere for Alice, go to page 227.

The last time you had a smoke you were in your teens. Ellen Bacon from down the road had "borrowed" her grand-dad's pipe and the two of you went behind the barn where no one could see and lit it up.

You got so giddy from smoking. It came on you quite gently. You were joking with Ellen about how baby lambs will suck on anything the size of a cow's udder teat, and how every farm boy within a hundred kilometres must know this. The both of you were laughing your arses off when your father caught you.

So when Sing hands the pipe over, you break out in a grin.

Sing smiles, encouragingly.

You lie down leisurely on the pillows and inhale. You only cough once.

You hand the pipe back and this is the way it goes. Back and forth. It's very soothing.

If only Ellen Bacon could see you now, you think.

It's unreasonably nice. A fireplace warming the room. Smoke curling into the ceiling. Lying around in soft, filmy robes.

As your head lolls on the silk pillows, you begin to feel at home.

You watch Sing take another pull. It feels like you'd been wandering around in Hell all evening, and that Sing is the only person you'd met who was willing to guide you out.

You kind of want to cry at his kindness.

The world is such an unlikely place. It is an unlikely story. Yet we all believe it. We all agree to it. And that's what keeps it turning. But where does the story go when it's not being told? You imagine it's where a flame goes after it's been blown out. Hopefully to be lit again at another time.

You giggle a little.

"A likely story," you say, or think you say.

You remember something from earlier that day — from the street. But it is coming back to you differently now. More dreamlike.

There was a man running a shellgame on the sidewalk outside a barber's. He had three thimbles, but as you're remembering it, they are giant thimbles.

He places a golden key underneath one of the thimbles, then starts moving the thimbles around at a great speed.

"Find the rabbit, find the rabbit," he mutters. You marvel at the dexterity it takes to move the thimbles about without them flying off into the street.

You follow the thimble the key is under with your eyes, and when the barker stops, you point to it.

He lifts the thimble, but there's nothing there.

You point at the next one.

Nothing.

He lifts the last thimble and it's empty too.

But where is Alice? You think. She's got to be somewhere.

The man grins, then opens his mouth. The key was under his tongue.

Turn to page 90.

"No," you stand your ground. "I shan't go."

"What?" Dodgson lifts his mask, confusion in his face.

"We must free *all* the girls."

Dodgson sighs, then steps back through the doorway and towards the beds. "Very well, I can carry exactly one more. Which one?"

You look at the sleeping girls. Each one a near duplicate of your own daughter. Each one very likely missed sorely by their parents.

"Choose one!" Dodgson insists.

You're unable to. Your heart breaks. For whomever you choose, eight will remain.

"Exactly," Dodgson says.

You shake your head, stepping through the mirror's doorway. Heartbroken, you refuse to look back.

Turn to page 231.

Edith leads you down one corridor, then another, skinnier one. After a few turns, you are completely confused, but the girl weaves around the palace wing like it's second nature, so you trust her.

You emerge from a tiny alcove into a large and magnificent garden.

It is so large you can't imagine why it would be called a *Secret* Garden. It'd be difficult to keep this place under wraps. It is only when you scan the perimeter that you see why — the garden is walled in on all sides. The only creatures who'd know it's here are the inhabitants and the birds.

"Why would little girls be out here, at night?" you whisper to Edith.

"Gardening," Edith answers.

"Gardening?! But for what?"

"Why, for anything that grows in the moonlight. Cheese. Nocturnips."

"Nocturnips?" you wonder aloud. "Are you certain that's the name?

"Of course I am."

"My dear, nocturnips aren't actually a real vegetable."

"Of course they are — I've *tasted* them."

"My dear, I'm afraid someone's been lying to you."

Edith gives you a sharp look, and halts, putting her hands on her hips. A perfect mimic of a vexed matron. "You've been here five minutes," she says, "who are *you* to tell me that things that I have *personally* tasted don't exist?"

You chuckle and throw your hands up in surrender. "My dear, you're quite right. My apologies."

This seems to mollify her and the two of you ven-

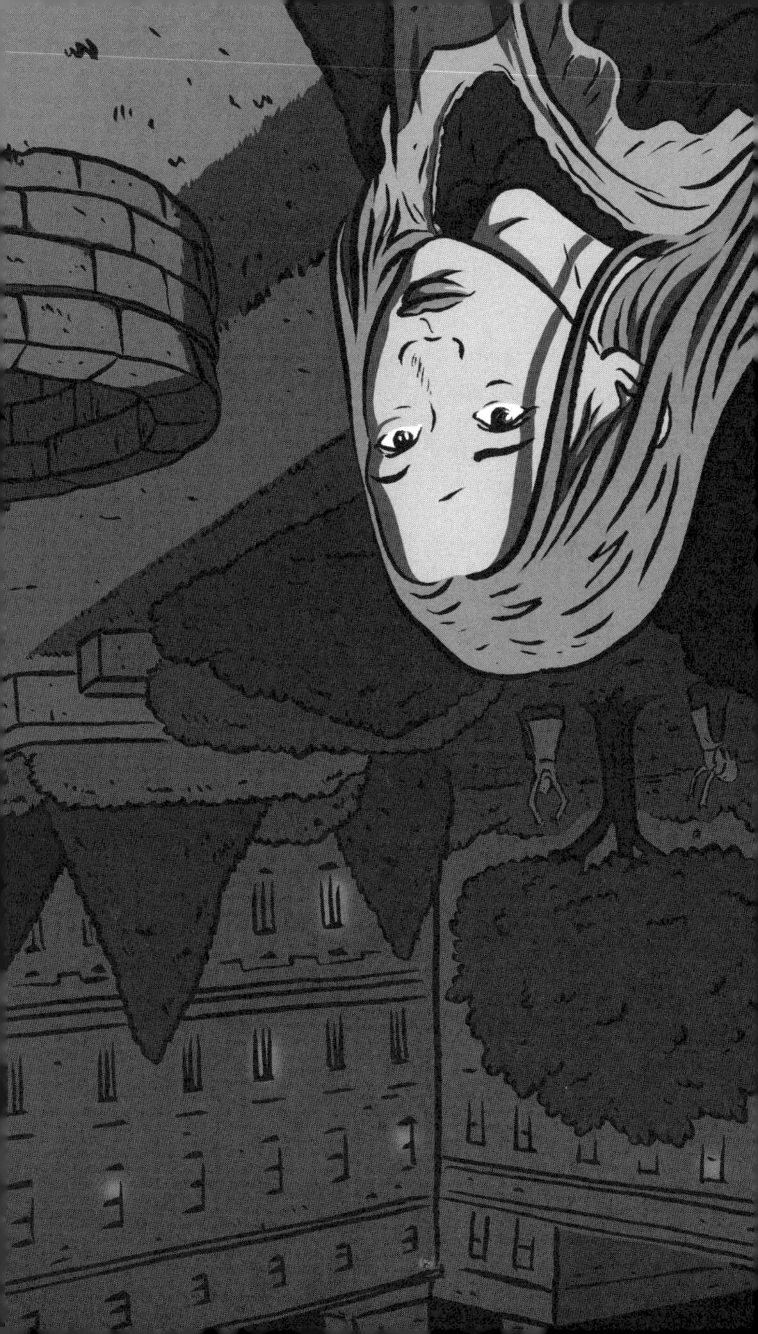

ture into the garden. You note the burbling of a large fountain, as well as an array of paths and carefully-manicured bushes radiating out from it. Off on the far end, you suspect you see the entrance to a hedge-row maze. To your right, there is a small well. And off to your left you see movement.

"Oh — are those some girls over there?" you ask.

Edith follows your gaze and clucks disapprovingly. "Naughty girls. They're not to be doing that."

In the moonlight, you see three girls gathered around the skinny trunk of a plumtree. One of them has managed to clamber up into the leaves and is shaking two branches which she's got ahold of quite vigorously.

As you hear the gentle thuds of plums dropping into the grass, you see a number of lights appear on the other side of the garden.

"Oy!" a male voice cries. "You girls — stop that!"

Three guards close quickly as the girls grab the fruits of their labour and scatter.

"Those are the Prince's plums!" another man yells.

The girls giggle and try to find shelter behind bushes and under benches while the guards spread out and begin searching the grounds.

Edith pulls on your hand. "You must hide!"

The well is right there. If you jump into it, turn to page 95.

If you turn right around and head back in the way you came out, turn to page 270.

"Wait! Stop!" you cry. You sprint to the lion, placing yourself between the hunter and the injured girls inside. "What are you doing? Have you gone mad?" You look at the surrounding servants, guards and girls. "These are little girls. Why do you all act as if this is completely normal. It's not! This is barbaric."

Shock, puzzlement, then outrage flashes over the face of the hunter. "What? *You're* the mad one." He points at the lion. "*This* is a monster!"

Reaching for the lion, you pull the head off of it, revealing the tousled hair of a girl. You exhale in relief that it's not Alice. But this girl's eyes are closed, and she's visibly hurt.

"She's alive!" you yell to the servants. "She needs aid!"

But nobody moves except the guards, who are all, wordlessly charging at you.

"Hold!" the hunter raises a gloved hand, and the guards stop mere strides away, poised to spring like cats upon a mouse.

The hunter turns to you. "This is my birthday, *not* yours!"

So it's as you suspected. This is the Prince.

"Perhaps *you* would like to be the lion next," the Prince sneers.

"No, I would not."

The Prince gets a gleam in his eye.

"Perhaps you would like to be the *hunter* next." You have a vision of yourself dressed as the hunter, being forced to shoot little girls and shudder.

"I will *not* play your games!" you snap.

"Who are you?" the Prince asks coldly. "You are not one of my servants. You are a mouse that has snuck into my house. You are an interloper."

"I am here for my daughter, Alice," you state imperiously. "If she's here, I want her returned."

A laugh escapes the Prince's lips.

"Occasionally it is refreshing for a woman other than my mother to make demands of me." Then he nods to the guards. "Take her."

The men in white masks surround you, dragging you to a cell with a single, small window.

You are left alone as it grows dark outside.

Turn to page 172.

You wield the rolling pin like a cricket bat and swing it at the figure's skull. With a solid *thwock* you make contact, and he goes down, falling flat on his face.

Edith takes a huge draught of air, then coughs, panting like a dog.

"Oh thank God!" she points at the figure. "It's a guard. From the palace. He'd come to kill me."

"Are you okay?" Dark bruises surround your daughter's neck. Edith nods, massaging it.

You bend down to turn the figure over, but Edith stops you.

"No, don't! He's my problem. Let me deal with him."

"Don't be ridiculous."

Edith takes the rolling pin from you and goes to strike the head again, but you stop her. "Have you gone mad?!"

"We must ensure he doesn't wake up!" Edith says, trying to push you aside.

You're both interrupted when the figure moans.

It's a woman.

Pulling at the hood, you see that it's actually a young woman.

Oh no.

Edith sighs, resignedly.

"Alice!" you cry, as you recognize the face of your own daughter. Even after six years you would know her. Even after a lifetime.

An hour later you sit with Alice and Edith in the parlour. Alice holds an oilskin bag of cool water on the back of her head, while Edith sits, arms crossed.

Alice reveals that she'd recently escaped with a

number of girls, and had made her way home only to find Edith usurping her place.

"I'd recognize you anywhere," Alice spat. Though Alice had only known Edith for a few hours six years ago, Edith had made quite the impression.

As hall monitor, Edith had wielded that power to lord over all the girls and compel them to do what she demanded. As a new girl, Alice had been hazed painfully and humiliatingly. And though Edith disappeared the next day, she had never forgotten the Prince's guard dog, attack dog and lap dog all in one — Edith.

"I thought you were dead," you tell your daughter. "That's why I left. I saw your name crossed out in the ledger."

"Edith was responsible for the ledger!" Alice yells. "All the names are in *her* script."

You whirl on Edith.

"Go!" you scream, pointing at the front door.

Edith is frozen. She shakes her head in denial.

"Now!" you stand up, yelling. "Before I lose my temper." Your heart pounding, your eyes welling, you watch your surrogate daughter of the last six years stand up and tread silently out of your house.

Then you sit back down and regard the girl you haven't seen in six years.

She's changed so much. But then, you have too.

THE END

As you emerge onto the dock through the cellar tunnel, you laugh out loud in relief.

Sing and his men are still there!

And now you see why: a full barrel of wine sits in the belly of the rowboat, alongside several huge wheels of cheese. They have another barrel on the dock, and look to be figuring out how to make it fit when you and Alice burst onto the scene.

"Thick as thieves you are," you smile at the three men. Never have you been so relieved.

Sing looks past your shoulder, as if concerned you'd been chased.

But the only thing chasing you is smoke.

Sing's nose twitches, like a cat's.

"Fire?" he asks.

"I'm afraid so," you nod. "I set them."

Sing mutters in Chinese to the men, and they abandon the second barrel, getting in the boat. Sing helps you and Alice board and finally gets in himself.

It's slow-going with the added weight, but the men row steadily and quietly.

Smoke fills the top half of the tunnel, and Sing urges you and Alice to keep your heads down.

Alice clutches you the entire journey back to the Thames, only releasing her grip once you've cleared the overgrown vines at the entrance.

Out on the river, you can hear the clanging of bells. A huge black plume of smoke rises in the distance.

"I do hope my friends got out alright," Alice murmurs. You want to reassure her that they did, but of that you can't be certain. All you know is that *she* got out intact.

At the first available dock, Sing and his men drop

you and Alice off, and you give them all the biggest and longest hugs you have. Then, it is such a beautiful day that you and Alice walk all the way home.

Turn to page 271.

As Edith comes down the steps, you stand aside, so she can see the box. But she's looking at you.

"Are you all right?" she asks. Your feelings must show on your face. You look away, down the hall. There are more boxes, more bottles.

When Edith sees the braids, she's puzzled. She believes they're wigs at first. But when she picks one up, and sees what it is, she drops it like a snake.

Her face crumples.

It's important that she sees the truth.

"This is what happens to girls here," you state quietly. "No Queen. No kingdom. This is what you get."

Edith is frozen in place, trembling, shaking her head.

Then she gags, and vomits on the floor. She brings her hands up to cover her mouth but she throws up again. She struggles to breathe normally.

"Do you see? Do you see why I need to find my daughter and get her away from this place?"

An ear-splitting howl claws its way out of Edith's throat, and she turns and starts up the stairs, still screaming.

"Edith, wait!" You chase after the girl. If she keeps screaming like this she'll bring the guards.

You chase Edith as she shrieks through the streets of Covent Garden and toward Shoreditch. All around you, the girls stir in their buildings and houses.

"Edith!"

Light spills into the city from a far door opening. It's as if dawn has come to London. But this one brings two giants on the outskirts. The guards draw their swords, surveying the scene.

"Oy! What's going on?" The guards spot Edith,

then swivel their gaze to you. "Who the bloody blazes are you?"

Light rakes the city from the north, from another open door. More palace guards. More swords. All the while Edith keens.

Your mind races through your options. At this rate, you'll be quickly surrounded. If you fight, they may simply spear you. So that's not an option.

If you decide to give yourself up, turn to page 139.

If you run, and try to backtrack your way to Sing's boat, spin and sprint to 195.

"Well," you begin, "if you must know..."

"I must," Lady Plumly says curtly.

You describe the girl to the best of your ability, mentioning the prominent mole on her left cheek.

Plumly nods.

"That girl's got a mouth as wide as her arse."

"What will happen to her?" you ask. "Will you punish her? She was merely attempting to aid me."

"It's none of your concern," Plumly says.

You open your mouth to protest, but then think better of it. Alice is your focus, you remind yourself. Alice.

"And indeed," Plumly continues, "regarding your missing child, I *have* been hearing things."

"Go on," you say.

Turn to page 26.

It takes you a long time to get to sleep. And when you do, you have a dream in which you are sitting with Lorina and Alice by the riverbank all those many years ago.

Hyde Park is busy, and you gaze at the courting couples walking in the sun. But then thick clouds roll in and cool the day.

Suddenly, a rabbit runs into view. Somehow, he is wearing a waistcoat, out of which he pulls a pocketwatch. Preposterous.

"I'm late!" he says frantically, bounding off. Talking animals? Madness.

Getting up, you follow him. But when you look back to see if Lorina and Alice see what you see, they are gone. There is nothing under the tree but a blanket, a picnic basket, a book and a daisy chain.

You turn back to the rabbit, but he is gone too. In his place are your daughters, but they are both facedown in the grass, unmoving.

"Alice!" you cry. "Lory!" You run to them, but already they have begun sinking into the earth, as if the grass were quicksand.

By the time you reach them the earth has almost fully swallowed them.

"No!" you scream.

You jerk awake.

"Eh?" Reg half-asleep, mutters at your movement.

Then you hear something from downstairs.

"Reg," you tap his shoulder. "I heard something."

"That was me," he says.

"No, from downstairs."

"Well, we do have another person in the house now."

"Why would she be downstairs?"

At this, Reg sits up in bed.

"Could it be a burglar?" you ask.

The two of you pull on your housecoats and your husband retrieves a cricket bat from the closet.

"Stay here!" he whispers, but you follow close behind, and Reg doesn't insist. You know that he is secretly grateful for your company.

As silently as you can, you creep downstairs.

Turn to page 262.

You blink blearily at the bars of your cell. It's morning. Your stomach growls like an angry lion. You can't remember the last meal you'd had.

In the distance, you hear a chanting. It's indistinct at first, but soon becomes clear.

"Off with her head! Off with her head!"

It goes on for what seems like hours, when two guards appear in their deadpan masks, unlocking your cell.

"Stand up," one of them orders.

"What's to happen to me?"

They laugh.

"Ain't you got ears to hear?"

The chanting outside drifts in unabated.

"But what have I done?"

Once you've stood, the guards manacle your wrists behind you, then place a thin black hood over your head.

You're marched through the halls until you are outside. You can't see much, only the area around your feet, but you can hear the sudden roar in the crowd as you appear. What must be a hundred little girls, all screaming for blood.

You catch glimpses of them. Little hands in white gloves. Some holding fans. One girl tries to peek under your hood, but is quickly pulled away.

The guards march you up several steps to a wooden platform where you are forced to your knees, and your head placed in a wooden stock. You try to call out, to protest your innocence, but are drowned out by the children's cries.

Then, as if someone had flipped a switch, the children fade into complete silence.

"Ladies and gentlemen," a woman's imperious

voice intones, "assembled guests — we are gathered here today to pick one lucky miss little who will be fortunate enough to — "

Here, the girls roar as one, as if rehearsed.

"Chop off her head! Chop off her head!"

You struggle against the stocks, but it's locked tight. You try again to voice your protest, but the guard knocks your head, making you see stars.

With your neck trapped like this, it feels stretched, like a giraffe's. It almost feels as if you could extend it, like a serpent, and fly up and around the courtyard. You can almost see yourself from outside yourself, kneeling on the wood, neck stuck like a silly ostrich.

"Who will be the lucky girl?" the woman says. There is a drum roll, then the crash of a cymbal. "Aha!" the woman continues. "It is Dinah!"

Polite applause from all the little hands.

Oh no, you think. Could Dinah be Alice? Upon arrival, she might have given them the cat's name.

"Dinah! Dinah! Dinah!" the chant grows and grows. In moments, you hear the girl's footfalls on the platform. She moves close, and a guard ushers her over to the guillotine.

"Awright, young miss," he says. "It's dead simple — you simply take this axe, an' chop the rope right 'ere."

Inside the hood, you clamp your eyes shut and wait for the end.

You hear a grunt of exertion, and a *thunk*, then a disappointed sigh from the hundred girls.

"I- I- I'm sorry," the girl says. "I missed. I'll try again."

Your heart stops.

It's her!

It's Alice!

You mean to cry out to her. You want to shout, "Mummy's here! Mummy's here for you! I love you!" But in a moment of clarity, you bite your tongue.

Whatever happens to your darling, you don't want her to spend the rest of her life wracked with the guilt of having been the one who killed her own mother.

So with Alice mere feet away, you stay silent and pray to God that the hood stays on your head, even as it tumbles down into the bucket.

As your tears stream freely, soaking the mask, you hear the axe slice through the air.

THE END

You duck into an alcove and try a door. It opens! Despite the sign that says, *No entry. Please be advised that the WC is on the other side of the courtyard,* you enter.

You find yourself in a long hall, and note the guard at the other end. Nonchalantly, you turn the other way. But you wonder if heading the guarded way might be better — there being something, or some*one* to guard.

"Oh! You startled me!" A woman in an apron emerges from a doorway, wiping her hands with a cloth. Then she bows, pointing back the way you came. "Ma'am, the ball is out in the courtyard."

"I was looking for the privy," you say, adopting the most posh accent you can manage.

The servant says, "It's the other side of the courtyard, ma'am."

"Isn't there one closer?"

"I'm afraid not."

Behind you, you hear the footfalls of the guard as he approaches.

Bollocks.

Together, they escort you back out.

Then you spot Dodgson in his dodo mask. Perhaps he's learned something.

Turn to page 244.

You and Alice sprint down the hallway toward the lit area.

This has to lead to an exit, you think. But the hall turns into a small sitting area and an outdoor balcony.

Oh no.

You look for stairs, but don't see anything. You begin to try doors one after the other when two guards appear at the end of the hallway.

You grab your daughter and move back to the balcony, looking over the edge. It's a surprisingly long fall. At least three storeys. But at the very bottom is a small clump of bushes. No feather mattress, that. Would it break your fall? Or would it break your neck? And what of Alice?

"Give up," a voice says behind you. You spin and see the two guards, blocking your way back to the hall.

You look over the edge. You have a dreamlike vision of your petticoats popping open like an umbrella and slowing your fall, saving you.

"Don't do it!" the guard says, as if reading your mind. The other guard has drawn a blade.

You take Alice around the waist, then hop up onto the ledge.

"Trust Mummy," you whisper to her.

"I trust you," she says, holding onto your forearm.

And I'll trust in the Maker, you think, taking a deep breath. You lean slightly backwards, the strong wind buffeting your back. If you just lean a little more...

Just then, the guard with the blade steps behind the other, pulling the guard's head back, and slitting his throat. The man is surprised, and tries to stanch

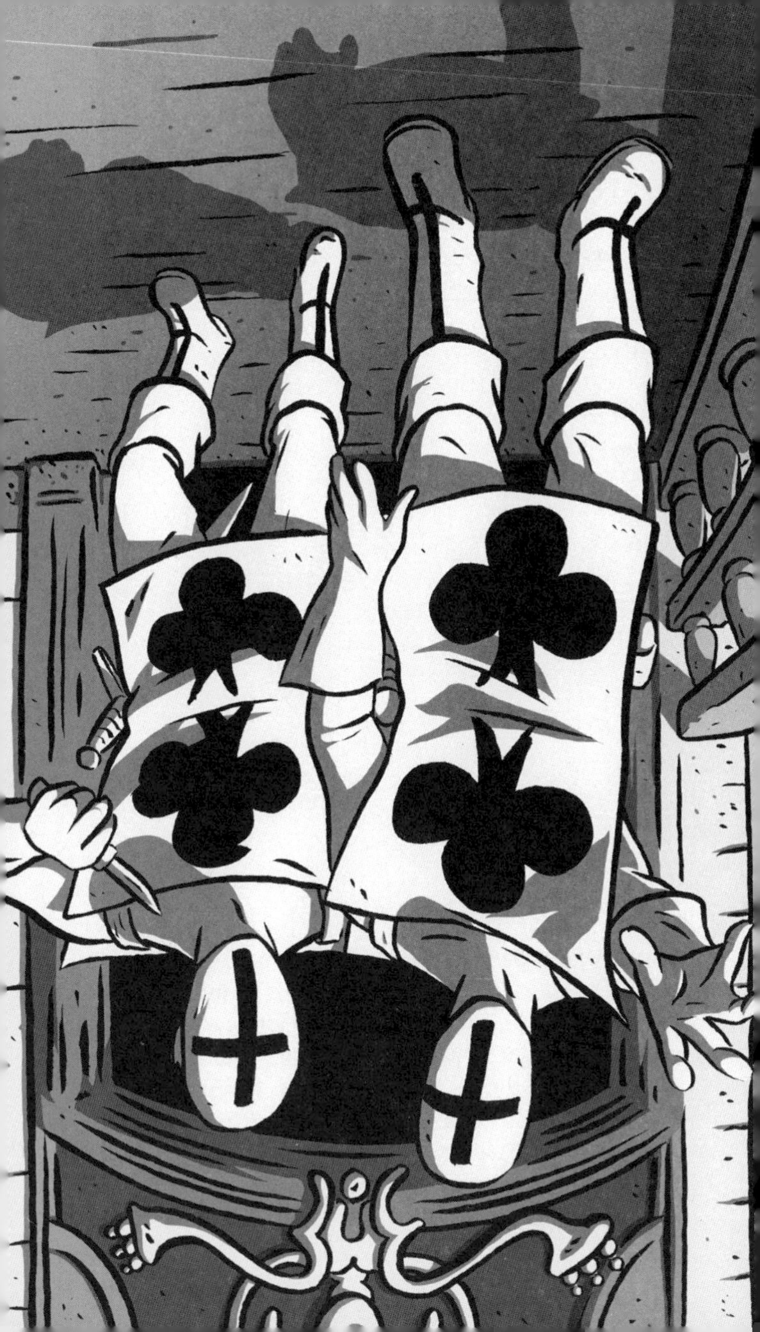

the sudden gush of blood with his gloved hands, but he quickly drops to his knees, then drops to his side, gurgling and writhing like a fish.

"What — ?" you whisper.

The guard flicks his blade to rid it of excess blood, then tilts his mask up.

It's Sing!

"Follow Sing," he says, offering a hand to pull you down.

Turn to page 253.

Edith hops from one foot to the other. "I don't know. It doesn't feel proper." The girl tries to haul the model closed but she hasn't the strength.

You step quickly down the stairs, discovering a long storage hallway. Cupboards and shelves line the walls, covered in junk. A doll's head. A saddle. A pepper grinder. Bottles of every size.

One in particular catches your interest and you lift it from the shelf. The pickling jar is filled with small white stones.

But in horror, you realize that they are teeth. All teeth.

On the floor, a wooden crate's cover is half-off and in the dim hall light, you think you see something else.

No. No.

You shove the cover aside and grasp a blonde braid. The box is filled with them. Hundreds of blonde braids, some still with pretty ribbons fastened.

Suddenly nauseous, you hold the wall for support. Gagging, you're close to throwing up. Of all the things you have seen so far, you think this must be the worst.

A noise from behind you.

"Well," Edith says, "I suppose a little curiosity never killed anyone."

If you quickly usher Edith back upstairs and close the palace up, turn to page 105.

If you want Edith to see the true nature of the Prince's Wonderland, turn to page 167.

After investigating all possible locations Alice could be, you stand with Edith in an alcove in the hall.

"I'm uncertain how to proceed," you confess to the girl. "I have to find my daughter, but it's impossible to check all the sleeping girls by morning — they're simply too spread out. And this doesn't even take into account other girls who might be with the — how did you phrase it?"

"The Jabberwock."

Edith taps her chin thoughtfully, then grins, "I have it! Tomorrow is the Prince's birthday celebration. There will be events throughout the day in the Garden. All the girls will be performing. If you find a quiet spot, you're sure to find her! There are occasionally new maids, so your presence won't look out of place."

"But it's *not* the Prince's birthday," you protest, puzzled. You explain that you know this because Reg's birthday is a week beforehand, and Reg's birthday was three *months* ago.

"That *was* his birthday, yes," Edith agrees. "But this is *also* his birthday."

"How is that possible?"

"Because every day is his birthday. And we have to do what the Prince wants on his birthday."

"Or what will happen?"

"Or it's off with your head! And out with your heart!"

You sigh. You wonder to yourself how many 'birthdays' this monster has celebrated. From everything you've learned, he has the capricious whims and the selfish temperament of a twelve-year old brat.

"If I am to witness these celebrations, I'll need a place to hide until morning."

Edith knows just the place. In the Dreamery, she takes you to a gentle hill just outside of the city. Lifting its velvet covering, she reveals a hidey-hole, coffin-sized, inside.

As you're clambering in, you hear Big Ben — the real one — chime distantly. How many hours was that? Well, it doesn't matter — by the time you wake, Sing will have left with his boatmen. As Edith rolls the velvet back over your hole, she whispers, "Good night, Hannah."

Edith's persistent poking wakes you in the morning. You climb out of the mountain to see the entire Dreamery now bathed cheerily in light from a glass skylight which you didn't see the night before. You scan the room for any girls, or guards.

"No need to fret," Edith says. "We're alone."

You yawn and stretch your back. It was cramped inside the mountain.

"I do, however, have some bad news," the girl says looking down at her hands. "I checked the ledger again, and there *was* an Alice. But the name was crossed out with red ink."

"Why would someone do that?"

"Sometimes when a girl is unruly, irredeemably so, the Prince sends her to the well. And her name is crossed out in red ink."

"The well? What is that?"

"Well, it's a well."

"But what sort of well?"

"It's a regular well."

"And what happens?"

"They're thrown in."

You're gutted. This was not the news you were

hoping for. "Do they drown? What happens?"

"Why, they fall forever."

"Nonsense."

"It's dug straight to China," Edith says.

"Impossible," you counter. "What about gravity? On the other side?"

"Well, they'd fall back, I suppose," Edith says.

"Where is this well? Is it the one I saw in the Secret Garden?"

"I don't know. It's just what the guards say. They throw unruly girls in the well."

You are doubtful there even *is* a well. You wonder if that's not just a story that the guards made up. More likely the girls are executed to prevent them from talking.

Heartbroken at this news, you sit back on the mountain. Could there have been some mistake? Maybe it was some other Alice.

If you stick to the original plan, and stakeout the Prince's birthday celebrations, hoping against hope there's been some error, turn to page 151.

If you decide to make your escape now while you can, go home and mourn your daughter on page 84.

If you want to see if Edith might consider escaping with you, turn to page 51.

You head upstairs, passing a man in a priest's collar and robe. That can't be right, you think. Why would a man of the cloth be here? At this hour? Perhaps he is merely meeting one of his parishioners — someone susceptible to drink, you imagine.

The upper floor has more tables extending around a central balcony which overlooks the bottom floor.

This might be a good place to survey the entire bar. You've got good coverage.

You tread over to the polished wood railing and scan downstairs, moving your gaze from person to person. You even scan around them, to see if they have a top hat crumpled down on a chair.

But then a top hat floats into view!

A man eases by the woman who stopped you at the door, making a beeline for the bar. There, he orders two quick shots, downs them, then heads back toward the exit.

Goodness!

You make your way down the stairs two at a time in your hurry to catch up with him.

Follow Top Hat outside to page 232.

The sun is perilously low by the time you get dressed and arrive at Hyde Park. After a day of vigorous movement, you feel simultaneously confined, and comforted by the hug of your corset.

"This way, Mummy." Lorina points toward a distant tree.

Well-manicured, Hyde Park is sprawling, full of fountains, woods, and pathways. At spots, statues are raised to memorialize prominent Englishmen. You'd never really paid much attention to them in the past, but tonight, in the dusk, they loom like gargoyles.

As you arrive, a pigeon flutters off. It'd been gnawing at the bread in the basket from the girls' picnic. You stand for a moment, breathless, as if Alice will somehow appear unbidden.

"It's as I left it," Lorina says, gathering the blanket and her book.

The spot the girls chose is beside a large manmade lake, which snakes its way through the park. At the base of the tree, you see the flattened grass where Lorina had slept. Beside it, a half-woven crown of daisies sits abandoned, blown apart by the wind. You can barely contain the sob in your throat.

You scan around, looking for more daisies, but there's no trail.

Once everything has been packed away, both Lorina and Maggie watch you, awaiting instruction. You wish Reg were here.

"We will do the most logical thing," you say. Pointing down one side of the snaking lake, you tell Lorina to search along the bank. "Maggie will go the other way," you say, "and I will venture into the park itself. We will go for twenty minutes, calling out continuously for Alice. Perhaps she is hiding. Perhaps

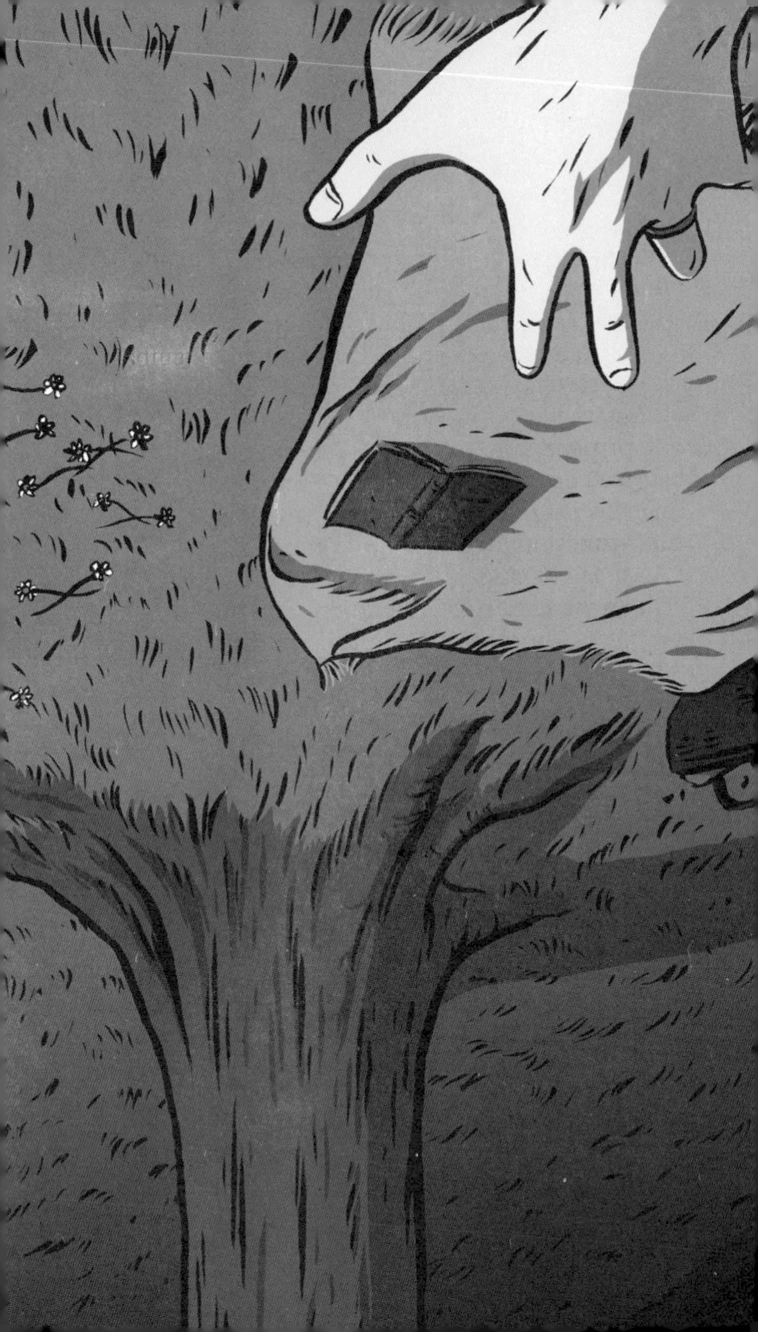

she is hurt. Then we return here. Am I clear?"

Your daughter and your housemaid nod, then you all start out.

This time of day, the park is sparsely populated. You pass a lamplighter, leaning his ladder against a lamp post.

"Excuse me," you say to the man as he climbs, "but have you seen a little girl? She's seven years old."

Striking a match, the man looks down at you, shaking his head. "Nay. Best get ye young'uns home double-quick," the man says. The gas flares, then stabilizes. The man closes the glass door on the lamp and starts back down.

"That is my intention," you say, moving on. What a supremely unhelpful gentleman.

For the next twenty minutes, you call yourself hoarse. You can hear the distant cries of Lorina and Maggie. In the dusk light, you look hither and tither for your daughter, but you only see couples sauntering in the evening.

Finally, you turn round and meet back at the tree. As you arrive, you are ever hopeful, but one glance dashes it. No Alice.

"Perhaps we missed her by a whisker?" Maggie says. "Perhaps the young miss made her way home?"

You nod. That is certainly a possibility. But in your secret heart you are afraid to believe.

"Maggie," you hand the picnic basket to your housemaid. "Take Lorina home. Hopefully Alice is there. Wait for Reg and tell him what's transpired."

"And you, Ma'am?"

"I'll keep looking."

Maggie frowns.

"Keep lookin'? All by ye lonesome?"

You nod, determined.

"An' when can we expect ye home?"

You shake your head. "I've no idea."

Maggie sighs, but does as you instruct. You watch the two of them tread off in the waning light. When they are nothing but small dots, you turn once again to the sound of the water lapping against the embankment. In the dusk, you can see the herringbone of wind on water, and feel the chill of the days getting shorter.

"Give us a copper?"

Jumping, you turn at the voice.

From behind the tree a vagrant in tattered rags appears.

You should have known he was there from the smell. Your nose wrinkles as the unmistakable scent of stale urine surrounds you. The man grins at you, his missing teeth a smattering of dark holes.

"A copper, miss?" He extends a grubby hand toward you.

Your gut is screaming at you to get away. His presence feels like an ill omen.

But then you catch yourself. Maybe the man saw something? This is his turf, after all. Could he have spied something helpful to you?

Perhaps you passed Alice on the way to the park? Perhaps she is already home and all this worry is for naught. If you decide to head home, turn to page 71.

However, if you decide to inquire with the vagrant about Alice, turn to page 54.

You run blindly, arms out in front of you.

"Help!" you cry as you hurtle through the fog. "Help me!"

In the lamplight, you can barely see a wall that leads to an alleyway. With no choice, you duck down it, pawing at its sides.

Halfway down, you stop. You try to calm your ferociously beating heart, and quiet your breath. You listen for footfalls, but hear nothing.

Perhaps you lost the thief?

Without warning, a forearm twines around your waist and a cold blade presses against your neck. You inhale sharply, but try not to move.

"So kind of you to find a place where we can be alone," the man purrs.

Then his hand moves to your neckline, pulling your cape open.

"Please," your voice comes out as a whisper. You swallow and try again. "Please, listen to me. I have money. I can — "

"Quiet now," the man deepens the pressure of the knife. "Hush, or I shall slit your throat into a smile so wide it should meet behind."

Even though you can't see his face, you can tell he is grinning.

You can barely breathe. You think you might faint. In fact, that might be a blessing.

As the man's hands drop towards your breasts, you hear a sharp *thock!*

The man's hands grow limp, then slide off your body like a cloak. The knife clatters to the ground.

You stand, unmoving.

Is this some sort of trick?

Then a different voice carries through the fog.

"You're safe now, madam."

In disbelief, you turn.

Though the light is faint, a man in a cricket player's uniform stands there, with a bat in his hand. On the ground in front of him is the cutpurse, unconscious.

"Oh!" you exclaim, grateful for the unexpected aid. "Were you on your way to a match?"

The man smiles confidently. "I am Batsman!"

"Well," you acknowledge, "you certainly must be an exceptional one."

"No," the man clarifies. "Batsman is my name."

"Your name is Batsman?" This puzzles you. Why is this gentleman's name what he is dressed as? That's as if your mother had named you Proper Englishwoman or some such nonsense.

"Indeed," the man half-bows. Then Batsman proceeds to tell you an astonishing story. One you are disinclined to believe.

Apparently, when he was a young boy, Batsman's family were moving from the countryside to the city. Their carriage was accosted by a highwayman, who brutally killed both his parents. Too young to do anything about it at the time, Batsman vowed to rid London of all crime and criminals.

"I wished to strike fear into the hearts of the cowardly cutthroats who would terrorize my fellow citizens," Batsman says. "Now I patrol this godforsaken Gotham by gaslight for beastly curs such as this joker right here." He nudges the unconscious man, who doesn't stir.

"Well I certainly appreciate your vigilance," you tell the man, "but why a batsman? If you truly desired to strike fear into the hearts of criminals, you might

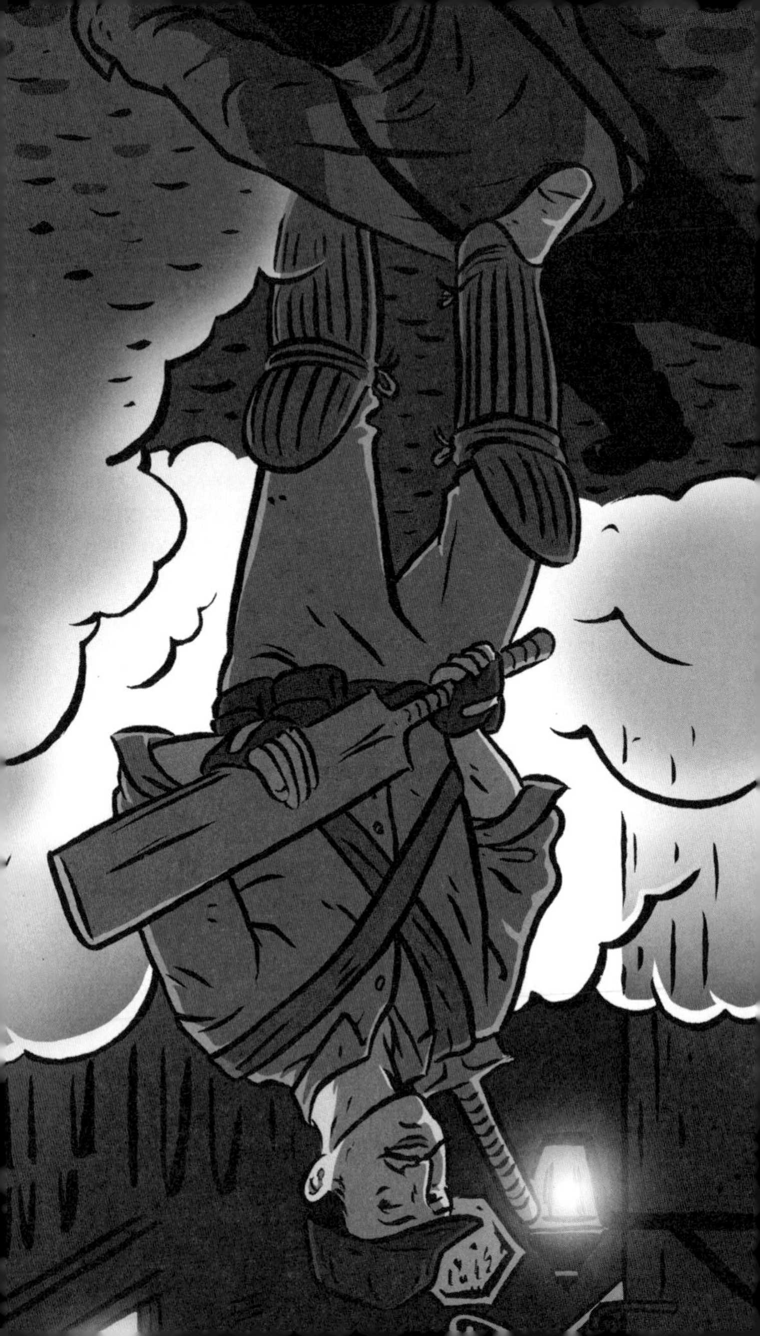

have chosen a more ferocious uniform."

Batsman looks offended.

"Such as what?"

"Well," you muse aloud. "Did you ever consider a bat?"

"A bat? Dress up like a bat? Are you mad?"

Then a vision of your cat Dinah as she's about to pounce on a bug comes to mind.

"Or a cat."

Batsman snorts in derision.

"The Batman? The Catman? Utter madness." Batsman bends down and rifles through the unconscious man's pockets.

This gives you pause. Is Batsman a thief himself?

"Twinkle twinkle little bat, how I wonder where you're at," Batsman sings to himself under his breath. Finding a small leather coin purse, Batsman tucks it in his own pocket and gets up. "Madam, I wish you a safe journey."

Then, brandishing his cricket bat like a cane, Batsman saunters off through the fog.

Shaken, but thankfully unharmed, you wander back to the street.

Continue to page 28.

You find some matches and light the candles on the man's table and desk, better illuminating the room.

Pacing along the shelves, you are immediately struck by the eclecticism of Dodgson's choices. Books on philosophy sit beside primers on mesmerism. The trashiest of penny dreadfuls beside fables for children. But one book stands out.

It's entirely handmade. Not only is the title hand-lettered on the spine, but the cover is carefully drawn and painted in.

ALICE'S ADVENTURES UNDER GROUND, you read.

You shake your head, disbelieving.

You open the cover and turn the pages. Absolutely *everything* is done by hand. It's clearly a labour of love by someone named Lewis Carroll, and with a shock you realize that it is dedicated to your daughter! Without question it is *her* full name!

For Alice Pleasance Liddell, it reads.

You are trembling as you turn the pages of this book. Who is this Lewis Carroll and why this particular interest in Alice?

You become aware of someone else in the room, and glance at the movement.

"Oh!" a woman stands at the entrance, holding a blue envelope. "I was expecting Mr. Dodgson."

You shut the book guiltily.

"I was just waiting for him myself," you reply with a confidence you don't feel. "Do you know if he's on campus?"

"I'm certain he is," the woman says, walking over to the table. She places the envelope on it, leaning it against the glass vial. "I saw him earlier today in the

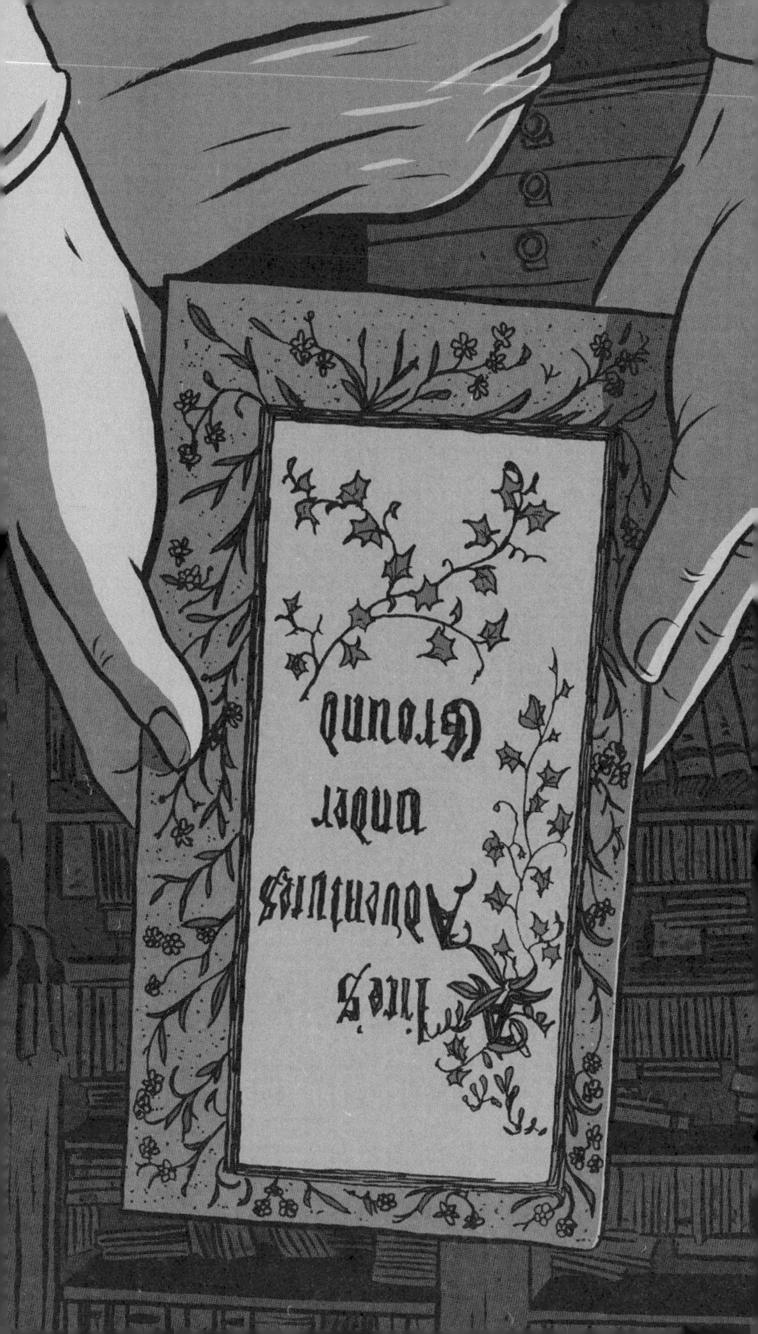
Alice's Adventures under Ground

garden." Then she glances at the book you're holding, and a smile breaks out on her face.

"Isn't it wonderful?" she says, "I saw an early draft of it."

"This book?" you ask. "But how? Do you know Lewis Carroll?"

The woman laughs. "You don't know about Lewis Carroll?"

You shake your head. "No. But I'd be very appreciative of anything you could tell me."

"You've never read his poems, or articles?"

"No," you reply. "Is he an instructor here?"

The woman can barely contain her delight. "My dear, Lewis Carroll *is* Professor Charles Dodgson. It's his nom-de-plume!"

You look at the book again. Why use a pen-name? Why write this book?

"Now if you'll excuse me," the woman smiles and waves goodbye.

You smile back until she's disappeared, then you examine the blue envelope. You pick it up. It's bulky. There's something inside. You read the return address.

My word.

It's from Buckingham Palace!

If you open the envelope, turn to page 202.

If, on the other hand, you decide to put the envelope back and read the book, turn to page 215.

The guards advance as quickly as they can through the city streets, taking care to leap over stray arms and legs, but you have a healthy head start and dash back the way you came.

They're not used to this. Years of indolence has made them slow. It's an easy job to watch over drugged, blindfolded girls.

You outpace them, and with a geographical sense that surprises even yourself, you manage somehow to find your path back to the pantry and the steps that lead to Sing.

You take the stairs two at a time, and when you arrive in the cellar, he steps out of the shadows, long metal bar in hand.

"Where Alice?" he asks, eyes searching the stairs.

"I've got guards behind me!" you cry, sprinting past him. "Run!"

But it isn't guards that make it to you first.

With a bark, a bloodhound leaps from the stairs and wraps its jaws around Sing's forearm. Sing swears in Chinese, then manages to beat it off with the metal bar, just as another dog snags his leg. He cracks this one on its forehead, dropping it.

You run through the tunnel with Sing only paces behind, limping. He's managed to lose the dogs but you hear urgent men's voices.

As you reach the gate that leads to the hidden waterway, Sing yells out in Chinese to the boatmen. When you emerge from the tunnel, the men are already aboard, oars in hand, ready to depart.

You take a running jump aboard, and Sing follows. He urges the boatmen on, and soon you are powering away from the dock.

But guards appear from the tunnel and instead of

swords, they're carrying crossbows.

"Down!" Sing screams, pushing you into the belly of the boat.

Bolts fly, one thunking heavy into the boat. A second hits a boatman. He doesn't scream. He just drops, the projectile jutting out of his neck.

Then Sing gasps. He clutches his shoulder, where his tunic is now blossoming a bright red. Scrambling, he moves back toward his fallen countryman and grabs the oar. With one arm, he tries to get you moving again.

But more bolts come. The man in front of you is hit. Then hit again. He drops.

Then Sing is struck once more. When the front of his shirt is scarlet he falls backwards, eyes open.

The boat slows and stops.

You sit there, shocked. You have never been this close to this much death before in your entire life.

The guards splash out into the tunnel and surround you, crossbows raised at your heart.

Go to page 172.

Forty minutes later you are wearing an elegant red evening dress and carry a duck mask in your hands. Festooned with feathers, its wide yellow bill flares out cartoonishly. Dodgson has a dodo's mask.

Anxious about Alice, you don't question why a bachelor don would have a woman's evening dress hidden away in his warren of rooms. Nor why he would have a variety of masks available on short notice. Strange men hoard odd items.

"Are you ready?" Dodgson pockets the invite and the key, placing them in the inside pocket of his red velvet jacket. "The carriage is here."

You merely glare at him.

"You- you- you're still angry with me," he says, more of a statement than a question.

"Furious."

"Well, you can be up- up- upset with me on the way."

The two of you walk out into the quiet of the Oxford night. A silvery half-moon casts the stately college buildings in a ghostly hue. You manage to hold tight your barely-contained fury until the two of you are safely in the carriage and on your way.

"Why her?!" It finally bursts out of you. "Why Alice?"

Dodgson looks down at his gloved hands, holding his dodo mask. He looks contrite and apologetic, but that does nothing to assuage you. He tries to explain his fascination.

"L- l- l- little girls are as close to *pure* at that age as they will ever be. She is so new on this Earth, she still c- ca- carries the warmth of the hand of the Maker."

You snort. Little girls are hardly pure. You think

back on Alice and Lorina's conniving ways to manipulate and cajole you and their father to get their way. You think about all the piss and shit and vomit you and their nurse, Ada, wiped up over the years. Only an unmarried Oxford professor of mathematics could believe that little girls are as pure as all that.

"They're not pure," you say. "They've merely had less of a chance to disappoint you."

"Th- th- there is another thing," Dodgson adds. "Around her, I hardly ever stutter."

You stare at this man, trying to decipher precisely what he is expressing.

"Do you intend to court her, Mr. Dodgson? Must I remind you she is only seven years old."

"No! No!" the man protests, waving his hands like he's treading water, "I only want to bask in her presence. Like a malnourished petal in the sun. I h- h- ha- have only the holiest, loftiest and n- n- noblest intentions!"

Something about the vehemence in his protest leads you to believe him, despite the circumstances.

"What is your relationship to the Prince?" you ask. "How did you meet him? Why was he compelled to do this 'favour' for you?"

Dodgson explains that he met the Prince through photography. Over the last year, as photography became more than a hobby, Dodgson would travel around London taking photos of well-known actors, writers — the glitterati. So when the Prince wanted portraits of himself done, Dodgson's name came up.

"It turned out that we had a mu- mu- mutual interest in little girls. And I showed him some of my portraits, including those of your d- d- daughters. I assure you I had nothing to do with Alice's d- d- disappearance. It was all the Prince's do- do- doing."

As the carriage sidles up to Buckingham Palace, you marvel at its majesty, even in the dark. You've never had cause to be this close to it before. Dodgson directs the driver to a modest side gate where both of you are let out. Just inside the gate, a palace guard stands, quiet and still as a statue.

Retrieving the golden key, Dodgson unlocks the small gate and gestures with a gloved hand.

"A- a- after you," he says.

You put on your duck mask, then step onto the palace grounds.

Turn to page 220.

Who is this woman? How is she here?

In a frenzied instant, you grab a brass statue of a mongoose and swing it at her head. Like a sack of potatoes she drops to the rug.

But Alice is screaming, which frightens you. The scream will bring others.

You bend down, trying to cover her mouth with your hand but she bites you!

You step back, like a rabbit bit by a python. But Alice takes this opportunity to jump up and out of the steamer trunk.

You swipe at her, but only manage to clutch the puffed sleeve of her petticoat before she tears away toward the corridor. "No, no," you mutter, chasing after her. Stupid, stupid.

The girl bursts out of the entrance to your warren of rooms and patters down the hallway, screaming. The dosage must not have been high enough. Alice should still be unconscious. It should have lasted until midnight.

You sprint into the hallway after her, but Alice has stopped screaming. She is sly enough to have gone quiet. When you encounter a break in the corridors, you aren't sure which way she went.

You grow nauseous. If Alice escapes and tells her story you will be scandalized.

And once the authorities arrive and see what you have hidden behind the curtain in your room, you will be arrested. Or hanged.

It was a mistake to take her. But your curiosity was ravenous. Mere watching, mere stalking wasn't enough. Not anymore. You were besotted by the girl.

You lived like a starving dog at the intersection of Curious & Curiouser.

For another hour you search, but Alice is gone. When you return to your room, you cover the woman's body with a blanket. It is only when you light a lamp do you recognize her. Alice's mother. My God. Who else knows she is here? How soon will they come for your head? You need to escape.

For a moment you consider drowning yourself in the Thames. You see yourself, like Millais' Ophelia painting in the Tate. Such a beautiful way to expire. But you fear they will catch you before you get your chance. They'd lock you up. You could never survive in prison. It's full of philistines and brutes. You would wilt.

Poison is faster. Quickly, you stir a fatal dose of arsenic into a cup of cold tea. The powder you'd kept for poisoning rats would now be your ignominious end.

Carpe Diem, you think, tossing the beverage back. *Carpe Tea Diem,* you smirk at the portmanteau as you wait for the poison to take effect.

You sigh. You'd always suspected that you were cut out for better things. But a single misstep and bad luck waylaid your historic provenance.

A sudden, unbearable pain seizes your stomach. When you spit up blood, another wave of pain drops you to your knees. As you lose consciousness you hear shouts out in the corridor, and approaching footsteps.

THE END

You recognize that it is a horrific breach of protocol to open another person's mail, but you have seen enough to make you very suspicious of Mr. Charles Dodgson, so with reluctance you take a letter opener from the table and slit the side of the envelope open.

Out slips a golden key. The card inside, delicately scented of rose petals, is an official invitation to a masquerade ball that very night. Scrawled on the card is a message.

"Hope to see you, my friend."

It's signed by the Prince himself.

You stare in shock.

Then something else slips out of the envelope, and it turns your blood cold.

It is a photo of Alice.

At least, you think it's Alice.

The truth is, you have never seen your daughter looking like this. She is smiling gently into the camera, but it looks coerced. Forced. Her eyes are half-closed.

Her hair is curled, and her face is painted with cosmetics. She looks older than her 7 years.

You are sickened. You turn the photo over and there's more cursive.

As a present, I've had my men invite your little lady friend.

A voice from behind.

"Oh! Who are you?"

You turn. It's Dodgson. You fling the photo at him. It's all you can do not to claw his eyes out.

"What is the *meaning* of this!"

The tall, skinny man stares down at the photo for a second before bending down to pick it up. He turns it around and reads the back.

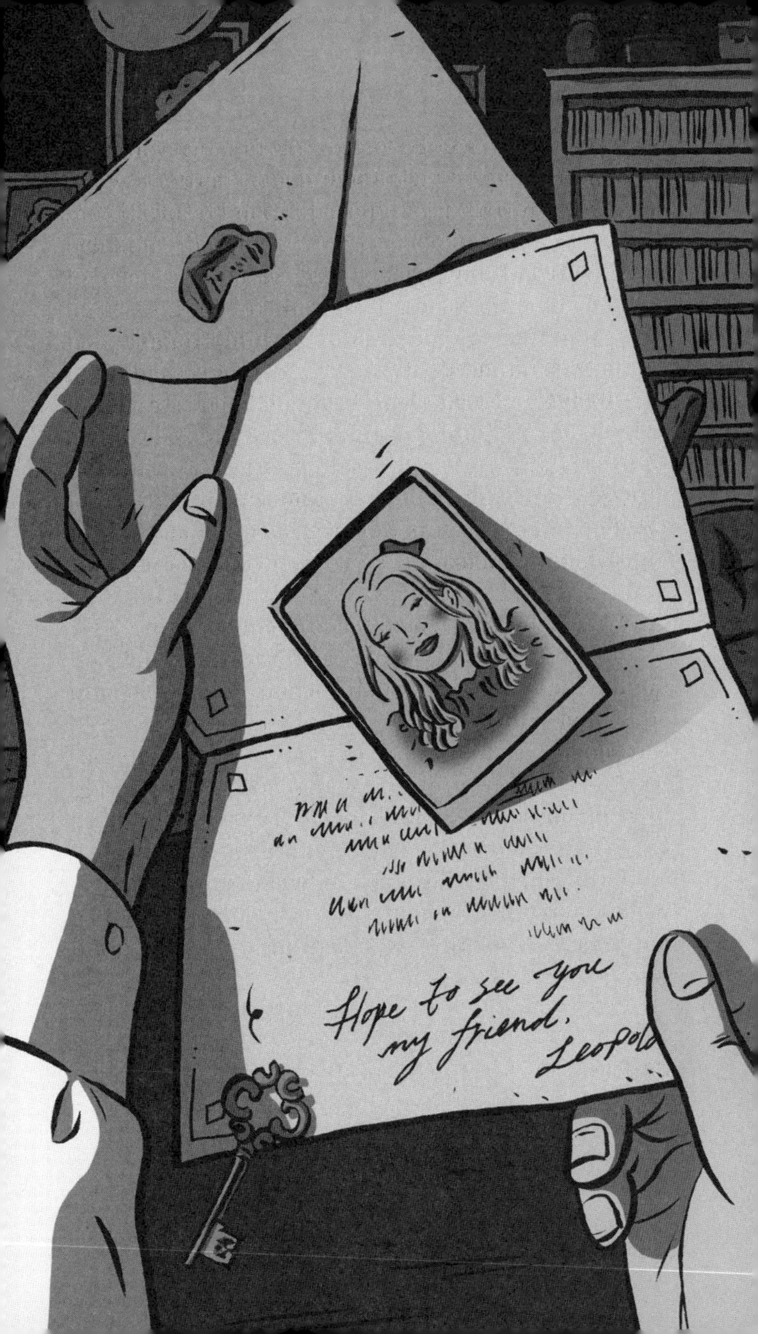

Hope to see you
my friend.
Leopol

"I didn't arrange this. I assure you. The Prince took it upon himself!"

Without realizing it, you've picked up the letter opener and are now wielding it like a knife.

"As a present?!" you step toward Dodgson and he backs away slowly, his hands up, trying to placate you. "My daughter is a *person!* Not a present!"

"Yes, yes," Dodgson agrees. "Let me — please, Mrs. Liddell, allow me the oppor-" Dodgson starts to stutter. For some reason this enrages you. You don't have time for this.

"The oppor-" he starts again.

You level your gaze at him, forcing yourself to be patient, to allow him to finish.

"The opportunity to r- re- redeem myself in your eyes, Mrs. Liddell."

There is no chance of that now, you think. But at the moment Dodgson seems to have you at a disadvantage.

"A- a- allow me to help you get your daughter back."

You want to kill the man. Truly you do. But you have so many questions that require answers.

If he can get Alice back unharmed, perhaps you will only stab his eyes out.

"What do you propose?" you ask coldly.

Turn to page 197.

Let's *not* play a game, you think.

Quickly, before the girls can use any of the dangerous tools, you find an exit into one of the sets, then sprint through them until you emerge in the inn room.

"Girls, get up!" you say with as much conviction as you can muster. "There's a fire!"

"Fire?" the older girl asks, frowning. "But we've heard no bell."

You move over to Alice, picking her up. She gasps when she sees you, but fortunately does not betray who you are.

"We must go!" you order. "Now!"

The older girl gets up and starts ushering the girls out.

"Hurry!" you shout, as they head towards the Performatory entrance. "Tell others! Fire!"

With some satisfaction you hear them echoing your alarm as they rush out.

"Mummy!" Alice embraces you, and you allow yourself a moment of relief. You choke out a sob and your eyes mist up.

"But is there really a fire?" Alice asks.

Lowering her to the ground, you grab the lamp oil and matchbox off the armchair. "There will be," you say with grim determination.

Moving back through the sets, you stop at a tree whose green leaves are made of paper and douse them liberally with the lamp oil, soaking the trunk for good measure. Then you light and toss a match.

"Mummy!" Alice cries out in alarm, as the wall ignites.

You grab her by the hand and hurry away.

"Abominable place," you mutter under your

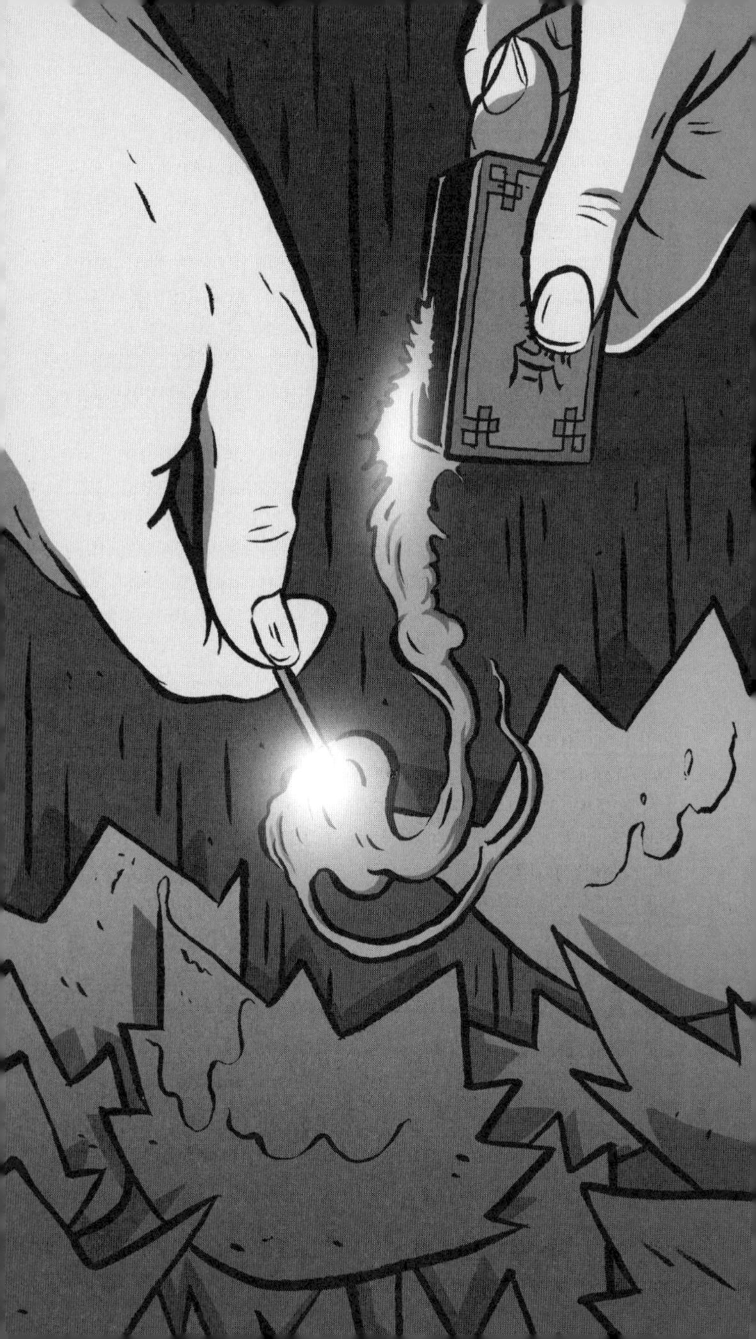

breath. As the both of you run through the sets, you're grateful that the girls heeded your alarm and the Performatory is blessedly empty. Still you check each room, even as they begin to fill with white smoke. You must be quick, however. You know that once the fire reaches the gas lamps, there will be excitement.

You stop in a milliner's shop and set a bolt of fabric on fire. You throw some of the display hats on it for good measure.

Now you hear the distant clanging fire bell.

As you help Alice down from the stage, two guards appear. You freeze for a moment, but they take no notice of you. Each carries a bucket, laden with water.

With Alice, you slip out into the hallway.

If you try to go out the guarded servant's entrance, turn to page 249.

If you want to take your chances with Sing's secret serpentine stream, head towards the cellar on page 165. He has surely gone by now, but you can be assured that that exit goes unguarded.

Springing out of the interrogation box, you dash towards Alice. A shocked gasp from everyone in the room. Taken by surprise, all the girls panic.

You grab Alice's hand while all the other jury members rush to get away, climbing up towards the back of their box.

But in their zeal to get away, their collective weight unbalances, then tips the entire box!

With a huge slam, bodies and chairs sprawl everywhere.

"Order! There will be order!" the Judge yells, banging his gavel. But he is hard to hear over the commotion. "Where are my guards?! Enforce order!"

By now, everyone in the room is panicking and trying to get out the doors. The guards trip over chairs and stumble over little girls.

"I will have order!"

In the confusion, you and Alice rush to the side door where two guards sit at a table, casually playing cards. They get up quickly, but overturn their table in the process.

Cards fly everywhere.

One tries to pick them up while the other guard lunges at you.

You dodge his extended grasp, then hurry out the side door, slamming it back in his face.

As he goes to open it again, you grab a chair sitting in the hallway and jam it under the doorknob.

"Out the other door!" you hear a voice boom in the courtroom. "Teams of two! Spread out! Find them."

You and Alice hasten down the hall. There are so many doors. You try one after the other, but they are all locked.

Then, the next door you try opens! At the same time, you spot an archway that leads towards a lit area that might just be an exit.

If you decide to open the unlocked door, turn to page 238.

If you head towards the lit area, move to page 176.

Dodgson marches over to a dining table then raises his arms. "L-l-ladies and gentlemen!" he shouts over the hubbub. "I will now attempt a feat of incredible dexterity and dimension!"

Everyone turns, but there is a laugh from someone in the shadows. "Dodgson," he calls out. "What are you on about?"

"I will now at- at- tempt," Dodgson takes a breath, "to pull this tablecloth out from underneath these dishes, without disturbing a single one!"

You start your escape. All eyes are on Dodgson.

The man in shadow laughs again. "Are you mad?"

"My P- P- Prince," Dodgson stammers, "I can do it!"

"He's sauced!" someone in the crowd shouts, to a response of laughter.

The Prince steps out of the shadows and toward the table. "All right, Dodgson. I believe you! But I wonder if you have as much faith in yourself. Would you care for a wager?"

By sticking to the walls, you've made it quite close to the passageway by which you'd entered. Fortunately, the Prince's offer of a wager has piqued everyone's interest, and the guards venture deeper into the courtyard. Enough for you to slip behind them, and out the exit.

"W- w- wager?" Dodgson says, uncertain.

You don't stop to see what Dodgson wagers. You make a beeline for a nearby Hansom Cab and pull your sleeping daughter into it. As the driver sets his horses going, you hear a loud clatter from the palace, then uproarious laughter.

Turn to page 259.

It pains you, but you hold your tongue.

"The valiant hunter steels his nerves," the announcer utters dramatically. "Aims..."

Boom!

The lion's rump is hit. Through the ringing in your ears, a soft cry is heard. The girl inside the costume twitches, then drops.

Everyone applauds as the Prince saunters over to the lion and places his polished boot on its back. You merely shut your eyes and stifle a sob.

But when you re-open your eyes, the Prince is staring at you.

You are the only one not rapturously overjoyed and clapping.

Quickly, you plaster a grin on your face and cheer the man, pumping your fist.

The Prince smiles, and he waves at the crowd. There is a line of grins on all the girls.

"I return triumphant!" the Prince cries, holding his rifle aloft. "Having slain monsters. Having faced immense dangers. Having dined with heads of state and Kings. I return from my grand tour of the world to..." He falters.

"War!" the announcer supplies.

"War?"

"Quite, you highness," the announcer continues. "In your absence, foul winds have gathered into a terrible storm. But with the experience you have accrued, the skills you have learned, you will wade into the war well prepared." You watch as the man in green whispers to an aide, who scurries off.

Another aide takes the rifle from the Prince and hands him a gleaming broad sword.

All eyes turn as massive doors to the courtyard

open and an army of girls dressed in pots and pans emerge. Their armour, crafted largely out of silver dinner trays, gleams in the sun. Each one of them carries a pot lid for a shield, and a candlestick holder for a sword.

It would be comical if you hadn't already watched the Prince kill two girls in cold blood.

You scan the faces of the girls for Alice, but they are all rushing forward, their pot helmets askew.

With a roar, the Prince meets the tide of enemy combatants. Many panic, dropping their shields in fright. The girls fight as best they can, but they are children, and an immense, terrifying man is coming at them with an actual sword.

But there!

At the back, faltering in the heaviness of her armour —

"Alice!" you cry.

At your voice, she turns to you. She can't quite believe it.

The Prince is whacking away at the girls. Fortunately, their armour keeps the sword from penetrating, but the blows still soundly knock them down.

You run to your daughter. Hopefully the madness of the battle will distract everyone from what you're about to do.

"Mummy," Alice whispers. "You're here!"

You start taking off some of the bulky armour. If you have to run, it will only serve to slow her down. But you're spotted!

"You!" the man in green shouts. "Stop!"

You grab Alice's hand and start toward the nearest doorway when three sharp bells ring in quick succession.

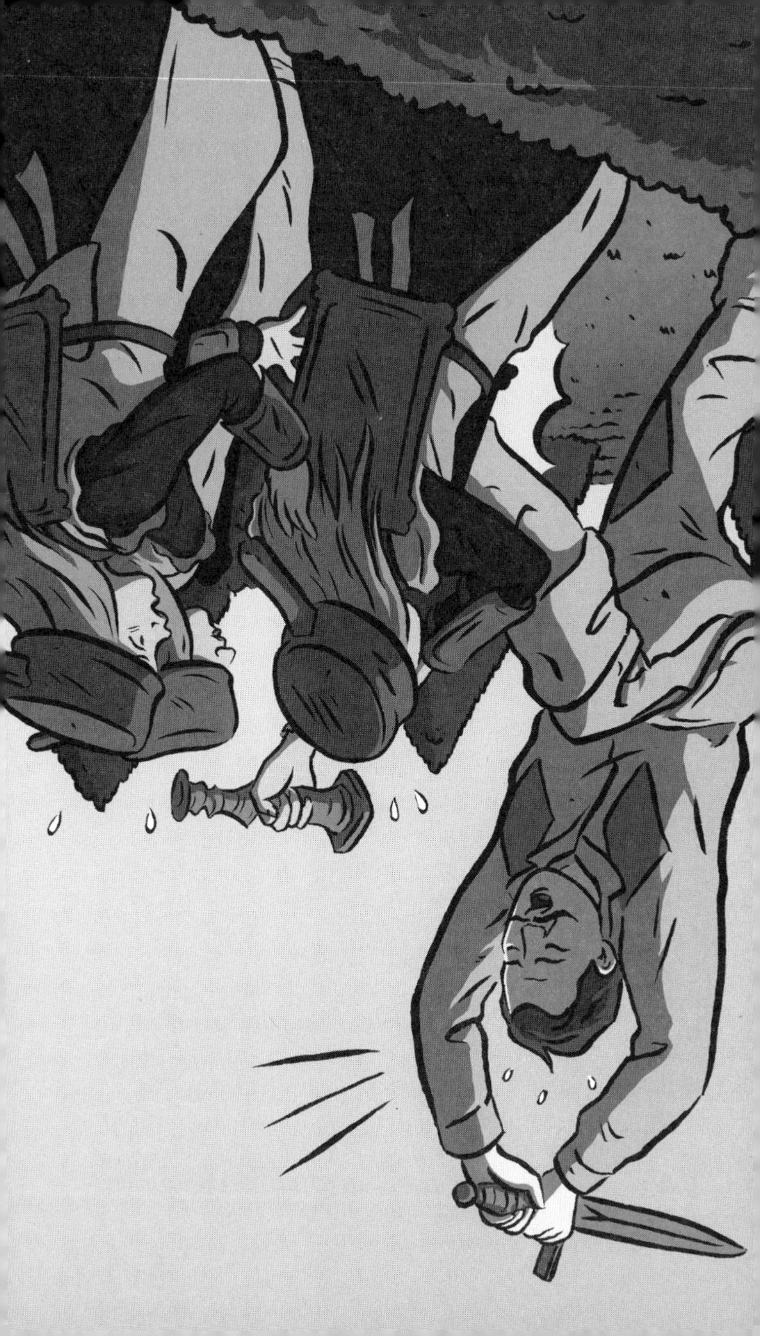

214

Ding! Ding! Ding!

You look back to see the announcer holding a brass schoolmaster's bell in his hand.

All the girls drop. The advancing army collapses. Every girl in the audience falls to the grass. Alice's hand grows limp in yours as she plummets.

"No!" you yell.

Alice lies on the ground, eyes open, staring up at you but she gives no indication that she can see or hear anything. Has she been mesmerized in some way?

Around you, the faceless guards advance.

What do you do?

If you give up, turn to page 133.

If you attempt to manufacture a plausible fiction for your actions, go to page 245.

If you tuck Alice under your arm and run, go to page 240.

Despite your curiosity, you decide that it would be too severe a breach of etiquette to read someone's private mail. So you light an oil lamp and sit down to read about *Alice's Adventures Under Ground*. But almost immediately, you are unsettled. It is about Alice's disappearance from the park into some kind of rabbit hole.

In another moment down went Alice after it, never once considering how in the world she was to get out again.

With trembling hands you shut the book and stare at it, as if the book itself were responsible for conjuring up real events. You blink, then open the book again.

In it, Alice is falling, but for miles. Is that some sort of clue?

Down, down, down. Would the fall never come to an end! 'I wonder how many miles I've fallen by this time?' she said aloud. 'I must be getting somewhere near the centre of the earth.

Even as you read it, you regard the book as if it were some kind of mystical artifact sent back in time. You are struck by an impulse to scratch out the ink and re-write it, sending Alice safely back home.

Much of the book is nonsense, of course. But you read it, rapt, as if it were really the story of where your daughter went. Then one passage — about a curtain hiding a passage to a secret garden — gives you pause.

You look up and around the room. When you first arrived, you gave everything a cursory glance, and you remember that there is a curtain cordoning off a corner of the room.

Putting the book down, you bring the lamp over to the curtain, drawing it back. Behind it, on a plaster

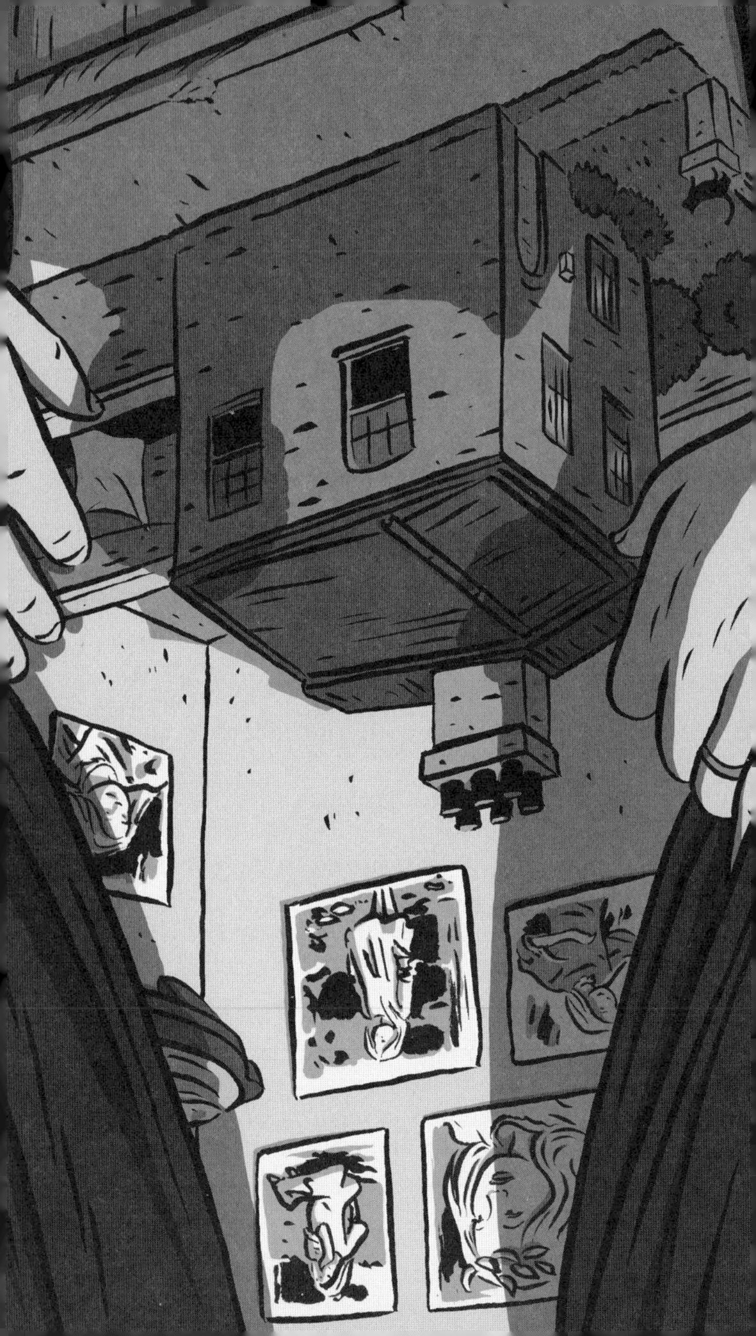

plinth is the most curious thing you think you have ever seen. It is a scale model of your home. Breathless, you bend down and examine it. The house is exact to a disturbing degree. There's even a tiny carving of Dinah, the cat, balanced carefully on the front post.

Above it, on the walls behind are blurry shots of Alice in the park, alongside more staged shots of Alice and Lorina that Dodgson had taken when on their day trip.

Nestled on a shelf screwed into the wall are some items you recognize: one of Alice's stockings. It had gone missing from the clothesline. You had assumed it had blown away in the wind.

A tiny white shoe that Alice had outgrown. You can't imagine where Dodgson had gotten that. You don't *want* to imagine. You are about to bend down and look in the windows of the house when you hear an intake of breath behind you.

"Who are you?!" Dodgson shouts indignantly, "Th- th- these are my *private* rooms!"

You spin on your heels and stare at the man. "You will explain yourself," you seethe.

Dodgson blinks at you. He doesn't recognize you at first. Then his eyes grow wide. He moves to the curtain, trying to draw it shut, but you don't let him. You hold the curtain where it is. You want this evidence against him obvious, in the open.

But in the struggle, the curtain rod is pulled off the ceiling and clatters to the ground!

Turn to page 224.

"Hello?" you squat down, placing your ear near the trunk. You tap it gently.

"Mummy?" The voice comes to you muffled, but it is her – without question!

Alice.

Your heart goes from still pond to river rapids in a split second.

"It's me! Alice! Oh my dear," you paw at the outside of the chest. "It's Mummy!"

You unbuckle the latches that fasten the lid, but it won't open. Then you see why: it's locked with a key. You look around. You search the table. No keys.

"Alice," you call to the trunk. "Mummy's looking for the keys. Are you all right?"

"It's dark, Mummy!"

"I know, I know," you say, moving to the desk, tossing pages here and there. You practically excavate the entire top surface of papers and letters, but no keys.

Then you open drawers one by one.

"Where am I, Mummy?" Alice cries. "I'm frightfully scared."

"I'm here," you call back. "Mummy's here. I'll get you out as soon as I can."

You fling drawer after drawer onto the floor, flipping them over to unearth their contents.

Finally, the clash and jangle of a ring of keys.

You lift them up.

But there must be forty keys here!

Going back to the trunk, you start with them, one by one.

"My dear," you mutter, "how did you end up here?"

Alice is silent. For the moment all you can hear is

your breath and the sound of metal struggling against metal.

"Alice? Mummy's not cross. Please tell me."

The story comes out in a torrent.

"Mr. Dodgson met us at the park. While Lory was napping, he told me that he had a treehouse. His very own private one – in the park! But we must get there in a steamer trunk! I went with him, and he gave me ice cream, but it made me ever so sleepy!"

Down to the last ten keys, it catches you by surprise when one works. At last!

You hear a *click* and you lift the lid.

Inside, lying on her back is your daughter. Tears streak her cheeks, a runnel of snot coating her lips. Her hair is horribly matted, but she is safe.

You half laugh and half cry when you see her.

You reach in to lift her out of that damned trunk.

But she is not looking at you, she's looking past your shoulder, her mouth an O of shock.

"It's Mr. Dod — " she starts.

Turn to page 200.

You tread down a narrow passageway, emerging in a beautiful outdoor garden. It is a lavish, opulent party, with everyone in their masks.

You've never been at a party this decadent. Wooden tables groan under the amount of food and booze on display. A small band sits in a corner and plays something by Bach. You'd heard it once before at a concert. You look over at them and are surprised to see that the band consists of young girls, barely into their teens.

"Mr. Dodgson," you say. "Have you been to one of these masquerades before?"

The dodo nose nods yes.

"Why the masks?"

Something slides against the bottom hem of your gown and you jump. Looking down, you note with relief that it's only a cat, festooned with a shiny red ribbon around its neck.

"O- o- occasionally it is pleasant to drop all titles and have an e- evening where you get to be someone else for a night."

For some reason you find the masks mildly threatening. Possibly if people's intentions were more forthcoming, you wouldn't find it so. "I shouldn't like a place where people lose their names."

One corner of the garden is lit by numerous lamps, and you see a painted backdrop against the wall. In front are chairs, books and wine. Flowers sit under bell jars. As you watch, a couple moves into the setting and the man takes the chair. The woman puts her hand on his shoulder, and a photographer begins the exposure.

In the other corner, opposite the band, is an all-girl choir. Their conductor is an older girl.

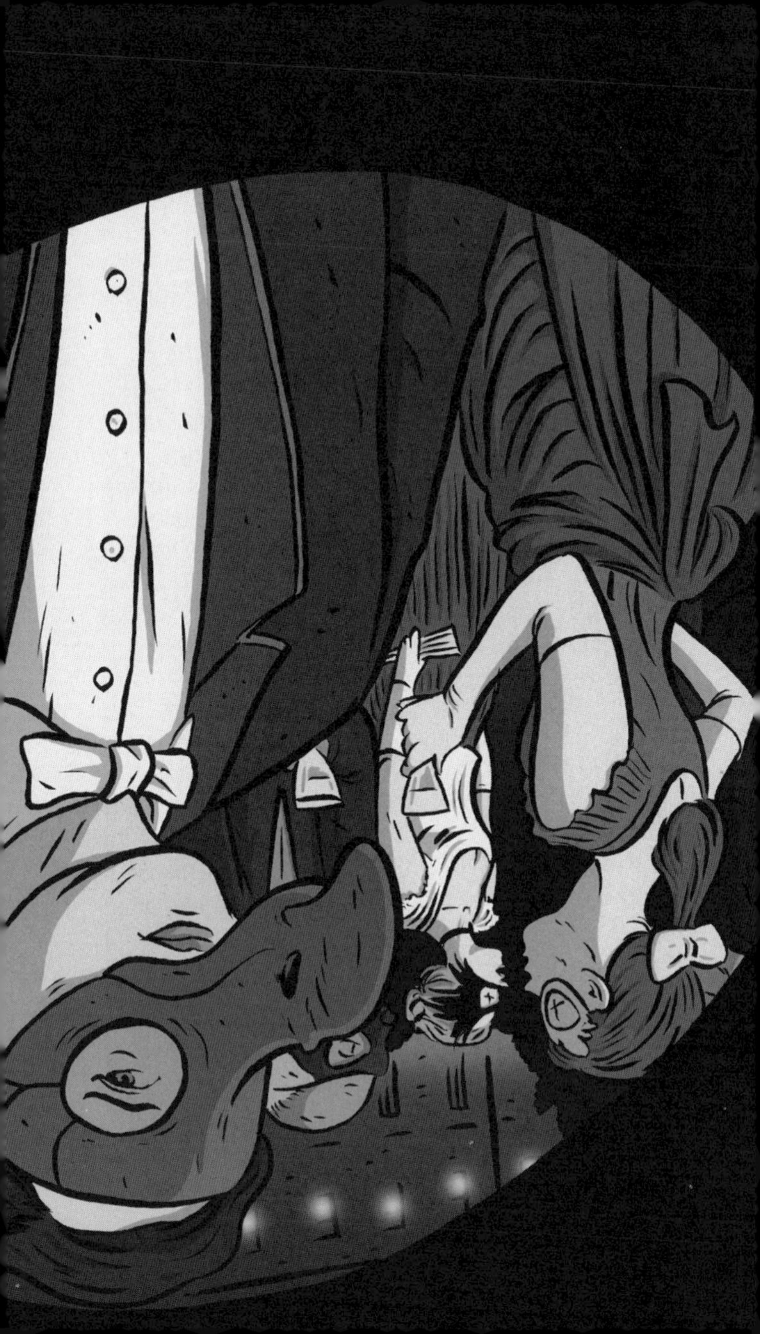

So, you think. Lots of girls here. But where is Alice?

Leaving Dodgson, you move along the periphery, stopping at a table to pick up an oyster. Served with vinegar, pepper and butter, you swallow it down, then have another. You love oysters. You only wish you were having them under less dire straits.

Along one wall of the courtyard, three little stages have three respective plays being enacted. You recognize the first one. It's Little Red and the Wolf. Against a backdrop of a forest, the girl playing the wolf stands on stilts and wears a long cloak, towering over the tiny girl in the red hood, and her basket.

Set on an island, the second play involves a group of mermaids. They sit on the beach, examining a crashed rowboat. A girl, dressed up as a sailor, lies unconscious on the sand.

The third play involves a unicorn standing in a fenced-in pen, on a farm. You can tell that there are two girls in the costume, co-ordinating their movements.

Looking over all the actors, you don't spot your daughter. You wonder if she might be in the unicorn.

"How delightful," you gush. "A unicorn! My favourite fantastical beast. Are there faeries about as well?"

The unicorn just stares back, nodding a little.

"So, yes?" you ask. You lift your mask up ever so slightly, so the unicorn can get a better look. You feel quite certain that if this were Alice that she would say something.

The unicorn remains silent.

"Do you speak?"

"I don't know," a girl replies through the unicorn

head.

"You just spoke."

"I know. But I don't know if I'm *to* speak. I *am* a unicorn after all."

"Expected to be seen and not heard. Is that it?"

The unicorn falls silent again.

"What's your name, dear?" you ask, then tap the rump. "And the name of your posterior friend here?"

The unicorn doesn't speak.

"Where are your parents?"

In response, the unicorn neighs.

A man in a green, velvet suit saunters over and smiles at you.

"Are you enjoying yourself?" he asks. "Would you like a drink?"

You move your mask back into place, nodding graciously. "I'm fine, thank you." Then you turn to the unicorn and say, "Well, *I* believe in unicorns, even if the world does not."

You walk away from the man in green. He unsettles you. Something is wretched here. You need to find Alice. What do you want to do next?

If you look for Dodgson, hoping that he's found some clue as to Alice's whereabouts, turn to page 244.

If you look for an unguarded doorway to duck into the palace, go to page 175.

If you decide to talk to Red Riding Hood instead, turn to page 243.

Dodgson backs away, leaning against a bookshelf. For the moment he seems mollified. Again, you point at the scale model of your house.

"I ask you again — what is the meaning of this?!"

The skinny man stares at the floor, eyes darting back and forth over the same square foot of rug. His tongue, like a cat's, sticks out and wets and re-wets his lips.

"Speak!" you bark.

"I- I- I- " the man stutters his first word but is unable to make headway into his second.

"This," you point at the model, "indicates an *unnatural* interest."

Dodgson nods.

"Where is she? Where have you taken her?"

The man looks up sharply, confusion on his face. "What do you mean?" he asks.

You watch him carefully, looking for any trace of deception, but Dodgson is genuinely shocked at the news.

"Alice has gone missing," you state.

"B- but where?"

"I was hoping you might tell me."

Dodgson blinks six times fast.

You describe the events of that afternoon, and the news sets the man pacing around the table. Distressed, Dodgson's fingers claw at his long, stringy hair.

"L- l- let me assure you, Mrs. Liddell, that I had nothing to do with Alice going astray."

Absently, Dodgson grabs the blue envelope off the table and rips it open. A golden key drops to the table with a clatter, which seems to snap the man out of his worrisome circling.

He slides the rest of the contents of the letter out and reads them, his face blanching.

"What is it?" you ask, nodding at the letter.

Without a word, Dodgson hands the crisp card to you. It is some kind of invitation to a masquerade ball at the palace that very night, personally signed by the Prince. You wonder abstractly why someone like Dodgson might be invited to a party so far above his station when he hands you something else. Something that stops your heart.

It is a small photograph of Alice. But Alice as you have never seen her. She is candied, wearing a silk party dress, her hair curled and coiffed, paint rouging her cheeks.

Breathless, you turn the photo around and see written on the back: I've had my men invite your little lady friend.

"W- what is this?!" Now it's you who's stuttering. You thought you'd seen it all, but this threatens to overwhelm you.

"L- l- let me help you," Dodgson says.

You want to claw the man's eyes out, but aren't sure if it will get you Alice back. All you can manage is a single, inchoate keening wail.

"Mrs. Liddell," Dodgson whispers.

Eventually, the noise that emerges from your throat stops and you manage to breathe out a question: "Do you know where Alice is?"

"I may. Let me help you g- g- get Alice home."

You don't trust the man to give you any aid.

"You can help me by supplying me with a photograph."

"A photograph?"

"Not this one," you spit, throwing the candied

photo of Alice on the floor. "It doesn't resemble her in the slightest. Another one. From another day. Scotland Yard requests one."

"The p- p- police? They are involved?"

Dodgson is hiding many things. At this point you know not what, having more questions than answers, but everything about the man screams guilt at you.

"W- w- will you trust me, Mrs. Liddell?"

You indicate the model of your house, the stolen items, the letter from the Prince. "How can I trust you?" Dodgson blushes, not daring to look at his shelf of prized possessions.

"Trust that I care more for your daughter," he says with a fierce determination, "than I care for m- m- my own life! I promise you — I can help you bring Alice home."

God help you, you believe him. But what other choice do you have? Tears of powerlessness fall from your eyes.

"When we have Alice home, you are to be gone from our lives," you point a trembling finger at the man. "Never contact myself, my husband, or my children ever again."

Crestfallen, Dodgson nods and shuts his eyes. He slumps, like a dead puppet. You'd almost feel sorry for him if your fury didn't blot out your compassion. Somehow this odious man had caused Alice to go missing.

"Agreed," Dodgson says.

"Now," you say. "What is the first step?"

"F- f- first of all — " the man says, indicating your simple dress, "you can't wear *that* to the party."

Turn to page 197.

You head back inside, keeping to the shadows.

By now you can fairly accurately navigate your way around, and you thread your way to the Performatory, where the gas lamps are lit and you hear children's voices.

Remembering the mirror that led to the secret passage, you soundlessly make your way in. Thankfully, no one is there, and you head down the dark corridor, stopping at each spy-hole, scanning each set for your daughter.

In a dress shop, you see girls trying on corsets. They're playing a game: helping one another with the tight lacing, they're seeing how small they can get their waists before they pass out. None of them are Alice, so you move on.

In a park scene, girls sit by a bubbling brook. Beside them are dozens of clear glass bottles, as if lifted from a pharmacy. They are busy writing notes, putting them in, then corking them closed. Once prepared, the bottle is dropped into the brook where it floats away, into the wall and through the corridor you're in. Curious, you retrieve them as they float past.

Help! says one bottle.

Another appears empty, but when you uncork it, you notice there is a little fluid inside. With the tip of your tongue, you taste the salty fluid. Could they be tears?

You read more messages. *I'm late!* says one. *Off with my head.*

The last one you pick up says *I am a leaf on the wind.*

You're curious where the bottles end up. You wonder if the brook is a circuit, and whether the bottles would float forever.

Next, in a set for a room in a cheap inn, complete with peeling paint and ragged lace curtains, an older girl sits with several younger ones. She rests in an armchair whose stuffing is bursting out.

"Say your love has left you," she addresses them. They sit on the threadbare rug in front of her, their backs to you. "How would you want to die?"

"I've heard hanging is quite quick."

"By pistol," another girl says. "Then I would throw myself in front of a runaway carriage."

"Silly," the older girl chides. "You'd be dead in an instant if you used a gun."

"Eaten by wolves. I read that in a book once."

"I'd tie myself to a stone and drown in the sea."

"Hit by lightning. I'd expect it to be quite shocking."

"What about you, Dinah?" the older girl turns to the only one who hasn't spoken.

Could it be — ?

"Nothing so dramatic as all that," a familiar voice says. "I'd probably die of consumption."

It's her! It's Alice!

The older girl stands up, walking to an ancient steamer trunk. She flips open the lid then pulls out a noose, a knife, a vial of poison, lamp oil and matches.

"Let's play a game, shall we?" she asks.

Turn to page 205.

You make your way to the bar, catching wary glances from other patrons.

What are they looking at? With a start, you realize that you are the outsider here. Merely because you are not some freakish scoundrel? Well, so be it.

Quickly you step up to the bar where a tall man with a trim moustache glances your way.

"What can I get you?" he smiles amiably.

"I'm looking for a man in a top hat."

"I don't reckon I know how to make that."

"It's not a drink."

"I know," the man says. "It was a jest."

You bite your lip. You are trying not to lose your temper.

"The hat is unusually large," you continue.

"That's what the ladies always tell me."

"Sir, I am quite serious!"

The easy smile disappears from underneath the man's moustache, and you are simultaneously grateful, but saddened at its passing.

"Top hat, eh?"

"Yes. Unusually large."

"We get a lot of those."

"He would have been seen just outside of your establishment."

The bartender sighs, exasperated. "Outside?" He shakes his head.

You fall silent. You don't know what you expected. The man must meet hundreds of patrons every night. How could he be expected to remember each and every person?

"You want a drink or no?"

Finally, you order a beer.

"Which kind?"

"Any kind."

The bartender laughs. "I wish all my customers were as easy as you," he winks. Then he pours you a pint, which you pay for and take back to your seat.

In the far corner of the pub, by the fireplace, stands a portly man in a waistcoat playing a mournful tune on a violin. You'd barely heard him, so loud was the conversation everywhere else.

You're unsure how long you'll stay.

Maybe you'll finish your beer and then head home. You consider canvassing the street. Perhaps someone out *there* saw something?

But just then, at the front entrance, a man with an enormous top hat steps inside. The woman with the evening gloves goes over to him and says something. Probably the same thing she said to you.

But Top Hat bends his mouth to her ear and whispers to her, touching her bare shoulder. She laughs and allows him to move past her to the bar.

There, the bartender greets him with a smile, and, without Top Hat saying anything, pours him a shot of whiskey.

You frown. Didn't the bartender say he didn't know anything about this man?

Top Hat downs the shot, then the bartender tells Top Hat something which causes him to frown. Top Hat looks around casually, then abruptly heads for the exit, back the way he came.

Follow Top Hat outside to page 232.

Dodgson leads you through a series of corridors. It's a narrow passageway, dirty and unkempt, obviously made for servants to thread their way through the palace quickly and discreetly.

In the end, you emerge from a doorway near the door where Dodgson gave the password. But this still leaves a whole masquerade party for you to carry your daughter through.

You are bound to get noticed, stopped, arrested.

"Is there another exit?" you ask Dodgson. "One closer to the gate?"

Dodgson shakes his head. He ponders your dilemma for a moment. Then he raises a finger.

"I h- ha- have it!" he says. "I shall provide you with a distraction. What do you think I should try?"

If you think Dodgson should pick a fight with a guard, turn to page 251.

If you think a better distraction would be if Dodgson attempts to pull the tablecloth out from underneath a table full of wine and glassware go to page 210.

If you think magic tricks will do the trick, turn to page 247.

As you exit the hall, you notice that a fog has rolled in off the Thames, making visibility low. You scan left, then right. Where did Top Hat go?

A shadow, he emerges out of a cloud ten paces down the street, and you set off after him.

While the heels on your boots aren't very high, they are still sharp enough to set off a cadence of harsh staccatos as you chase after the man, so you deliberately slow your gait, putting the weight on the front of your feet.

You are unsure what you should do. Simply confront the man? Ask him about Alice? Or follow him? In the hopes that observing what he does and where he goes can provide some clue as to his identity.

Top Hat turns a corner and enters a laneway. It's only after you round the corner when you realize something: while you have been following Top Hat, Top Hat has been following *someone else*.

Far down the laneway a gentleman with a cane is tottering along, and Top Hat was keeping pace with him, but is now closing fast.

You get a terrible feeling in your gut, and under a gas lamp you witness Top Hat break into a sudden sprint. He takes the hat off, jamming it down over the head of his victim! A flash of metal as Top Hat stabs the man in the gut. You inhale in surprise.

"No!" you cry out.

Top Hat spins, eyes glaring dangerously. He holds his knife out, slick and red with blood.

You stare in horror.

As he advances, you realize that you might have committed a grievous error drawing attention to yourself like this.

"He deserved it," Top Hat growls.

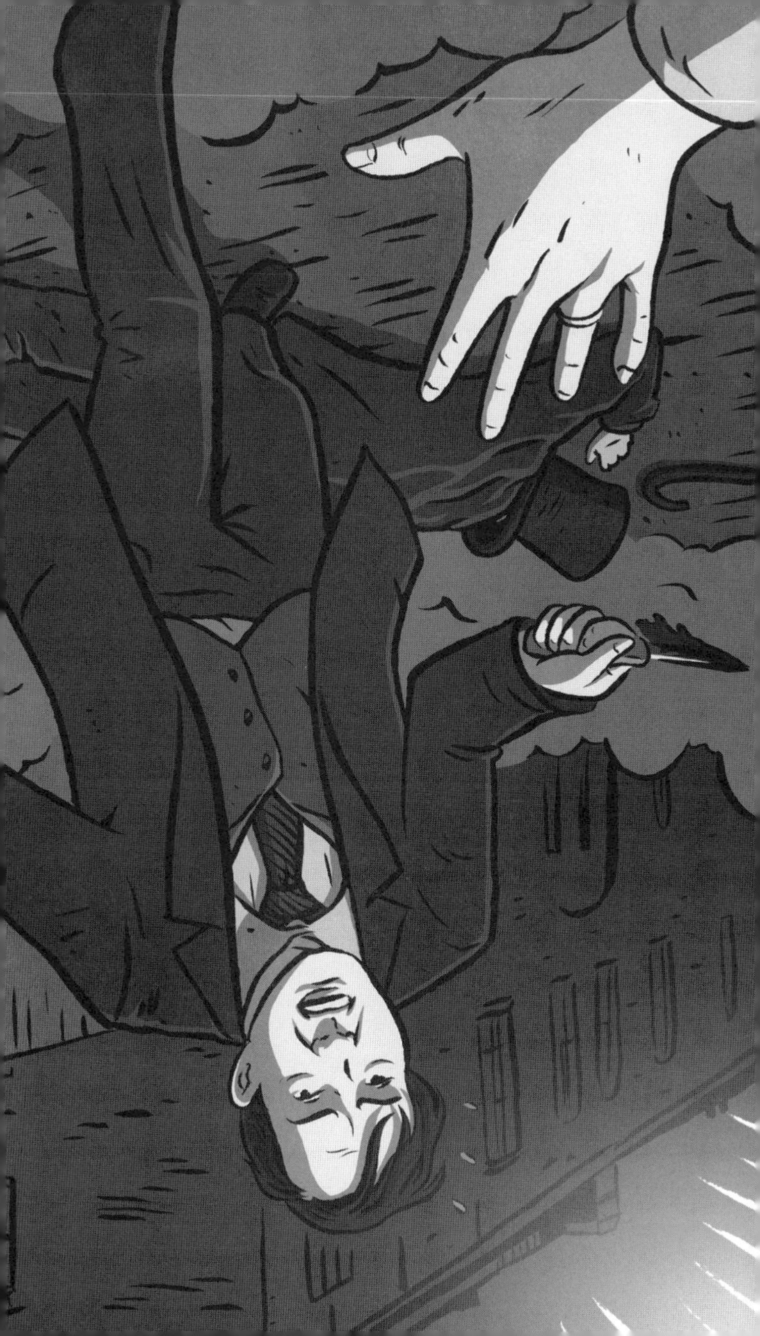

"Who could deserve that?" you ask. You can't help yourself. You know you should run, but you want to know why, and if Top Hat can tell you what happened to Alice.

"You've no idea what that man has done," Top Hat says.

On the ground, the man breathes his last breath, his gurgling wheeze coming to a halt.

"You're right," you concede. "I don't. And actually I don't care," you change the subject with no preamble at all. The circumstances were unusual, and you are desperate enough to make them more so. "I wanted to ask you something. You spoke to my daughter the other week outside of the Tiger-Lily. She's only 7. She's fair of hair. Her name is Alice."

Now it's Top Hat's turn to be mystified. He stares at you a moment, wondering if this is some sort of trick. Finally he responds.

"Aye," the man nods. "Why? What of it? I was warning her, that's all."

"About what?"

With a quick flick of his wrist, Top Hat whips excess blood off his blade, then produces a red silk handkerchief from an inside pocket and wipes it clean.

"About what?" Top Hat raises an eyebrow. "Well, what have little girls got to be frightened of?"

You wait a moment, expecting Top Hat to answer his own question.

"I say again — what have little girls got to be frightened of?"

"You're asking *me?*"

"Well weren't you a little girl once yourself?"

As Top Hat speaks, you come to the slow realiza-

tion that there's something queer about him. It takes you a moment but when you finally see it, you can't unsee it. You're so shocked, you blurt it out.

"Why — you're a woman!"

Top Hat flinches, as if it were you who were holding a knife.

"Aye," Top Hat admits. "What of it?"

"Answer your own question yourself, then! What have little girls got to be frightened of?"

"The answer is, what *haven't* little girls got to be frightened of?"

That strikes you as an absurdly pessimistic view to take on society.

"So, you were warning Alice to be frightened of absolutely everything, is that it?"

Top Hat looks up and down the alleyway, then directs her attention back to you.

"I used to work these streets meself," she says. "Painted face, tits out, the whole deal."

"You?" It's hard to imagine Top Hat as a prostitute. She's so imposing in her crisp black suit, starched white collar.

"Aye," she nods, retrieving her rumpled top hat from her victim. You shoot a glance at the man's face. Pasty, white, eyes ghoulishly half-closed. "Until one night I was beaten so brutally I could eat naught but gruel and treacle for weeks."

"Oh I'm — "

"You would know this yourself," Top Hat says, punching the hat back into shape from the inside.

"*I* would?"

"An unaccompanied woman? In this neighbourhood? This time of night? You know how this looks. You understand how it's perceived. How you would be blamed were anything to happen to you."

You fall silent.

"But as a man, I go unmolested. No one questions my presence. Not even when I slip up behind them and stick a shiv in between their ribs."

"So you said all that? To Alice?"

"Not in so many words, no," Top Hat says. "But that was the gist."

"How did my daughter get this?" you say, producing the matchbox.

Top Hat squints at the box, then leans back.

"I was having a smoke. Alice liked my box of matches, so I gave it to her."

"Well, now Alice is missing. Would you know anything about *that?*"

"What?" Top Hat looks genuinely shocked.

You tell Top Hat about the park, and how you found the matches, and you watch as she shakes her head.

"Predators everywhere," she mutters, lifting the hat and putting it back on. "I know naught about Alice, but I have been hearing whispers, rumours."

"What rumours?"

"Girls are disappearing. From alleyways, parks. Public places — even some private."

"How many?"

"Who knows? From paupers to princesses, simply gone."

You're unsure you can handle it right now if Alice's disappearance was part of some larger group of disappearances. It's all you can do to handle *hers* right now.

"Can you help me?" you ask Top Hat. "Forgive me, but you seem to know the underworld. Is there anything you can do?"

"The underworld?" Top Hat grins at your characterization, then shakes her head. "Not interested."

"But you're — "

"What I *am* is not interested."

You sigh, exasperated.

"But," Top Hat lights a cigar and puffs it, her smoke mingling with the thick fog. "I might be able to direct you to someone who *can* help you."

"Who?"

Top Hat doesn't say, but she gives you directions to the East End — Limehouse. There's a storefront in the Chinese district, near the ports. It's actually not too far. It's walkable.

"And they'll help me?"

"No idea."

"Can I mention that you recommended me?"

"No bloody way."

"Then how can I know this isn't an enormous waste of time?"

"You can't."

"Then what use is your advice?"

Top Hat smirks, turns, and walks into the fog.

"Welcome to the underworld!" she calls over her shoulder.

Almost on cue, it starts raining. Not heavy, but steady and unrelenting.

As you start on the way to this storefront, you consider Top Hat's ingenious disguise. Any witnesses would describe a man, but Top Hat could go home to collapse the hat and pile on the petticoats. It's rather brilliant.

Turn to page 144.

238

The moment you step into the small, darkened room, you realize it's a mistake. But there are already footfalls in the hallway, and it's too late to flee without being spotted.

"Curses," you whisper under your breath, urging Alice inside. Beside a dustpan and mop, you huddle with your daughter on the floor.

"Get this door open!" a guard shouts somewhere down the hall. Then a moment later, "It's clear."

This happens several more times. It'll only be a matter of minutes before they find you.

Perhaps you and Alice can go quickly from the broom closet towards the lit area. You wonder if both guards are investigating each room, or if there's only one left out in the hallway, watching.

"Try the broom closet," a guard says. The door opens easily and a guard looks in, his shadow falling over you both. Alice tenses in your arms.

Maybe you could grab the broom and spear the man! Make one last dash.

But the guard does not move, or raise the alarm.

"See anything?" the other guard asks.

The guard standing over you shakes his head, then points towards the lit area. "Balcony," he says.

"Right," the other guard replies. You hear his footsteps fading.

Still, this guard does not move. Does he have something more nefarious for you in mind?

Without a word, he removes his mask.

It's Sing! You could kiss him you're so glad to see him.

"Follow Sing," he says quietly.

Go to page 253.

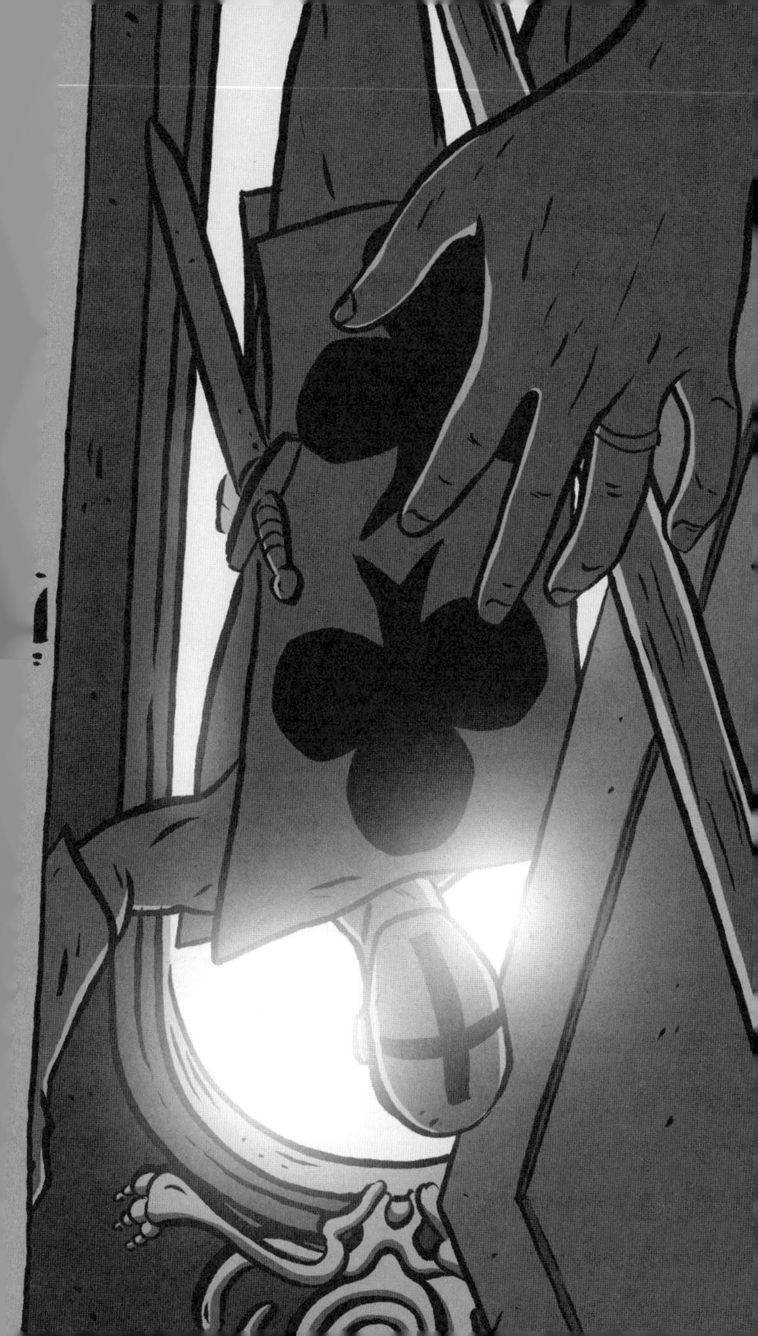

Heaving Alice up, you tuck her under your arm and run. You can't move very fast, but the guards have difficulty getting to you, having to dance around all the prone bodies.

You run into the palace and follow your gut. You have to make directional decisions based on pure instinct.

Behind you are the heavy footfalls of the guards. They're calling to one another when they spot you, triangulating your location, blocking off your escape routes.

But you recognize the area you're in! This is the pantry where you first arrived. What luck! Moving quickly down the stairs, you end up in the cellar.

"Sing?" you whisper, hopefully.

But he's gone. You move through the tunnel to the waterway, but there's no boat.

You stand at the edge of the pier. You consider swimming, but with Alice still drowsy from whatever hypnotized state she was in, that would be impossible.

Still, you have no other choice.

You plunge in, holding Alice's head above water.

The freezing cold water hits you like a horse, knocking your breath away and immediately sending your teeth chattering. What's worse — you lose your grip on your daughter! You dive after her, but the water is dark as ink.

When you finally return to the surface, Alice is gone.

"Alice! Alice!" you scream through a mouthful of water.

When the guards finally appear behind you, you're grateful.

"She's in the water!" you tell them frantically.

You stand in their custody as two guards dive into the water, and after several anguished moments, one of them emerges with your daughter.

The best sound you'd ever heard is her coughing up Thames river water.

Turn to page 139.

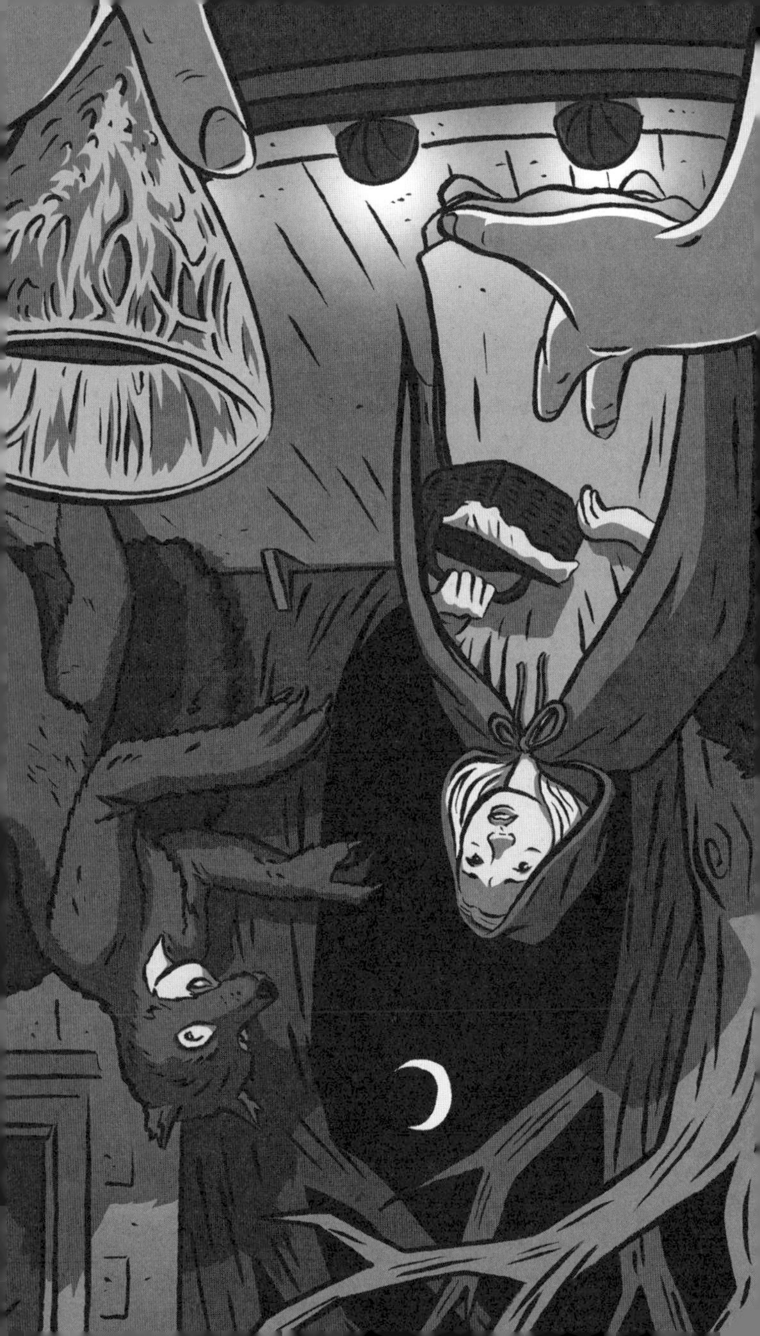

You move back to the Dark Forest stage, picking up a glass of wine from a servant's tray. When you're certain the man in green is focused elsewhere, you call to the actress.

"Little Red!"

She is pretending to be intimidated by the encroaching trees.

"Oh, the wood is dark and deep!" she says.

"What's your name? Your real one?"

"And I have a basket full of bread and sweets!" she says. "That I must bring to Grandmother."

"Don't you have a name?"

Finally the girl looks at you.

"My- my name is Little Red," she says, then flashes you a grin.

"Your actual one. What do your parents call you?"

The grin disappears, and the girl looks uncertain.

"I'm Matilda," she says. It comes out in a rush.

"Matilda what?" you persist. "What is your full name?"

"Matilda Gamble, miss."

The wolf stalks over, hissing "What are you doing?! We're to stay in character."

Matilda points at you, whining, "Well she asked!"

You become aware of Dodgson at your side, hand on your arm.

"I've found her!" he mutters. "L- l- let me take you to h-h- her."

Turn to page 265.

Dodgson chats amiably with the photographer in the corner, taking photos of the guests.

"I f- f- find that paper intolerable," Dodgson says, waving his hands dismissively. "Doesn't hold a print. I go through far too much selenium f- f- fixing it afterwards."

"Mr. Dodgson," you say, taking his arm. "Might I have a word?"

"Mrs. Liddell, I was just — "

Then the photographer grasps you both, urging a photo of the two of you together. You take a quick glance at the portraits he has arranged around himself, as evidence of his work. Most are of famous luminaries, but one catches your eye: three girls together. They are grinning so fiercely that their teeth resemble white picket fences. The girls' grins are such a contrast with the rest of the photo that they seem almost to float unsettlingly in mid-air.

"Now, the exposure will take time. You'd need to remain as still as you can manage."

You decline the photo. You are afraid of what it might show despite the duck mask — white hot fury.

Dodgson excuses the both of you, then takes you aside.

"I've found her," he whispers in your ear. "Come with me."

Turn to page 265.

Surrounded by the guards, you wait as the Prince strolls over.

"What are you doing?" he asks quietly. Somehow the man manages to be even more menacing the softer his tone.

"I- I noticed the girl's outfit was ill-fitting, you see — falling apart."

"You shall address the Prince as 'sire'," the announcer says sternly.

"My- my apologies, sire."

"Ill-fitting?" the Prince looks down at Alice, and the pile of armour on the ground behind her. "Falling apart?"

"Indeed, sire," you say. "I was aiding her in re-fastening it."

The Prince clucks his tongue, and murmurs, "I must speak with the armourer and fitter about this then." He raises his voice, looking at an aide. "Such shoddy craftsmanship. Off with their hands!"

"Their hands, sire?" The announcer says, a twinkle in his eye. "Then how shall they fix the costumes?"

"With their feet! And their mouths!" the Prince retorts. "They shall help one another! We are better together!"

"Make it so!" the announcer orders, and the aide runs off.

The Prince turns away and walks back to the front of the unconscious army. You breathe a sigh of relief, and the announcer rings the bell again. As one, the girls come to, finding their feet and slowly rising. Like the eyes of the Hydra blinking into wakefulness, soon they are all standing at attention again.

"Let the fighting continue!" the announcer yells, and the Prince re-takes his broadsword.

You help your daughter up and take her inside, but the announcer follows you.

"Turn around," the announcer orders. "*You're* not Mary-Ann, are you?"

"Who is this Mary-Ann?" you ask nonchalantly, tightening your grip on your daughter's hand. "Truly, I must meet her one day and see how closely she — "

You take off running, carrying Alice.

But the announcer had taken the precaution of signalling a couple of guards to follow, and they quickly chase you down.

Surrounded, they take Alice away from you and throw you into a cell.

You scream in anguish at having been so close to your daughter, and having her taken away.

From the cell's barred window, you watch the bright day turn into night.

Turn to page 139.

Dodgson advances to the centre of the courtyard then calls for everyone's attention.

"If it pleases the Crown," he says, "I w- w- wi- will now perform feats of magic!"

"Finish a complete sentence, first!" someone calls out.

Dodgson blushes, but soldiers on.

"For my f- fir- first trick, I will require a top hat. Sir, might I borrow yours?"

A partygoer in a long cloak obliges.

Then Dodgson walks slowly over to a white cat, in its red ribbon, sitting on the edge of a table.

"I shall make this c- c- cat, disappear before your eyes!"

All eyes are now on the man, and you begin moving, keeping to the shadows and the courtyard's walls.

But as Dodgson attempts to lift the cat, it protests, howling.

Everyone laughs.

"I shall — "

The cat claws at Dodgson! But doggedly, Dodgson hangs on, now using both hands. An unearthly yowl and the cat is a blur, knocking Dodgson's dodo nose to the side, scrambling upside-down. Dodgson swears as he's scratched.

This is great entertainment for everyone involved, and you are relieved to see the guards at the exit gate venturing out from their posts into the courtyard for a better view. Quickly, you slip past them and towards the exit gate.

You take one last look back and see Dodgson with his mask hanging askew around his neck, cheek bloody.

"Get in!" he mutters, jamming the hat on the cat.

"How preposterous!" someone cackles. "A cat in a hat!"

You don't stop to see if Dodgson can do it. You make a beeline for a nearby Hansom Cab and pull your sleeping daughter into it.

As the driver sets his horses going, you hear more laughter, and Dodgson screaming.

Turn to page 259.

Never did you imagine the fire would spread so fast. Soon, smoke fills every hallway and room. You're lost, but you just follow the little girls. They run like rats off a sinking ship. You trust in their knowledge, and they find the stairwells for you, leading you in the right direction.

But you see the Prince in his hunter's uniform turning down the hall ahead. He carries a handbell, and he rings it sharply three times.

Ding! Ding! Ding!

Immediately Alice drops to the ground. As do a couple girls near the Prince. The man keeps running, ringing the bell again and again.

"Alice!" you cry. Your daughter's eyes are open, but they are glazed and unseeing, as if she were mesmerized.

After a few moments of trying to rouse her, you realize it's no use. You have to carry her.

As you pass the other girls on the floor, you're filled with a terrible regret — that you can't save anyone else.

When you get down to the servant's entrance, two guards stand there, alarmed.

"Mary-Ann!" they shout at you. "How bad is it? Is there any news?"

"It's desperate," you say, never stopping. "You need to go help. The Prince needs more men."

"But we're not to leave our post," the other guard protests.

But when the first guard gets up and starts running, the second quickly lets you out, then follows.

As calmly and as quickly as you can, you carry Alice away from the burning palace.

A huge plume of black smoke rises up to the sun

behind you.

You don't stop until you're all the way home.

For a full day and a half Alice remains unconscious. You deliver water to her mouth with an eyedropper. She only awakes when the front door is accidentally slammed by the wind.

Turn to page 271.

"Are you sure?" Dodgson is apprehensive when you make the suggestion.

"Positive," you say, grateful for the darkness, unable to keep the smile from your lips.

You watch from the shadows as Dodgson walks up to a guard in the middle of the courtyard.

He says something to him, and the guard says something back, but then Dodgson brings himself to his full height.

"D- d- did you just make fun of my s- st- stutter?" he screams, outraged.

"No, sir."

"I think you d- d- did!" howls Dodgson. "Apologize!"

"My deepest apologies, sir."

"No! On your knees!"

"Sir?"

"I demand you apo- apo- apologize on your knees!" Dodgson points at the paved stone floor.

After a moment, the guard gets on his knees.

You start out for the exit, hiding Alice against your side nearest the wall, keeping to the shadows.

Nobody notices you. Most of the partygoers have quieted, and are raptly watching the spectacle.

Dodgson starts slapping the guard. He slaps so frenetically that the guard's mask flies off.

You are almost at the exit gate when a silhouette turns toward you.

All too late, you realize that it's the Prince himself who's spied you.

He points at you, shouting.

You run, but are quickly surrounded.

"You dare! You dare steal from the Crown!" he screams into your ear as you're held by the rough

hands of the guards.

He bites off the skin of the enormous turkey leg he's munching on, then bashes you in the face with it, knocking your mask off. Then it comes back the other way, clubbing your temple.

With your fading consciousness, you can't remember where Alice is. You might have dropped her.

The next blow drops you.

Turn to page 172.

Sing scampers down the hallway, and you start to follow, but Alice holds you back.

"Mummy!" she whispers. "It's a Chinaman!"

You sigh. You wish Reg never used that term around the house. At this point, when he'd realized you weren't following, Sing stops and turns.

"I know dear," you say, "but he's one of the good ones."

Alice glares at Sing suspiciously, but you tug on her arm. You don't have time for this. In the distance, guards shout to one another, their voices nearing.

"You are, aren't you?" you ask Sing. "One of the good ones?"

Sing cracks a smile, shrugs, then tries a door.

Now that you consider it, you wonder how Sing acquired the guard's uniform he's wearing.

Sing takes off a glove and rolls up his sleeve. On his tightly muscled forearm he's traced a map. Swivelling his wrist, you see another map drawn on the back. He pops open his palm. A third map. He scans it briefly, then points. "We go."

Sing drops the mask back over his face. Moving down the hall, you hear him counting doors in Chinese. He pushes one open, leading to a stairwell, which the two of you hurry down.

Along the way, Sing grabs one of the oil lamps from its wall sconce.

"You've been here the entire time?" you ask. "You could have found a way to get word to me."

The man shrugs again.

"Not *whole* time. Sing go home. Sleep. Smoke. Come back."

At the next landing, Sing looks out into the hallway where a long red carpet extends the length of it.

He douses it with lamp oil, then drops a lit match onto it, where it quickly bursts into a good-sized conflagration.

"Down," he says, urging you back into the stairwell. You descend another flight and Sing gathers more oil lamps. On the next floor, he sets tapestries alight as you charge down the hall.

"Is the boat here? Can we escape that way?"

Sing shakes his head. "Two men — lots money."

"They were too expensive?" you say, incredulous. At this point, you'd have paid anything to have an easy escape route. "You couldn't have owed them a favour?"

Following his maps, Sing leads you down one hall, then another. At one point, he pushes you into an alcove where the three of you stand motionless while three guards rush by with blankets and buckets. A distant clanging signals the fire.

Sing leads you through the kitchen, then outside into a courtyard which houses the stables.

When he enters a stall to take a horse, the stable-boy comes out to see what's unsettling the horses.

"What's goin' on?" he starts to say, but when he sees Sing, he straightens up. "Oh! The Prince's guard!"

Sing nods at the boy, then points at another horse. "One more."

The boy hurries to lead it out of its stall.

Sing helps you and Alice mount one horse, then gets on the other.

"You don't want saddles?" the boy asks, confused. But then he hears the fire bell. "Oh! There's a fire somewhere."

Sing points into the palace. "Inside. Go help."

"Yes, sir!" the boy grabs a wash bucket and runs.

Sing slaps your horse's rump to get it going, then digs his knees into his own.

"Yah! Yah!"

You sit, holding tightly to the reins, Alice clinging to the horse's mane. Sing leads you to the main gate where two bored guards look up in surprise. When they see Sing's uniform, however, they straighten up.

"Open!" Sing yells at them, and they rush to comply.

You gallop the horses out into the park that surrounds the palace, startling passersby and bystanders. But they barely give you a glance, drawing each others' attention back to the palace.

You chance a quick glance over your shoulder.

Thick, black smoke billows from broken windows on the top floors and the angry orange flames lick up its sides.

You hurry off the palace grounds, and it's not until you're over a small bridge that spans a serpentine brook that you finally feel safe.

"Where home?" Sing asks, when you rein the horses in for a moment. You direct the way, and together, you and Sing gallop through the streets that bring Alice back to her doorstep.

Finally, when you are all standing in front of your house, Sing raises his mask again and looks at your daughter.

"This is Alice?"

"Alice," you say, nudging her forward. "I'd like you to meet Mr. Sing Sang-Song. Without him, Mummy would never have been able to get you home."

Alice seems chastened by the dramatic escape and raises her hand for a shake. "Very pleased to make your acquaintance, Mr. Song."

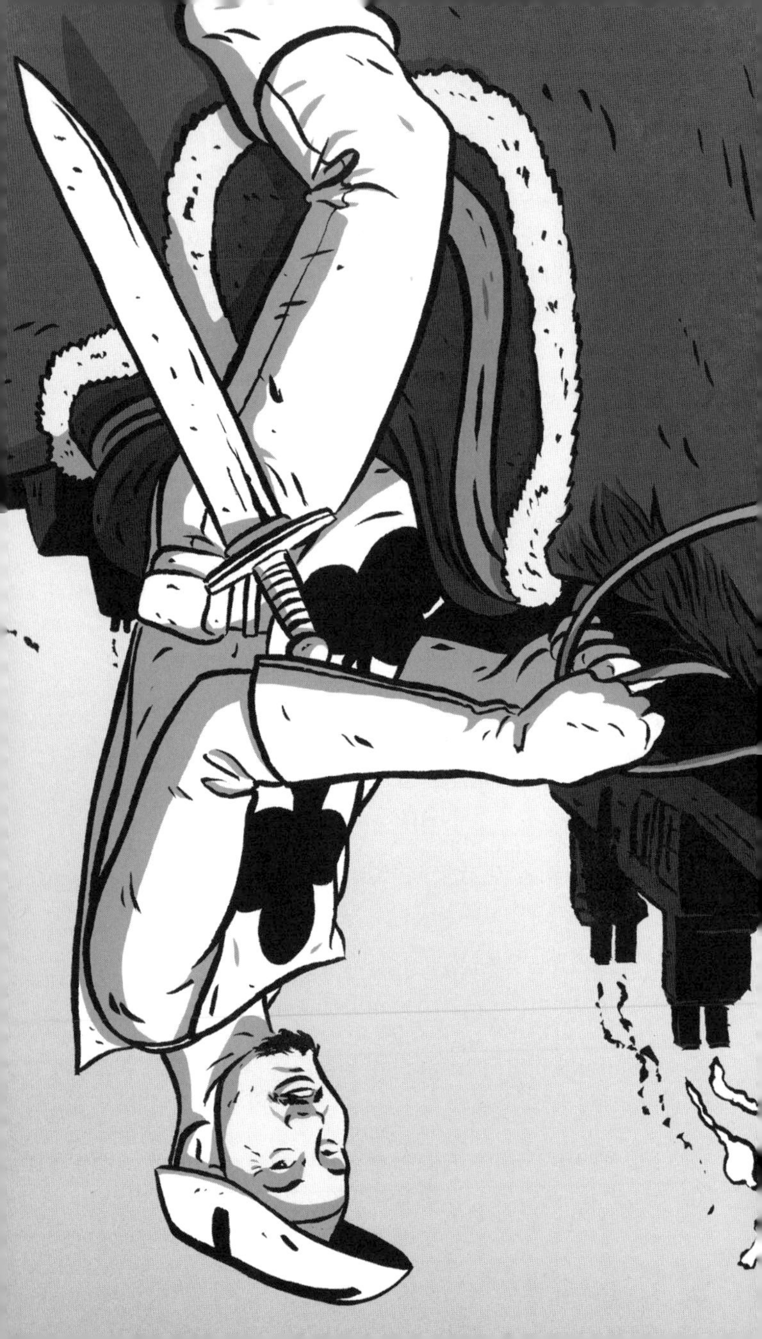

He shakes her hand, then turns to you. "So lots fun."

You give the man a deep, enduring embrace. You know how this must look to any nosy neighbours, but you don't care. You think you might cry.

After a moment, Sing extricates himself.

Slapping one of the horses' flanks, he sends it rushing off down the street. Then Sing gets back on his own horse. He turns to you, does a nonchalant neck roll, winks, then flips his mask down.

Alice has climbed the front yard fence so she can get a better look and waves her hand at him as he rides off.

Turn to page 271.

With a trembling hand, you give the man your purse.

He snatches it away, then withdraws the knife.

The man disappears into the fog and you hear rapid departing footfalls.

With a delayed reaction, you start hyperventilating. Needing support, you move toward the misty glow of a streetlamp and clutch at its steel trunk.

You close your eyes and try to catch your breath.

You need to be inside, you think.

In the gloom, you move towards the first lit storefront you see. Opening the door, a little bell tinkles.

"We're just closing," a woman announces, but then she sees the look on your face. "Oh dearie, are you ill?"

"I just — " You reach out to take support from a wooden table.

The room is spinning.

As you faint, the woman manages to catch you.

Turn to page 62.

Many years pass.

Charles Dodgson sends numerous letters full of his profuse apologies, but you burn them all in the stove.

You are haunted by the girls left behind. Each tender face in its bed. Where were *their* saviours?

You feel powerless, and weep bitter tears at the thought of men, and their power, and all that they do. You remind yourself that this is the brutal history of the world, no matter what reforms conscience recommends.

For the next several years, you keep an eagle-eye on your children. The carefree days are over.

Alice, for her part, is changed. It's difficult to describe exactly how. In a million tiny ways. Similar to winter arriving — there are innumerable signs. You can't pay attention to them all. But the change is in the aggregate.

Dodgson dares to release a book entitled *Alice's Adventures in Wonderland*.

"The nerve!" you rail when you find out. "The cheek of the man!" You hurl plates around your kitchen. Then weep as you pick up the shattered porcelain shards.

It almost overwhelms you when the book becomes a sensation, selling out its initial print run in days. Dodgson is in all the high society papers. Always an ambitious socialite, now he is unbearable.

You will never know to what extent he was responsible for brokering Alice's kidnap. You will never know the full extent of his knowledge of the Prince's activities, and what Dodgson tacitly approves, enables or facilitates by his silence or full participation. You will never know.

And it's too dangerous to investigate.

As much as you want to go back and get the other girls, a Prince is a force of nature. It's best to stay out of their notice. To quarrel with a Prince is to invite disaster. You dye Alice's hair black. No more photographs.

Even more years pass.

Lorina marries a barrister, and Alice is betrothed to an American businessman. Maggie leaves to go back to Birmingham to take care of her ailing parents, and decides not to return. Then a few years after that, Reg dies one afternoon of heart failure. You survive off his pension from the college.

More years pass. You live for the few visits from Lorina and Alice and their families. Especially your grandchildren. When they play in your back yard, you always stay out there, keeping an eye on them, but you're unsure why.

Sometimes you remember a pretty ball you were invited to so long ago. When was that? You remember that everyone wore exotic masks. There were such darling, talented girls. Such performances. You try to tell your daughters and their grandchildren about this party, and they merely nod their heads, smiling.

"There was even a Prince in attendance!" you tell them.

"Of course there was, Mum," Alice says. She holds your wrinkled hand and stares at you with an unusually intense look.

More years pass.

A friend tells you that Lewis Carroll has died. "You were acquainted with him, were you not?"

"Oh yes," you say, "I knew him."

Your friend leans forward. "Really? In what capacity?"

"Why, it was my daughter Alice that he based his famous book on!"

Now your friend is full of questions, and you are more than happy to supply answers.

"He sent me many letters," you say. "I think I still have some of them somewhere. They're bound to be worth quite a bit someday."

Your remarkable daughter Alice, who became his obsession, now has become the world's obsession. You smile beatifically at your friend, feeling your chest swell with pride.

"She is the *real* Alice," you say. "The original."

THE END

Alice has lit a single candle on the dining table to help her see.

She carries a pillowcase in her hands, bulging with items.

"What is the meaning of this!" your husband roars.

Startled, Alice drops the pillowcase underneath the dining table, shoving it out of sight with her foot.

"I- I- " she stutters. You can see her mind working, trying to ascertain how much we saw.

"Why are you stealing from us?" you say. "You're not Alice at all, are you?"

"Mum! Dad! It's just that I've been poor for so long. I needed some items to reassure myself. In case something happened."

"Sit!" you point at a dining room chair and Alice dutifully obliges. The girl starts weeping, but now your dander is up. You don't believe her remorse for a moment.

"Who are you?"

"I'm Alice," the girl protests unpersuasively. "I'm your daughter."

"You're a liar and a thief," you state. Behind the girl, Reg glowers, ensuring she does not escape. "How *dare* you play on our emotions."

But the girl continues her claim that she is Alice.

Then you get an idea. It's an evil one, but the circumstances have inspired you.

"No one knows you're here, do they?" you state flatly.

A look of concern flashes through the eyes of the girl.

"Somehow, you'd heard about our daughter's disappearance, and decided to use that knowledge to gain our trust. Isn't that so?"

The girl falls silent. No more fake tears. She is just watching you.

"But people go missing all the time," you look up at Reg, and his brow is knitted. He isn't sure you mean what you're intimating. "What's one more girl?"

She starts to bolt, but Reg grabs hold of her.

"Tell me what you know," you say coldly, "or you won't be seeing the inside of a cell. You will be seeing the inside of a coffin."

The girl struggles a little against your husband, but then whispers, "Aye, I'll tell you."

A year and a half ago, the girl met Alice in a lace factory, where they both worked, and became friends. Over time, Alice confessed to her that she'd had another life that might have been real, or might have been fiction. It'd been so long ago that she wasn't sure.

Alice wasn't always an orphan. She'd had a family. A mother and a father and a sister. And a housemaid named Maggie in a house with a back yard. And a cat named Dinah.

"She believed she was an orphan?" you interrupt.

"She became one," the girl explains. "Years ago, a vagrant asked for her help to find his rabbit. But he stole her. Tried to raise her as his own. And eventually she got away, but not before he put the fear of God in her. She was afraid, you see, she'd get into trouble. For going with him in the first place. So she ended up on the street, where someone found her and brought her to an orphanage. She was still there when the lace factory came a'callin for more hands."

"Is she there now?"

The girl looks down at the woven placemat on the

table.

"There was an accident," she says.

"She's dead?" your voice breaks.

"Aye."

In front of you, Reg slumps.

"Which orphanage is this?"

The girl tells you everything. The name of the orphanage. How her friend had ties with the police, and how the girl took all the clues Alice gave her and found the missing person's report on her.

"That's how I knew where to find you two," she says. "I had this dream. That *I* could be Alice. That *I* could be from a loving home, have this rich life in a house with a back yard. Cat named Dinah."

Picking up the pillowcase, you look at its contents.

China. Dishes. Two brass candleholders. A silver letter opener.

You hand it to the girl and tell her to go.

"What?" the girl looks confused.

"Go!"

The girl rushes off into the night.

Over the next few days, you and Reg go to the orphanage. Heartbreakingly, it is only a fifteen minute cab ride from where you live. You claim Alice's things and find out where she is buried. In her personal items, you discover her journal, where she details her attempts to find you again, though she is constantly hounded by the nagging notion that you were all merely a dream she once had.

THE END

Dodgson leads you to a corner of the courtyard overgrown with trailing vines, then opens a door almost hidden by leaves. But the moment you step inside, a guard is there. The guards here are all clothed in white. Black playing card clubs emblazon their chests, and they wear blank masks, with only slits for eyes.

"Party's t'other way," the guard mutters.

"Bandersnatch," Dodgson says, in a quiet whisper.

"Of course, sir," the guard says, then lets you pass. The two of you move a little ways down the darkened hall and arrive at another door and another guard.

"Jabberwock!" Dodgson barks, getting in the man's face.

The guard steps aside, then the two of you go in.

"What was that all about?"

"Each password has its own p- per- personality that must be performed."

You find yourself on the observation gallery of a large, round room. Various masks hang on the walls at intervals. Moving to the railing, you see ten tiny beds below, all covered in satin bedsheets. A single blonde girl lies in each one.

Your eye moves from one to the next, scanning for —

"Alice!" you cry. When you finally see her your heart has been tight with so many hours of longing that you practically sob.

"Shh!" Dodgson hushes you.

"Are they slumbering?"

"In a m- m- mu- manner of speaking."

"Can she hear me?"

"They are sedated."

"Why?"

"They are n- n- new arrivals. New arrivals are usually set asleep. They're always unruly."

"New arrivals? From where?"

"Various orph- orphanages around the city."

"They come to the palace? This is madness."

"Hard to believe, I realize, but this is, in fact, L- L- London's *largest* orphanage."

"Except," you jab a finger towards your sleeping daughter, "that that one *has* a mother — me!"

"And for pu- pu- putting you in this situation, I do apologize," Dodgson says, demure.

"I don't want your apologies. I want your help! Now how do I get down there?"

Dodgson leads you around the railing to the other side, where a spiral staircase takes you downstairs. At the bottom, you might as well have been in a toy shop. The shelves are covered in toys, games, dolls and puzzles.

You rush to your daughter. Someone's painted her face, and curled her hair. Outfitted her in a light blue silk dress. You shake her gently.

"Wake up, dear," you stroke her face. Though she breathes steadily, she doesn't wake.

"Please," you start gently slapping her cheek. For a moment her eyes flutter open, but then they close.

"What was she given?!" you demand.

"It's just a sedative. It's supposed to be h- h- harmless!" Dodgson says, pulling at the frame of a giant mirror on the wall. Behind it is revealed a secret doorway into a dark passage.

"Where does *that* lead?" you ask, gathering Alice up in your arms.

"It's the servant's corridors."

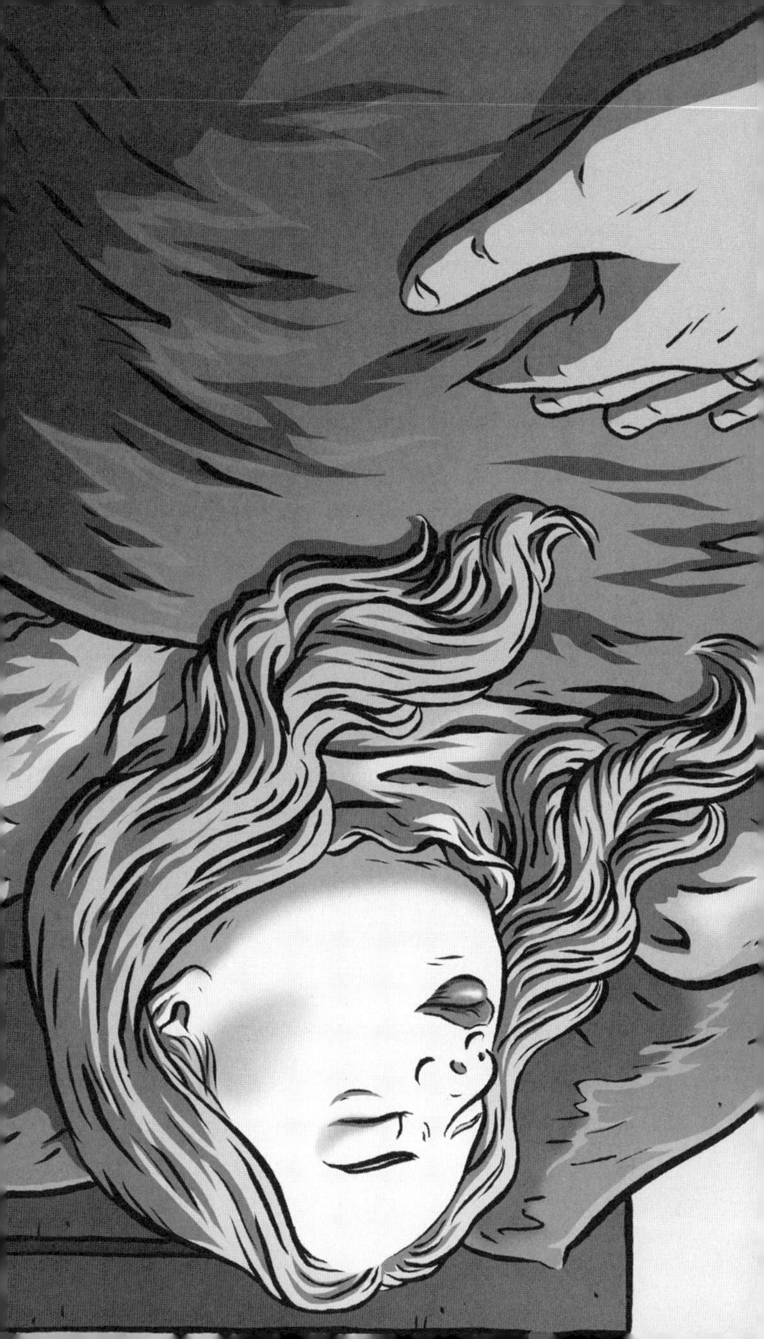

You begin to step through, but pause. "What about the rest of these girls?"

"They're orphans."

"No. I don't believe that. If my Alice wasn't an orphan, what are the chances that they are?"

"There's n- no- nothing to be done n- no -now."

"They were brought here. They can be sent home."

"This is their n- new home, now."

"The Queen stands for this?"

"The Queen wants the Prince to be h- happy. It is his b- bi- birthday, after all."

"Then he is a poor Prince," you mutter, tears in your eyes. "And she is a wretched Queen."

"Come!" Dodgson beckons. "We must leave!"

If you refuse to leave without the other girls, turn to page 157.

If you step into the corridor and leave with Alice, go to page 231.

"No," you tell the girl, "but I seem to be a little lost. Might you be able to help me?" As the girl approaches, you bend down on one knee, to be closer to her level.

"Who are you?" she whispers. "You don't belong here. You have to leave!"

"I'm looking for my daughter. She's a young girl about your age. Very pretty, like you. And I have good reason to suspect that she might be here. I'm wondering if you might be able to help me?"

The girl's brow knits cutely. You can tell she wants to help you, but is afraid she'll get in trouble.

"What's your name?" you ask kindly. "My name is — "

But from the end of the hall you hear heavy footsteps coming down a spiral staircase. Low voices and a glow portending the imminent arrival of palace guards.

Oh, no.

Turn to page 134.

"Well, that was exciting," you mutter.

You shut the door to the garden behind you, grateful to be out of the guard's area of surveillance. But sad that you weren't able to get a closer look at the girls.

Back inside the palace hall, tucked inside an alcove, Edith asks you where you would like to go now.

If you haven't yet checked out the Dreamery, turn to page 124.

If the Performatory is still a mystery to you, go to page 106.

If you've already investigated both, turn to page 180 to consider your next move.

Days later, the newspapers report that much of the palace is unrecoverable. What's more — citizens around the palace were puzzled regarding the dozens of identical little girls milling in the courtyard in the midst of the blaze. Who were they?

A photographer who was taking a picture of the palace at the time managed to get a shot through the bars of the front gate. Much of it is blurry, but there are several girls who are in sharp focus. And when it was printed in the newspaper, families across London came forward, identifying their missing daughters, taken from schoolyards, sweet shops, slums.

This enormous scandal threatens to topple the Crown, but the families are contacted and quietly threatened or paid off. Meanwhile, Queen Victoria mourns the death of her fourth, and youngest son, the Prince, who perished in the blaze.

Years pass.

Lorina marries a barrister who litigates against unscrupulous pharmacists who try to pass off well-water as consumption remedies. Meanwhile, Alice continues at school, showing a remarkable facility for drawing. She speaks little about her time at the palace, but over the years it leaks out in drips and drabs and comes to form a picture that corresponds to your own experience of the wretched place.

Then one evening, just after supper, there is a knock on the door.

"Who could that be?" Reg frowns. "Weather's bloody awful."

Indeed, it'd been raining all day and into the night.

When you open the front door, light spills out and

bathes the man standing there.

"Sing!"

Older, his goatee flecked with grey, he clutches his side, his vest wet with rain but also blood.

"You're hurt!" You go to bring him in when you notice someone else in your yard. A young Chinese woman stands in a man's coat, carrying a bundle in her arms.

Sing looks back at her and nods his head, urging her forward. She glances around warily, then joins him at your door. They are both soaked to the core.

"Who's this then?" Reg barks, coming up behind you.

Sing manages to smile, then through gritted teeth says, "Sing need favour."

THE END

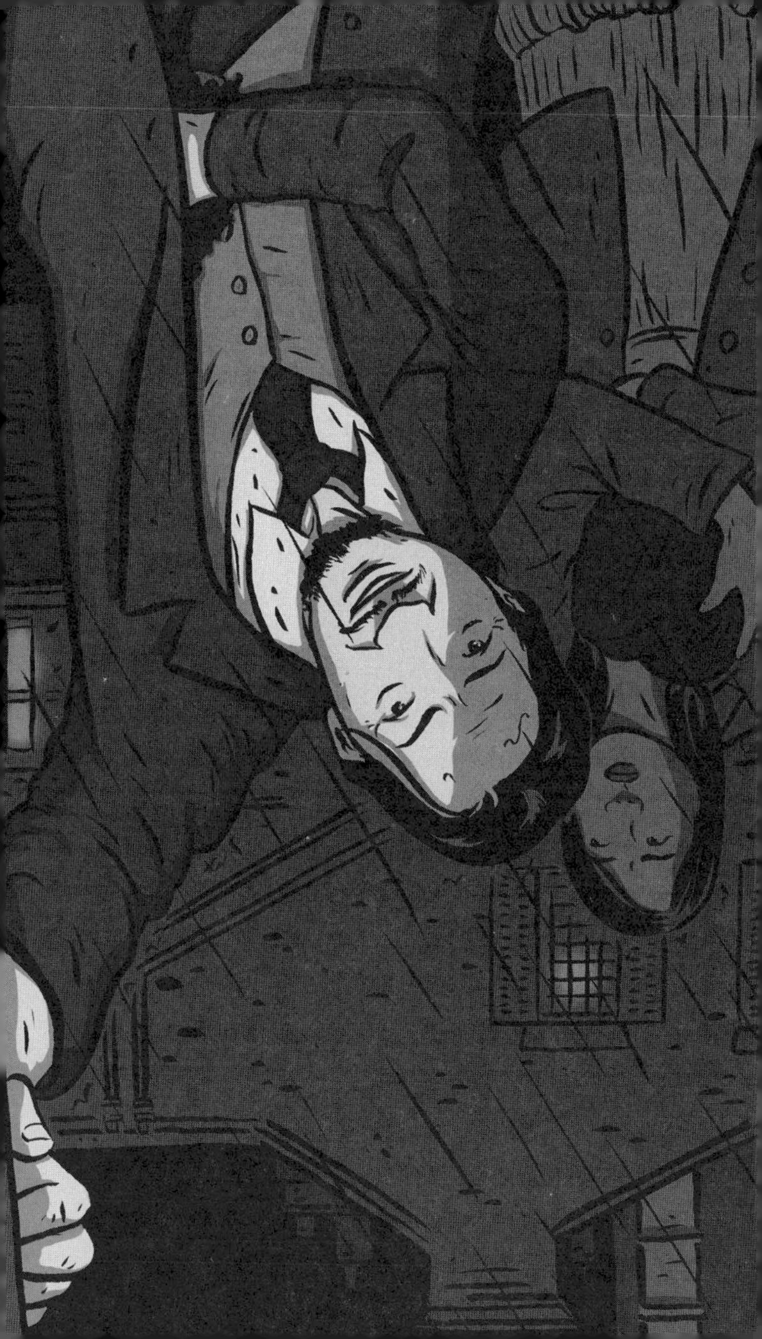

"Wake up, Alice dear!" said her sister. "Why, what a long sleep you've had!"

"Oh, I've had such curious dreams!" said Alice, and she told her sister, as well as she could remember them, about all these strange Adventures of hers that you have just been reading about.